Collide

Maria V. Ciletti

COLLIDE
© 2010 BY MARIA V. CILETTI

ISBN 13: 978-1-935216-14-8

First Printing: 2010

This Trade Paperback Is Published By
Intaglio Publications
Walker, LA USA
WWW.INTAGLIOPUB.COM

CREDITS
EXECUTIVE EDITOR: TARA YOUNG

COVER DESIGN BY TIGER GRAPHICS

Dedication

To my mom, Donna Infante. Although Alzheimer's disease has taken part of you away from me, it can never touch the part of you that is in my heart forever.

In memory of Amy Zucco. Although you lost your battle with breast cancer and were taken from us way too soon, having the privilege of taking care of you during that difficult time has meant so much to me. You and your wonderful husband, Joe, and beautiful daughters Brooke and Hannah were the inspiration for this book.

Acknowledgments

To my family: my brother Mike, Annette, Kayla, and Sara. My sister Traci, David, Jacob, and Katie. Aunt Lou, Aunt Patty from Arizona, and Uncle Ralph. I couldn't ask for a better family.

To Nann Dunne, for your excellent editing and encouragement in the beginning stages of *Collide*.

To Tara Young, for your excellent editing in the final stages of *Collide*.

To the staff at the McKinley Memorial Library, for their help in research for this book.

And last but not least, to my partner Rose, the love of my life—forever.

Prologue

Of course, being so close to each other was what started it.

Renee Cardone and Anna Maria Castrovinci lived next door to each other in the east end of Niles, Ohio. They had been best friends since kindergarten at St. Vincent's School. At recess, they used to walk hand in hand on the playground and seldom found the need to interact with the other children. All through grade school and junior high, one could always be found close by the other.

They played T-ball, took dance lessons, and attended birthday parties together. They joined the Girl Scouts, but that was short-lived because Renee didn't like the outfit. When they got older, they played softball on the same team up until high school, when it supposedly wasn't cool for girls to play sports anymore. Their parents treated them like they were sisters instead of friends. Often one of them would tag along on the other's family vacation, whether it was a weekend trip to Lake Erie or a two-week car trip to Renee's aunt's house in Phoenix, Arizona.

When they were sophomores in high school, at a sleepover after a friend's Sweet Sixteen party, the giggly girl talk turned to kissing boys. Some of the girls had done it, and some even had gone to second base. But neither Annie nor Renee had done anything like that. They sat back and watched as two of the more experienced girls put on a kissing demonstration. Among the peals of adolescent girl laughter, Annie and Renee sat motionless. Renee's heart pounded in her chest as she watched the two girls kiss.

Later that night as they lay on the floor in their sleeping bags, Annie's voice was barely a whisper in the dark. "Do you want to try it?"

"Try what?" Renee asked, even though she knew what Annie meant.

Renee heard the whirl of a zipper being unzipped. Her pulse quickened as she felt Annie come closer to her. In the dim glow of the streetlight that shone onto the family room floor where they had bunked down for the night, Renee could see the longing in Annie's eyes.

Renee's body trembled. She looked away, unable to meet Annie's gaze. "I wouldn't know what to do."

Annie reached up and gently lifted Renee's chin. "Close your eyes," she whispered.

The kiss was soft and sweet, and Renee was surprised at how much she liked it. Tingling sensations cascaded through her body, giving her a sense of pleasure she had never known before. When it was over, they lay next to each other in their own separate sleeping bags, holding hands. Renee lay awake for a long time, unable to quiet the excitement she felt deep inside.

Renee's gut feeling was that what they did was forbidden, but as time passed, the kissing experiments continued. Even though their attraction for each other felt genuine and pure, they were being raised as Catholics, and guilt hovered over them. After all, it was a sin, right?

Chapter One

It was a cool rainy April night in Annie's attic bedroom when the kissing led to more intimate experimentation. Scared and excited at the same time, Annie and Renee would find hiding places where they could be alone. "The game," as it would become known, was nothing like anything Renee or Annie had ever experienced. The only rules to the game were that it had to be done in secret, and afterward, not a word was spoken about it.

Renee's heart fluttered wildly in her chest when Annie was near her. Although a good two inches shorter than Renee, Annie's compact strong body, silky chocolate hair, and warm, easy smile elicited a magnetism toward Renee that she felt powerless to resist. As time went on, their kisses became more fervent as Annie's tongue sent shivers of desire racing through Renee's veins. Renee could hardly breathe as it was, but when Annie reached under her T-shirt and caressed Renee's small breast, she felt as if her legs would collapse underneath her. Annie caught Renee around the waist and pulled her to her. Renee slid her thigh between Annie's legs and could feel the heat of Annie's passion as she held her close.

"Annie..." Renee whispered, trying to catch her breath. Her chestnut hair disheveled around her perfectly oval face. She placed her palms onto Annie's heaving chest.

Annie gazed into Renee's tawny brown eyes and ran her thumb across Renee's taut nipple.

Renee tried to fight the exquisite feelings.

"Annie, we've got to stop."

Annie smiled as she flicked her thumb over Renee's nipple again. "You don't like this?"

The sensation sent currents of desire through Renee. She closed her eyes and took a deep breath, trying to regain her composure. She opened her eyes and saw the look of desire on Annie's face. She stepped back, loosening their embrace.

"What is it?" Annie asked. "Did I hurt you?"

"No. It's just that…"

"What?"

"We shouldn't be doing this. It's wrong."

"How could it be wrong if it feels so right? Anyway, no one knows about it but you and me."

"But what if someone finds out? What then?"

"No one is going to find out."

"How can you be so sure?"

"Because nobody thinks anything of two girls who are best friends and have sleepovers."

Renee lowered her head in despair.

"Hey, what is it?" Annie lifted Renee's chin. "I thought you loved me."

"I do love you."

"Then that's all that matters."

A soft moan escaped Renee's lips as Annie kissed her again. What's the use, Renee thought as she let what Annie was doing to her sweep her away. When they were finished, Renee tried to rationalize that it was just a phase they were going through, but her guilt always got the best of her. It got so bad that after they would be together, Renee would force Annie to make a pact that this would be the last time, but even that wasn't enough to keep them apart.

Although she did love Annie, how could she and Annie have gotten into this "unnatural" relationship? Everything she was taught in Catholic school about "these" kinds of relationships bought you a one-way ticket to hell. She was afraid that there weren't enough Hail Marys or Our Fathers to wash away this kind of sin. Not that she would have the courage to confess such a thing to a priest, even one from another parish. Not only that, what would her parents think? What would their friends think?

Annie, the bolder of the two, seemed resigned to the fact that this was more than a phase. She spoke often about Renee leaving home with her after graduation so they could begin a life of their own.

"Pretty soon, Reen, we can get out of this place and go somewhere where we don't have to hide. Wouldn't that be great?"

Renee smiled weakly. "Sure," Renee said, but the thought scared her to death.

That's when things started to change. Renee, intent on living a life acceptable to society, began to date Tom Del Fino. She needed something real in her life and knew Tom could give her that. Tom played on the football team. He seemed nice, and Renee knew he liked her, as she would catch him looking at her in chemistry class. Tom asked Renee to the homecoming dance, and she said yes. When Renee finally got up the nerve to tell Annie about her plans, it nearly broke Annie's heart.

"How could you?" Annie asked tight-lipped.

"Annie, my dating Tom has nothing to do with our relationship," Renee said. "What you and I do together is great, but it just isn't reality. I read in *Cosmopolitan* that sometimes girls do these kinds of things until the real thing comes along." At that moment, Renee regretted everything she had said because by the look on Annie's face, she knew she had hurt her deeply.

"I don't know about you, Reen, but for me, this is real."

"Annie, I'm sorry. I never meant to hurt you. It's just that…"

Annie waved her hand in front of Renee's face. "Don't bother. Go. Go be with your boyfriend. Go find your 'normal life.'"

After several tearful days of not speaking to each other, Renee couldn't stand it any longer and finally went over to talk to Annie. She walked across the backyard and, as usual, let herself into Annie's house through the back door. Once in the kitchen, she ran into Mrs. Castrovinci, who was slicing eggplant and tomatoes for dinner.

"Is Annie home?" Renee felt her face heat up. She could feel Gianna Castrovinci's scrutinizing gaze on her. Renee was afraid that Mrs. C could read her mind and know that she and her daughter did things—unnatural things—and that she too would be angry with her but for different reasons.

"She's a up in her room," Mrs. Castrovinci said in her Italian accent. She set the knife on the butcher-block counter and wiped her hands on her apron.

"Can I go up and see her? I need to talk to her," Renee said, trying to calm the nervousness in her voice.

"What a happened between you two? She won't even come a down to eat. I hope a it's not over something stupid like a boy."

Renee shook her head. "I said something, and I need to apologize to her." Renee looked at the floor, unable to meet Annie's mother's gaze.

"I hope a you two can patch a things up. That daughter of mine is a skinny enough, she can't afford to miss any more a meals."

With that, Renee bounded up the stairs two at a time. She found Annie lying facedown on her bed.

"Hey," Renee said.

Annie turned over and lifted her head. "Hey."

"Look, Annie, I'm sorry. I never meant to hurt you." Renee paused, searching for the right words to explain how she felt. "It's just that…what we do…we shouldn't be doing it. It's not normal."

"But you said you loved me, and I love you. What's changed?"

"Nothing's changed. I do love you, but…"

"But what?" Annie pulled herself up and sat cross-legged in the middle of her bed. Her face was creased from her pillow, and Renee couldn't help but think how adorable she looked. Renee walked over and sat on Annie's bed. She reached up and tucked a loose strand of hair behind Annie's ear. "But nothing," she whispered, then leaned in and kissed her.

Even though Renee appeared to be "officially" dating Tom all through high school, she continued to see Annie, as well. Rendezvous masqueraded as best-friend sleepovers or late-night study sessions. To make things look legitimate, Annie and Renee attended Tom's football games and sat together as they cheered Tom on. To make things even more convincing, Annie started to date boys, too, although those relationships were few and far between.

After graduation, Annie got accepted at Mount Holyoke University. She broke up with her latest fake boyfriend and begged Renee to come with her to South Hadley, Massachusetts.

"We could stay in the dorm for a while, then get a small apartment off campus," Annie pleaded.

Renee considered running away with Annie. But a lot of things held her back. First, she had no plans to go to college. Her family couldn't afford it for one thing, and because of the work program through the high school, she got hired on at the library and loved working there. She also had a hard time leaving Tom.

Even though what she and Annie had together was wonderful, Renee couldn't see herself living that way. After all, she and Annie weren't gay. They had boyfriends, for Christ's sake. Renee knew Tom loved her, and she was very fond of him. She thought that in time, she would learn to love him, too. She also knew that he could offer her the respectable life she wanted and her family expected of her.

Tearful arguments erupted when it came time for Annie to leave for college and Renee refused to go. Both of the girls' families were confused as to what all the upset was about. Neither girl was talking.

"What's a matter for you? It's a like you a married, you and Renee," Annie's mother would shout at Annie when she would come home inconsolable. "Get over it, bambina. You go to that fancy school, and you have a no trouble making new friends. I bet there are a lot of nice girls there. You don't need a Renee. You'll see."

It did feel like a marriage to Annie. She loved Renee very much. But now they were getting divorced, so to speak, all because of Renee's stubbornness and her inability to let go of her family's expectations.

After Annie left, Renee buried her feelings for Annie and continued to date Tom. Tom's love and devotion helped fill the void. Soon after Annie left, Renee and Tom got married and built a respectable life together.

Occasionally, Renee felt an odd twinge when she saw or met an attractive woman, but surely that didn't mean anything. That part of her life was behind her. She and Tom had a good marriage and two beautiful daughters. Then fate slapped them in the face and changed Renee's life forever.

Chapter Two

Renee Del Fino sat at her kitchen table among the half-eaten, Saran-wrapped casseroles and veggie trays and poured herself an Amaretto on the rocks. While most families were planning picnics and get-togethers this sunny Memorial Day weekend, she was planning her thirty-seven-year-old husband's funeral.

For the first time in days, actually for the first time in months, the house was quiet. No health care worker barging in with medical supplies or medications. No constant hiss of the oxygen concentrator.

The hospital bed that sat in the middle of their living room for two months had been dismantled and taken away, along with the wheelchair, bedside commode, and over-bed table that housed her husband's water glass, plastic pink pitcher, and numerous bottles of narcotics and anti-emetics.

Her family life as she had known it had been stolen—disturbed and interrupted by nurses, home health aides, physical therapists, and later on, the entire hospice team. Oh, she was grateful to all of them. If it weren't for them, she never would have gotten through this ordeal and neither would her girls.

She swirled the sparkling ice cubes in her glass and took another sip of the amber liquid. Her insides warmed as the liqueur slithered down her throat and into her stomach.

Tom Del Fino had gotten sick the previous fall. What he had thought was the flu ended up being pancreatic cancer. The first time Renee saw her six-foot-three, two hundred thirty-pound husband cry was when they sat in Dr. Michaels's office and he told them the devastating news. She saw Tom cry once more when they told their daughters, Lindsay, sixteen, and Sara, fourteen, that this

Christmas might be their last together as a family.

In an instant, just when Tom and Renee could enjoy some of the freedom of not being tied down to the kids 24/7, their lives had changed.

Dr. Michaels had told them Tom had six months to live at best and to go home and put his affairs in order. There was no cure for pancreatic cancer. The only treatment was to keep him as comfortable as possible. Dr. Michaels assured them that everything that could be done would be done. He scheduled Tom to see an oncologist and start chemotherapy to buy him some time. Hospice was mentioned, but Tom and Renee declined, unable to get their minds around the inevitable. Hospice? We don't need hospice. That's for people who are…

After the appointment, Tom and Renee sat in the car, barely able to breathe.

"Did he just tell me that I only have six months to live?" Tom asked.

Renee nodded, unable to find words.

Tom shook his head as they sat there looking through the windshield at a flock of geese flying low overhead in the metal gray November sky. Their honking sounded like an ominous message.

"What are we going to do, Reen?" Tom's voice, barely a whisper, sounded choked.

Renee reached across the front seat and took his strong hand into hers. "Whatever we have to."

To cope with the unthinkable, Tom focused more on their daughters' well-being than on his impending death. In the coming weeks, he and Renee met with attorneys, oncology specialists, social workers, and the benefits coordinator for federal employees. They drew up a will and set up trusts for the girls. At the time of Tom's death, the house and the car would be transferred into Renee's name.

When they spoke to the benefits coordinator at Tom's workplace, they learned that Tom was eligible for a small pension, which would also be transferred to Renee upon his death and that the girls were eligible for health insurance until they graduated from college. The coordinator helped Tom file for disability benefits and told him that he had a life insurance policy through the Postal Service that was worth two hundred thousand dollars. That would be a great help since Renee was working only part time at the library.

"Sounds like I'm worth more dead than alive," Tom said as they pulled out of the parking lot of the post office.

"Don't say that," Renee said. "It's morbid."

"But it's true." Tom grasped Renee's hand. "At least I know you and the girls are taken care of."

Tears splashed down onto their joined hands. Renee was terrified. She didn't want to lose Tom. She didn't want to admit that this could be real. She looked down at her husband's strong hand. They had a wonderful life, two great kids, and a great marriage. Why was it all ending now?

After graduation, Renee worked full time at the local library. Tom went to Youngstown State University and held a job as a walk-on mail carrier at the post office. Before the winter quarter started, he was offered a full-time position. He took it and never finished his degree in economics. A year later, he and Renee were married at the side altar of St. Vincent's Church.

Lindsay was born four months before Tom and Renee's first wedding anniversary, a secret they kept from the girls by telling them they were married the year before their actual wedding date. Sara came along exactly twenty-four months after Linz.

Renee stayed home with the girls until Sara started all-day kindergarten, then she returned to her job part time, reshelving books. She could get out of the house and feel productive and be home by three o'clock when Sara and Lindsay got off the school bus.

When the girls were four- and six-year-olds, Tom coached their peewee soccer games. He looked like the Incredible Hulk in the middle of those little kids, trying to teach them how to kick and pass the ball. He'd pick them up two at a time under his massive arms as they squealed with delight. He'd carry them over and gently set them in their assigned position of forwards or midfielders. Yes, that was Tom Del Fino, the gentle giant.

After every soccer game, whether their team won or lost, all the kids went to Dairy Queen for a treat because at that age, that's what it was all about: fun, no matter if you won or lost; if you had fun, it was a good game.

The Del Finos did everything together as a family. Now Tom was gone, and it felt like the core of their lives had been ripped out.

Renee was alone for the first time in her life. She had gone from her parents' home right into married life with Tom. Now she had a big empty house to take care of and two teenage girls to raise. The thought paralyzed her.

She drained the rest of her nightcap and headed upstairs to bed. The girls had gone to bed hours earlier, exhausted from all the emotion and heartache that losing a parent brings.

She flipped on the bedroom light and there it was: their bed. She hadn't slept in it since Tom passed away; in fact, it had been weeks since they both shared that bed.

After Tom's last hospitalization, they gave in to the fact that he couldn't make it upstairs to the bedroom anymore. The hardest thing to admit was that they needed help. But they called hospice, and in a matter of hours, a hospital bed and everything else they needed was set up, turning their spacious living room into a functional hospital room. Once everything was in place, Renee slept on the couch every night, not far from Tom in case he needed her.

At the end, Tom could barely speak or lift his head and sip water from a straw. Renee had to turn him in bed every two hours to prevent his body from getting pressure sores and his lungs from filling with fluid. She kept a urinal propped in his groin to keep the sheets dry.

He had suffered several strokes during his illness. The first one occurred on New Year's Eve, sending Tom to the hospital where he spent the first three days of 2006 in intensive care. He recovered enough to come home, but he had limited use of his right side. He was admitted to the hospital eight more times: twice for recurring strokes and several times for adverse side effects from the chemo. The chemotherapy agent he was receiving, 5 FU, had a name that sounded more like a curse word than a lifesaving medication. Maybe it got its name for what it was supposed to do to the cancer, or maybe it got its name from the horrible side effects the patient had to endure.

Renee leaned against the doorjamb, unable to even walk into the room. Too many memories lingered there: the first night they made love in this bed with six-week-old Lindsay only a few feet away, asleep in her bassinet; their New Year's tradition of snuggling in bed before midnight to watch the ball drop on TV; and the last time they made love—three, no four months before. Even then, Tom was too weak to be an active participant. Renee took matters into her own hands, so to speak, but was still afraid she might hurt him. It made her heart ache to think about it.

Although Renee was still pretty numb from the events over the last few days, she wasn't ready to contend with the searing loneliness she felt. For nearly seventeen years, she had been used to the warmth of a familiar body sleeping next to her. Now Tom's side of the bed was cold and empty. She turned off the light and went back downstairs.

Her eyes burned and her head buzzed as she settled into the recliner and flicked on the TV. Not much on this time of night, but at least it was noise. She was afraid of the night, afraid to be alone, afraid of what the next day might bring. That was when thoughts of Annie erupted for no good reason. Renee immediately squashed those thoughts as she had no business thinking of her at a time like this. After all, she had just lost her husband, the father of her children. What she and Annie had couldn't compare to what she had with Tom…Right?

Renee closed her eyes. The previous few days reeled through her head like a bad movie trailer she couldn't turn off.

The day of Tom's passing, he slept off and on but never seemed to get into a deep restful sleep. His morphine pump showed that he was getting the maximum dose of two milligrams an hour, but that didn't seem to be giving him much relief. Renee called the hospice nurse to see if she could get him more pain medicine. The nurse told her she would get in touch with Dr. Michaels to increase his dose.

Lindsay and Sara took turns sitting at their father's bedside, holding his hand, trying to comfort him. But he seemed more agitated at their presence as if he didn't want them to see him that way. The girls were upset, as well.

"Lindsay, why don't you and Sara go out to the mall for a while? I'm sure you both could use a change of scenery," Renee said.

Lindsay's face lit up. "Really, Mom? Is it okay?"

"Yes, it is, honey. Take your sister and go have a little fun. You two have been a big help today. You deserve a break."

Renee slipped Lindsay forty bucks and warned her to share with Sara. Both girls seemed pleased to be relieved of their duties.

Tom looked into his daughters' eyes, seeming to memorize their faces as the girls crouched next to him. Lindsay and Sara kissed their father goodbye like they did every time they left the house, not knowing that this time would be the last.

Once the girls left, Renee lay next to Tom. His head rested on her breast. She stroked his sweaty dark hair and told him everything was going to be all right. She whispered to him that he was a good father and a great husband, and even though it was the most difficult thing in the world to do, she did what the hospice nurse advised her to do. She told Tom that it was okay for him to let go. Tears streamed down her face as she kissed his forehead and told him she loved him very much.

"Reen, I'm...so sorry," Tom whispered, his voice nothing more than a puff of air.

"Sorry? Sorry for what?"

"Sorry that I got sick...sorry that I have to leave you with all this." Tom took in a gulp of air. "Sorry I won't see the girls..."

He began to cough uncontrollably. Each breath wracked his body. Renee grabbed his glass of water and made him drink. He lay back on the bed, his chest rising and falling unevenly with his labored respirations.

He finally closed his eyes and lay peacefully in her arms. Tears trickled down his stubbled cheeks. The oxygen that flowed through the nasal cannula hissed, the only sound in the room.

Tom's breathing changed, becoming quieter and shallower. He seemed more relaxed now, and a sense of calm swept over Renee. She lay with Tom, watching the local news on TV with the volume turned down low. By the time *NBC Nightly News* with Brian Williams came on, Tom had slipped away.

His last breath was a deep sigh. His last words to her, a whispered "I love you, Reen," would ring in her heart forever.

Renee lay very still, bargaining with some unknown force in the universe, that if she didn't move, if nothing changed in the room, it wouldn't be true, Tom wouldn't be gone. Her heart pounded. Anxiety-filled thoughts rifled through her head as she lay there holding her dead husband. It wasn't until an hour later, when *Everybody Loves Raymond* came on that she gave up on the fantasy and got up.

Tom lay motionless in the rumpled sheets, his head lolled to the side. His eyes were half shut, and his skin was a waxy white. Renee removed the plastic nasal cannula and noticed that his nasal septum, the stretch of skin that separated his nostrils, was paper thin. She shut off the oxygen compressor and tossed the cannula and the tubing onto the floor. She stood in the middle of the living room, terrified as reality set in, and covered her face with her hands.

That was the last thing she remembered of that day. The rest was a blur. She didn't remember the paramedics coming to take Tom's body to the hospital, where he was pronounced dead, or how her parents showed up out of the blue, like they received a call from heaven that now was the time Renee would need them the most. Nor did she remember Lindsay and Sara returning home and telling them that their father was gone. No matter how hard she tried to recall the events of that day, it was still a blur. Maybe that was a blessing.

The next morning, Renee had driven downtown to the funeral home to make Tom's arrangements. Jim Caruso, the eldest of the sons in Caruso and Sons Funeral Home, helped Renee with the dismal task of planning Tom's funeral. Never in her wildest dreams had she ever imagined she'd be planning a funeral for her young husband. Renee's parents stayed at the house with Lindsay and Sara. Renee didn't think the girls should go through the ordeal of picking out a casket for their father.

She sat in Jim's cramped office that hadn't been redecorated since JFK was assassinated. She always thought funeral homes were creepy, and now it felt creepier sitting in this place where her husband lay on a cold slab somewhere in the basement. The knot in her throat grew tighter.

Arrangements had been made for a Catholic service and burial in the Catholic cemetery within walking distance of Renee's house. She found comfort in that. She usually passed the cemetery on her morning walks. The same walks she had neglected once Tom's health had taken a nosedive. This would be reason enough to start them again.

She signed the papers and handed over a check for ten thousand dollars, payment in full for Tom's funeral. She thanked Jim Caruso for his time and headed home.

Her house was bustling with activity when she arrived. The aromas of spaghetti sauce and chicken soup and fresh baked bread permeated the air. She walked through the living room where Lindsay and Sara sat watching a movie with some of their friends from school. Lindsay sat on the couch with Justin, a new boy who had just moved to town right before the school year started in the fall. He and Lindsay worked on a project for school together a while back and seemed to hit it off pretty well. Now it seemed Justin was a permanent fixture at her house most days. Justin seemed like a nice kid—polite and all.

With Tom being so sick, Renee hadn't paid much attention to their budding relationship. Were they sitting close...maybe too close on the sofa? Oh, heaven's no. They're just kids.

Her mother, Angie Cardone, and Mrs. McKenzie, Renee's next door neighbor, sat at the kitchen table sipping coffee and eating nut kolachi.

"Reen, you look like hell," Angie said. "Here, sit down. Have some coffee." She pulled out one of the kitchen chairs and Renee sat. Her mother poured her a cup of coffee and dumped three packets of Splenda into it, the way Renee liked it. "Try some of this kolachi that Rose Moderelli brought over. She made it this morning. It's wonderful." Angie sliced off a piece and put it on a white paper plate.

Renee took a bite, and it stuck in her throat. She took a sip of coffee to wash it down.

"Everything set for tomorrow?" Angie asked.

"Yes, the limo will be here at one o'clock to take us to the funeral home for the family viewing. I'd like it if you and Daddy could ride with us."

"We'll be here. Besides, I told your father that I was going to stay here tonight. I didn't think you should be alone on the night before Tom's funeral."

Renee's throat tensed up. "Oh, Mom, you don't have to. Me and the girls will be all right. We have to get used to being on our own sooner or later."

"Better later than sooner. It's already been decided. I'm staying."

Renee didn't argue. She knew she'd never win.

Each time the door opened, someone was bringing in food. People Renee hadn't seen in years seemed to just appear, expressing their condolences.

As the afternoon turned into evening, the crowd diminished until only Renee, her mom and dad, and the girls were left. After cleaning up the kitchen, Angie sent her husband home with specific instructions to pick her up at ten in the morning so she could go home and get dressed for the calling hours. She kissed his forehead before he left, and Renee couldn't help envying what they had together. Their marriage had lasted over forty years and was still going strong. Why was hers so prematurely interrupted? What did she do to deserve this?

Angie slept on the couch while Renee took the recliner. She was amazed at how quickly her mother fell asleep. Renee lay in the dim room listening to Angie snore and watching the shadows on the wall from the streetlights. No matter how she tried, she just couldn't sleep. Feeling frustrated after several hours of restlessness, she forced herself to get up and move. The day would be difficult for her and the girls. She needed to get a grip and hold it all together for her family's sake.

She went into the kitchen and made some coffee. As the coffee brewed, she looked around the room. Memories arose of the day she and Tom bought this place. Lindsay was barely a month old. Renee carried her in a papoose pack slung around her neck as she and Tom toured the house, a big old two story that needed a lot of work. But the price was right. They moved in two weeks later. A month after that, the furnace and hot water tank simultaneously croaked. Renee remembered sitting on the basement steps, crying her eyes out, not knowing where they would get the money to fix them. But Tom, as always, came to the rescue. He knew a guy who knew a guy, and by the end of the day, the furnace was up and running. Heat blasted through the cavernous air ducts, and they were the proud owners of a new hot water tank.

She and Tom had bought this house with the intention of living here for the rest of their married life. Who knew it would end this soon?

"You doing okay?" Angie entered the kitchen, rubbing sleep from her eyes with the heels of her hands.

"Yes, Mom, I'm fine." Renee poured herself a cup of coffee. She lifted the coffeepot, and her mother nodded. She filled a cup with steaming coffee and slid it across the table.

Renee looked at her mother and smiled. Her hairnet was askew on her head.

"What?" Angie asked.

"Your hairnet. It's crooked. I can't believe you still wear that thing," Renee said, still smiling.

Angie reached up, removed, and replaced the black net, tucking the loose strands of salt and pepper hair underneath the elastic band. "How's that?"

"Better."

The two women drank their coffee in silence. When they finished, Angie collected the cups and placed them in the dishwasher. She returned to the table and slipped her arms around Renee's neck, holding her close.

Feeling her embrace, Renee couldn't hold back the tears. It was the first time she had cried so openly since Tom's death.

"I'm so sorry, honey, that this has happened to you…so sorry,"

Angie whispered into the top of Renee's head. Renee could feel her mother's body tremble as she cried, too.

"Mom, I don't know what I'm going to do." Renee's voice was ragged and uneven. "Tom took care of everything, and now…"

"Shh…everything will be okay." Angie rocked her and stroked her hair.

"How can you be so sure?"

"Because no matter how bad it gets, it always works out." Angie sat in the chair next to her. She handed Renee a paper napkin to wipe her tears.

"I wish I could be so sure." Renee took the napkin from her and blew her nose.

"I know, honey. There's no explanation for these things. You just have to trust that it will be okay, and it will."

Renee pulled another napkin from the stack in the middle of the table and dabbed at her wet eyes. Angie rose and bustled around the kitchen, loading the dishwasher, wiping off the counters.

"Why don't you go upstairs and take a shower? The girls will be up soon. Maybe I'll make those pancakes I used to make for them when they were little, you know the ones with the Mickey Mouse ears," Angie said as she hunted through Renee's cupboards for the griddle pan.

"I think they'd like that." Renee got up and moved toward the stairs. Standing on the first step, she looked back through the kitchen doorway and watched her mother crack eggs into a large glass mixing bowl. "Thanks, Mom."

Angie looked up and smiled.

Chapter Three

One o'clock came, and the black limousine pulled into Renee's driveway right on time. The last time Renee rode in the back of a limousine was two years earlier at Tom's mother's funeral. The time before that was when Tom's father's passed away, two months before Lindsay was born. Renee wore a simple black sleeveless dress with sensible black heels. Lindsay had dressed in a black and gray jumper, and Sara wore her navy blue pleated skirt and white short-sleeve blouse, the outfit she was confirmed in only a few short months earlier. The girls looked exhausted, their eyes red-rimmed and glassy. Renee put an arm around each of them as they walked onto the front porch and down the steps to the driveway. They climbed into the limo along with her parents and headed to Caruso's for their first viewing of Tom.

Once at the funeral home, the driver came around and opened the door. Renee's father stepped out first and helped each of them out of the car. Jim Caruso met them at the back entrance.

"Is everyone here?" he asked.

Renee nodded.

"Step this way please."

Jim led them into the main chapel, where Tom lay. They walked up to the casket with Lindsay on one side of Renee and Sara on the other. Renee pulled the girls to her and could feel them trembling.

Sara and Lindsay sobbed uncontrollably at the sight of their father lying in the bronze casket. Renee pulled the girls closer, burying their faces into her chest, feeling their bodies wracked with sorrow.

"Shh, shh. It's okay," Renee whispered. She walked them

over to the gold lamé chairs that lined the far wall of the funeral chapel.

"Sit here a minute." She knelt between the girls, trying to hold herself together, as well as them. Sara's and Lindsay's eyes were wet and swollen from crying. Jim Caruso appeared quietly at Renee's side with two paper cups of water. He offered them to the girls, and they each took a sip.

"I need you guys to be strong today, okay?" Renee bit back her own tears. "I know this is hard, but we have to get through this. We have to…we have to do it for Daddy."

Lindsay and Sara nodded.

They sat stoically next to Renee as the first of the mourners came in. After about an hour of accepting condolences, Renee had come to the conclusion that most people didn't really know what to say in these situations. Many people came through and said they were sorry for Renee's loss, which was the respectful thing to say. But then there were others like the woman who was a friend of Angie's. She came through the line, took Renee's hand, and told her what a good job she did taking care of Tom. Then before moving on, the woman said, "At least you're young and can get married again."

Renee didn't know what to say to that. How was that supposed to be comforting? Was her being a young widow some sort of consolation prize? But that wasn't the worst of it. A pack of nuns from the church convent arrived.

One by one, each nun expressed her condolences to Renee, which included sentiments such as "God needed him more than we do" and "He's with the Lord now. You should take comfort in that." As each nun passed, Renee's numb sadness steeped into anger.

God needed Tom more than we did? For what? I really need him here with me and our family because I don't think I'm strong enough to pull off this charade much longer of pretending that I have it all together.

Renee remembered the final nun from her elementary school days. She was the school librarian and, as Renee remembered it, was elderly even then. The ancient librarian nun took Renee's hands into hers. Renee looked into watery crystal blue eyes, which looked enormous through thick-lensed glasses. The nun's head shook, and she smiled before she spoke. "My dear, I know you're mourning the loss of your husband, but you must know that God has a plan for everything." She squeezed Renee's hands. It took every bit of resolve Renee could muster to keep her emotions under control.

He has a plan? Well, I wish he would have clued me in on it, so I could have prepared better. And why did his plan have to include taking my husband and my children's father away? Did God think about the pain our daughters would feel and all they would be missing out on without their father? Who was going to take them to the father-daughter events at school and who was supposed to give them away at their weddings? With all due respect, I don't think God really thought this one out.

Renee reminded herself where she was. She smiled politely, nodded, and bit the inside of her cheek to keep from saying what was really on her mind.

As the calling hours came to a close, she couldn't help feeling disappointed that the one person she wouldn't have minded seeing hadn't showed up. Oh, well, what did she expect? After all, it had been seventeen years since they had spoken. Renee hadn't thought about Annie in a long time, and it seemed odd that she came to mind now.

The next day, St. Vincent's Church was packed as Renee and her daughters walked down the center aisle behind Tom's casket. The three of them sat alone in the front pew of the church. Renee's parents sat behind them. It comforted Renee to know they were there in case she lost control or something.

Father Carlo gave the eulogy, which seemed appropriate. He had known Tom since he was an altar boy. His words were kind, and Renee was sure they were meant to be uplifting. She was too numb to take any of it in.

She began to feel claustrophobic, like the entire congregation was closing in on her. Some people, she was sure, pitied her, being left alone with two young daughters to raise. But it was her self-doubt that made her feel like she was suffocating.

The choir sang "Amazing Grace," and Father Carlo sprinkled holy water over Tom's casket in the sign of the cross. Renee felt light-headed as she sat in the pew with Sara tucked under one arm and Lindsay under the other. A few more swings of the smoking censer, and thank God, Tom's funeral Mass would be officially over.

Jim Caruso appeared at the front of the church and escorted Renee and her girls down the aisle, which, to Renee, felt like a ten-mile hike. With each step, it became harder to breathe.

A hand touched her arm. "Are you all right?" Jim asked.

"I'm feeling a little closed in. I'll be okay. I just need a little air."

Once outside, Renee took a big gulp of fresh air. She glanced at the beautiful cloudless, cobalt blue sky. How could her world be ending under such a beautiful sky? Jim opened the door of the black limousine and helped the girls and her inside.

Renee's heart hurt and her head throbbed. It made her angry that as the funeral procession made its way through town, she noticed that the rest of the world went on with their lives while hers was falling down around her. You're never entirely prepared for the death of someone you love, she thought. Grief inflicted a sense of losing yourself in a way you feel you will never be found again.

After the graveside service, the limousine driver drove Renee and her family home. Friends and relatives gathered for the dinner that her mother, her aunts, and some of the women from the neighborhood had prepared. Renee slipped an apron over her black dress and helped serve the more than thirty people who had come to her home after the funeral.

Serving her guests made her feel a little better; it let her feel useful, and the mindless task of dishing up pasta and meatballs gave her heart and mind a break from the heavy feeling of sorrow she had been burdened with for the last few days. Lindsay and Sara seemed to be doing better, too, which gave Renee a ray of hope that eventually they would all be okay.

As the evening wore on, family and friends peeled away, going back to their homes and unchanged lives. By midnight, the girls had gone to bed and everyone else, including Renee's parents, had gone home.

Finally alone, Renee finished washing the last of the Tupperware containers someone had brought wedding soup in. She wiped down the kitchen counter and shut off the light.

Without bothering to change out of her funeral dress, she sat in the recliner and closed her eyes. Her head hummed from weariness as she told herself she would just sit here a minute or two, then go up to bed, or at least go up and change clothes. She wasn't ready to sleep up there yet. Would she ever be?

She drifted off and finally settled into a deep sleep. But she found no comfort. That night, she had the cruelest dream of all: that none of this had happened, that Tom was alive and well. In the dream, their family was having a picnic in the park. The girls were little, and they were giggling and frolicking in the lush green grass while Tom and Renee lay on a blanket, watching them play. The dream seemed so real that Renee thought she felt Tom touch her. He kissed her gently on the lips and stood to play with the girls. The sun, a butterscotch disc in the sky, was warm and bright as Tom played with the girls, scooping them up in his strong arms and spinning them around, all laughing, until they fell down from dizziness.

Renee walked over to where they lay in the tall grass. The laughter had stopped. When she looked down at Tom lying there in the grass with his daughters around him, his skin was ashen and stone cold and his eyes were blank as he stared toward the sky. She covered her mouth with her hands to suppress her scream.

"Mom?"

Renee bolted up. Her heart pounded and her face was wet with tears.

"Mom, are you okay?" Lindsay knelt next to the chair.

Renee wiped her face with the palms of her hands and shook the sleep from her foggy head. "Sure, honey, I'm okay. How are you doing?" She pulled Lindsay up and into her lap. Lindsay's long legs dangled over the side of the chair.

Lindsay shrugged. "I don't know. Do I really have to go back to school in the morning?"

Renee knew that the best way to help her daughters heal from this tragedy was to get their lives back to as normal as possible. School was their regular routine, and besides, there were only six days of the school year left. "Why don't you want to go, honey?"

"I don't want the kids to stare at me like I'm some kind of charity case."

"You're not some charity case. Your father died. The kids in your class feel bad for you and don't know what to do or say."

"I still hate it. I hate how I feel, and I hate it that he died." Lindsay started to cry.

Renee held her tight and rocked her in her arms like she did when Lindsay was a newborn.

I hate it, too, baby...but it's the hand we were dealt. I wish I had more answers for you, but I'm new at this, too.

Renee tucked Lindsay's head under her chin and kissed the top of it. "I don't think you missing one more day will make much of a difference." Renee stroked Lindsay's silky chestnut hair. "I'll call the school office in the morning and let them know you won't be back until next week. I'm sure they'll understand."

Renee and Lindsay slept in the chair until the first morning light seeped through the mini blinds. How dare another day start again? She extricated herself from beneath Lindsay's long, lithe body and padded into the kitchen to make coffee. The sunlight in the room turned shadowy, then bright as she filled the glass coffee carafe with cold water that she dumped into the back of the Mr. Coffee. Almost immediately, the soothing aroma of coffee filled the room.

She sat at the kitchen table, taking her first sip, when she saw Sara come down the stairs rubbing the sleep out of her eyes. At fourteen, Sara was built like her father: sturdy with strong legs and a thick waist that never seemed to taper like Lindsay's did at Sara's age. She had a mouth full of silver braces and a head of wild, curly brown hair that was a tangled mess every morning.

"Morning, honey," Renee said.

"Morning," Sara said in a soft, low whisper. She pushed her hair out of her eyes and plopped down into the chair across from Renee at the kitchen table.

"What's wrong with Lindsay?" She glanced toward her sister curled up in a ball, sound asleep in the recliner.

"She had a rough night," Renee said. "How about you? How are you doing?"

"Okay, I guess. I keep having bad dreams. That Daddy's hurt and we can't find him to help him." Tears formed in Sara's chocolate brown eyes...her father's eyes.

"Oh, honey, it's okay. I think that's pretty normal to have those dreams, considering everything you've been through."

Renee reached across the table and took Sara's hand into hers. "Lindsay's upset about going back to school. Are you scared, too?"

Sara nodded and wiped her tears away.

"Maybe we can do something fun then, just the three of us."

For the first time in days, Sara smiled.

"Now go in the living room and wake your sister up. I think it's time the Del Fino girls had a little fun."

Chapter Four

The drive from Cleveland took a little over an hour. Dana Renato spent practically the whole time on her cell phone, switching back and forth between the contractor who was renovating the house she and Risa bought five years earlier and her lawyer, who was fighting the lawsuit that could cause Dana to lose the house altogether.

She and Risa had planned to renovate the 1940s kitchen back to its original style. The huge O'Keefe & Merritt gas stove with the side Grillevator broiler, however, had been sitting in a crate in the garage for over two years. They also had planned to turn the downstairs bedroom into an office for Dana, but Risa got sick before the project had been completed. Both rooms had been construction sites for more than three years.

When the contractor told Dana they had run into yet another problem that would require the utilities to be shut off, he suggested it would be better if Dana found some place to stay while the rest of the renovations took place. Hearing this and hoping to ease some of Dana's frustration, her publisher suggested she relocate to Niles for a while to do research for her new book. All expenses paid by the publisher, of course.

Dana thought the publisher was crazy. First of all, Dana was leery of leaving the contractor there alone. Not that she thought he would steal anything, but it seemed he had a work ethic of "out of sight, out of mind." If Dana didn't check in with him every day or so, he'd easily get distracted. What could she discover in Niles about the mob that she couldn't find in Cleveland? But she agreed to the move anyway. Now that Risa was gone, no one in Cleveland would miss her.

Dana arrived at the apartment complex where her publisher had rented a small furnished studio apartment for her. The place smelled musty from being closed up. She walked through it and opened the windows—both of them—to air it out. She tossed the one suitcase she had brought onto the hide-a-bed sofa and set her laptop on the oak Poe table that sat next to it. She found an outlet and plugged in the computer to charge the battery.

Dana sat on the sofa and looked around the room that would serve as her home for the next few months. A heavy sadness engulfed her. She didn't want to be here. Not only had she been uprooted from her spacious home in Cleveland Heights where she could hide away from the world, but also this place reminded her of the first apartment she had shared with Risa.

She and Risa Demarco had been seniors at Cleveland State University when they met. Risa was an early child education major, and Dana majored in journalism. It was an exciting time for them. Risa was finishing up her student teaching, and Dana had just started an internship at *The Plain Dealer* in Cleveland. They met at a Pride event in The Flats and became fast friends. Quickly, their friendship blossomed into a loving relationship that lasted over fifteen years.

They had only been in their new home a year when their lives were turned upside down. On a hot Saturday afternoon in August, Risa and Dana were spending a leisurely day around their Italian-tiled swimming pool. Dana watched as Risa swam the length of the pool underwater, then emerged in the deep end. As she grabbed onto the stainless steel pool ladder and pulled herself out of the water, Risa looked like a *Sports Illustrated* swimsuit model. Her body glistened as water streamed off of her sun-kissed skin. Dana grabbed a towel, wrapped Risa in it, and pulled her close.

"You look so beautiful when you're wet." Dana kissed Risa eagerly. Risa's hands slipped around Dana's waist and inside her swimsuit.

"You're pretty wet yourself," Risa said with a wicked smile.

Dana grabbed Risa by the hand and led her through the French doors that opened from their bedroom to the back patio. She stripped off Risa's wet bathing suit and laid her down on their bed. While Benny Mardones crooned over the outside sound system, they made love.

"Reese, what's this?" Dana asked as she stroked her hand over Risa's left breast. The skin on Risa's small breast was hot to touch and had an orange peel texture to it.

"What?"

Dana propped herself up on one elbow. "This...here...it's all red and inflamed. Does it hurt?"

Risa sat up and looked down at her breast. "It's been sore for a few days. I just thought it was a spider bite or something." Risa touched the reddened area. "Ooh...it is tender." She pressed over the area again and again, but nothing changed. It was still painful and hot and hard. Risa's expression turned serious. Fear hammered in Dana's heart.

She drew Risa into her arms. "Maybe it's nothing, just a skin infection or something. Call and make an appointment with Dr. Fletcher on Monday. We'll find out what it is and get it taken care of." She stroked Risa's honey-colored hair.

Even at that moment, Dana had a deep disquieting feeling that whatever was going on with Risa wasn't good.

Three days after her appointment with Dr. Fletcher, Risa was scheduled for surgery. The exam and breast biopsy showed inflammatory breast cancer, a rare but very serious aggressive type. Risa's cancer was Stage IIIB, which meant that the tumor had spread to other areas of her body, such as the lymph nodes and chest wall. Risa's lymph node biopsy showed three positive lymph nodes, meaning the cancer could have spread anywhere.

Risa endured a bilateral mastectomy. She wanted the cancer out of her body immediately. As a preventative measure, they removed both breasts and the three positive lymph nodes.

She suffered through three grueling months of chemotherapy and six weeks of radiation therapy. She was fit from all the tennis she played in high school and college, and she was a fighter. She accepted the ravages of her cancer treatment as something that had to be endured. After all, what was the alternative?

The chemo caused her silky, shoulder-length hair to fall out in clumps. She tried several wigs but finally opted to wear only a

Cleveland Indians baseball cap after allowing Dana to shave off the patchy remnants of her hair.

For a little over a year, the treatments seemed to be working. Risa's hair and strength returned, and she even went back to work, but only part time, substituting in a kindergarten class whose regular teacher was out on maternity leave.

Then one morning as they were getting ready for work, Dana came out of the bathroom and found Risa lying on the floor unconscious. Fear paralyzed her, but she managed to break through it and dial 911, never leaving Risa's side. By the time the paramedics arrived, Risa began to wake up.

"What happened?" she asked.

"I don't know," Dana said. "I heard a crash, and when I looked out to see what caused it, you were on the floor."

One of the paramedics mentioned that Risa looked a little dehydrated and might need to be admitted for some IV fluids. They helped her onto the gurney and carried her down the two flights of stairs. Dana followed behind the ambulance in her car.

Once they arrived at the hospital, nurses and doctors swarmed the gurney. Apparently, Risa had lost consciousness again in the ambulance. They wheeled her off into a curtained treatment bay while a frantic Dana stood outside of the exam area. Dana tried to listen and make sense of the orders one of the doctors called out while they worked on Risa. One was for a neuro consult.

Neuro consult? Why would Risa need a neuro consult? She has breast cancer. There's nothing wrong with her brain. Dana paced outside the cubicle as nurses and doctors rotated in and out of the exam area. Finally, a young doctor came out to speak with her.

"Are you with Ms. Demarco?" he asked.

"Yes, I'm her...uh...we live together." In spite of their commitment ceremony, they had no legal bond. Because of this, Dana might not be told what was going on with Risa. She had known this from before when Risa had her first surgery. The surgeon who was going to do her mastectomy refused to speak to Dana about her condition, something about a HIPAA law or privacy issue. After that, they had living wills and medical powers of attorney drawn up. But everything happened so fast that morning, Dana forgot to bring the papers with her.

"You're not a family member?"

"No, but I have her medical power of attorney." Dana prepared herself for the struggle she expected to ensue when she didn't have the documents with her. This time, she was pleasantly surprised.

The doctor took Dana aside and spoke to her about Risa's condition.

"I'm Dr. Remy." He shook Dana's hand. "I've evaluated Ms. Demarco, and it appears that her sudden loss of consciousness was due to a seizure. I've called in a neurosurgeon to take a look at her."

"Okay," Dana said. "Why would she have a seizure? She's not epileptic."

"She told me she has metastatic breast cancer. Is that true?"

"Yes."

"I'm afraid that the seizure may be an indication that the cancer has spread to her brain."

Dana felt like she had just been kicked in the stomach. "So what does that mean? More chemo? More radiation?" Dana asked desperately.

"She might require surgery. There's no chemotherapy for brain cancer."

"Surgery? What kind of surgery?"

"It depends on where the lesion is. If it's in a place that's operable, they'll try to remove it or radiate it. If it's not, the surgeon will put a shunt in her head to keep the fluid that's caused by the tumor off her brain and give her some quality of life."

"*Some* quality of life?" Dana snapped, shaking.

"I'm sorry, Ms.…."

"Renato. Dana Renato."

"Ms. Renato, if Ms. Demarco has any family, now would be a good time to notify them of her condition so decisions can be made."

"There's nobody but me…here anyway. Her dad lives in Phoenix. She hasn't spoken to him in years."

"You might want to give him a call. Maybe he would want to know his daughter's critically ill."

A nurse approached them. "Dr. Remy, Dr. Parker is on line two."

"That's the neuro guy." Dr. Remy put his hand on Dana's shoulder. "I'll let you know more after I speak to him."

"Thank you, Doctor, I appreciate it."

After thirteen hours in the emergency room, which included a spinal tap, copious amounts of blood work, and a CT scan, Dr. Parker revealed that Risa's cancer had spread to her brain, her spine, and the left lobe of her lung. He explained that without treatment, she had six weeks at best. With treatment, which would include a shunt being placed in her head, as well as chemo for the lung mass and radiation to her spine, she could buy herself a year, maybe two.

How could this be happening? Dana listened to the doctor explain the risks and complications involved if Risa decided to go on with the treatment.

Risks and complications? Was he crazy when the alternative to not undergoing treatment was certain death?

Never in Dana's life had she felt so helpless and hopeless. Her life partner, the love of her life, was dying right before her eyes, and she was powerless to help her.

Risa signed the consent forms, agreeing to the treatment Dr. Parker prescribed. They took her to surgery that night and put the shunt into her head to keep the fluid off her brain, preventing any further seizures. Dana sat in the family waiting area alone and watched the sunrise through the floor-to-ceiling windows. Dr. Parker emerged from the operating room around six in the morning. Dana's eyes burned as she listened to him recount the procedure. He assured her that Risa did well and that she could probably take her home later that day. He suggested that Dana go home and get some rest.

"Can I see her before I leave?"

"Sure," Dr. Parker said. "She's still pretty out of it, but you can talk to her. She can hear you."

He walked Dana down the carpeted hall to the recovery room area. Before they entered the room, Dana donned a surgical mask and paper gown.

Risa lay on her side, bundled in green surgical sheets and blankets, still asleep from the anesthesia. Half of her newly grown hair was shaved down to stubble again. The shunt that lay just under her scalp was a noticeable bump. Dana touched her cheek. Her skin was pale and cool, but the heart monitor above her head beat steadily, reassuring Dana that for now, Risa was all right. Dana wanted to kiss her, but always aware of what was considered appropriate in public, she held back.

"Reese," she whispered.

"She's going to be out for a while." The nurse attending to Risa wrote something on a metal clipboard attached to the foot of the bed. "You look like you could use a little sleep yourself."

"Will someone call me when she wakes up?" Dana asked.

"Yes, we have her contact information here. Someone will call you the minute she wakes up and is on her way to her room."

"Thank you, I'd appreciate that."

The nurse walked out of the curtained recovery bay.

Dana bent down quickly and kissed Risa on the cheek.

Risa's eyes fluttered open. She tried to focus them on Dana.

"Hi, honey." Dana stroked Risa's face. "The doc said you did great."

Risa forced a weak smile.

"You rest. I'm going to go home and get some sleep, too. I'll be back in a few hours to take you home," Dana whispered into Risa's ear. "I love you, babe."

"I love you, too." Risa's voice sounded raspy and faint.

The nurse returned to Risa's bedside and hung another glass bottle of IV fluid. Dana left the recovery room and headed home in the bright morning light. Once at home, she couldn't shake the awful feeling that had been gnawing at her ever since they took Risa to the emergency room. She knew that someday she might be walking into this house alone without Risa forever.

Dana lay on the couch and closed her eyes. Her head throbbed from fatigue. Sleep came almost immediately, a dark dreamless sleep.

Just before noon, the phone rang, startling her awake. She glanced at the caller ID and noticed the call was from University Hospital. She grabbed for the phone.

"May I speak to Dana Renato, please?" the female voice said.

"This is Dana."

"Ms. Renato, could you please come to the hospital? There's been a change in Ms. Demarco's condition, and her doctor would like to speak with you. If there are any other family members, the doctor wants to speak to them, as well."

Icy fear practically stopped Dana's heart. She raced to the hospital, running red lights and blowing through stop signs. She reached the second-floor conference room, where the woman calling from the hospital had told her to meet Dr. Parker.

Dana stood when the conference room door opened. She barely recognized Dr. Parker when he came in. He had changed from his surgical greens into an expensive, navy blue pinstripe suit.

"Ms. Renato, I don't know how to tell you this…"

Dana's knees buckled. Dr. Parker didn't have to finish. She already knew in her heart that Risa was gone.

Dr. Parker explained that Risa developed a blood clot, a pulmonary embolism, he called it, that lodged in her lung. He assured Dana that Risa didn't suffer. He said she probably wasn't aware anything was wrong. They tried everything they could, but nothing helped. She was pronounced dead at 11:15 a.m.

Dana remembered the pain, the actual searing pain she felt in her body at the loss of Risa. She felt like she had died, too. Wished she would have because there wasn't much sense in going on without her. Risa was her life.

Dana had walked around in a thick haze during the days that followed. She felt like her chest would explode with all the sorrow she carried in her heart. She existed under a heavy weight of guilt for not being with Risa when the end came. She knew she would never forgive herself for letting Risa die alone.

Their friends Julie and Cindy stayed with Dana while Risa's arrangements were made. Dana got up the nerve to call Risa's father to tell him of Risa's death, and he agreed to come for the funeral. Although money was no issue when it came to making Risa's arrangements, it angered Dana when Risa's father made it quite clear that he had no intention of contributing to the expenses.

Risa's father and mother had been divorced since Risa was three. She lived in Cleveland with her mom while her father and his girlfriend, now his wife, moved to Phoenix. Risa described her father as a guy who couldn't hold a job for more than six months. He liked his beer and other men's wives.

After Risa's mother had filed for divorce, she and Risa enjoyed a modest life in a tiny apartment on the west side of Cleveland. Her mother was working full time at Lakewood Hospital as a nurse's aide at night and attending Marymount School of Practical Nursing during the day.

One frosty winter morning, exhausted from the demands of work and school, Risa's mother fell asleep at the wheel of her GMC Gremlin and crashed into a utility pole. She died three days later from her injuries. Risa was fifteen.

After her mother's death, Risa was shipped to Phoenix. She hated leaving her home and friends in Cleveland, she hated Phoenix, and she hated living with her father and stepmother. She would never belong there. They made her feel like she was imposing on their lives.

Risa's father didn't know what to do with her. After all, the last time he saw her was the day she started preschool. Risa stuck it out, though, trying her best to stay out of her father's way and keeping mostly to herself. She did make some friends at school. During softball tryouts, she met Shannon, a half-Italian, half-Mexican beauty with silky black hair that almost reached her waist, and they became instant, inseparable friends. Because of Risa's home situation, she sought solace at Shannon's house, sometimes spending entire weekends there. They did all the things normal teenage girls did: shopping, going to parties, and talking on the phone for hours at a time. But one hot summer night after a Stevie Nicks concert, together in the front seat of Shannon's parents' Oldsmobile, they became more than friends.

Their attraction for each other caught both girls by surprise. Their lives seemed to open up to any and all possibilities. Through high school, they sneaked time together whenever they could. But in the fall of their senior year of high school, the girls' luck ran out. Risa's father came home unexpectedly one afternoon and caught Risa and Shannon together in a compromising position on Risa's twin bed.

By the look on her father's face, Risa was sure if he had a gun he would have shot them both dead. Her father was furious at the evidence of what his daughter had become, and all hell broke loose. He threw her out of the house and told her he never wanted to see her again. Risa gathered her things and moved in with Shannon's family until she graduated from McClintock High School.

The very next day after graduation, she and Shannon packed up Risa's old Cutlass and headed east. They applied and got accepted at Cleveland State University, and the two girls lived in the dorm together their first two years of college. However, by their sophomore year, their relationship started to fizzle, and by Christmas break, Shannon dropped out of school and moved back to Arizona.

Two years after her breakup with Shannon, Risa met Dana, and it was love at first sight. The funny thing was that neither of them was looking for love. Risa liked her independence. Of course, she dated but never anything more serious than a one-night stand or two.

Dana was still recovering from her most recent breakup and had vowed she would never again let anyone that close to her. At least until she met Risa. In her heart, Dana had known Risa was the one for life.

Now that life was ended.

Risa's father and stepmother came for Risa's funeral, which surprised Dana because they'd had no contact with Risa since the day they tossed her out. Dana offered them a place to stay at her and Risa's house, but they declined, opting for a room at the Econo Lodge just off the highway.

Dana made the funeral arrangements without any input from

Risa's father. Even though she asked only for his opinion, he wanted no part of it. It was a simple funeral service with the minister from the Unitarian church officiating. Most of their friends from the community and Risa's school colleagues attended. The most heart-wrenching part of the funeral was when Risa's kindergarten class walked in with pictures they had painted for her. Each child filed by her casket and laid a watercolor picture at her feet. There wasn't a dry eye in the place. Dana made sure that those pictures, as well as Risa's commitment ring, stayed in the casket with her.

After the funeral, Dana contended with the frustrating work of settling all the legal matters that come up when your spouse dies. Risa's dad returned to Phoenix, but not before he questioned Dana about Risa's assets, especially the house. This terrified Dana. Even though Risa and Dana had wills drawn up and left one hundred percent of everything they owned to each other, there were still some things, including their house, that could be contested by Risa's family because of Ohio's constitutional amendment banning gay marriage. The ban made unenforceable in Ohio courts any arrangement that approximates marriage. So because Dana and Risa had no marital rights in Ohio, half of the house was fair game for any of Risa's next of kin.

Dana sat on pins and needles every day waiting for the phone call from Risa's father inquiring further about this loophole in the law. The house meant a lot to Dana. They had put everything they owned into it. This is where she and Risa shared their lives. Dana didn't want to have to fight for the right to keep it. Especially with Risa's father, who had shunned his daughter because of who she was.

Sure enough, three weeks after Risa died, Dana received a certified letter in the mail from the law firm of Orlando, Reminger, and Cline stating that Mr. John Demarco was contesting his daughter's will and was suing Dana for Risa's portion of their home.

That was three years earlier, and the case was still grinding its way through the courts. Dana hated living in limbo. For three years, she had put off the work that needed to be done to the house, waiting for the lawsuit to play out. It didn't look like things would be concluding soon, and she was tired of living among torn wallboard and sawdust. She decided to finish the renovations. She had put her life on hold for too long all because of a greedy old man whose only contribution to Risa's life was having a small part in bringing her into the world.

The next hearing was in six weeks. She'd let her attorney worry about the details; she'd paid him well enough. She was mentally too exhausted to put forth any effort in the fight, and all the legal proceedings did was give her a headache.

She had come to Niles to write, her only solace in life now that Risa was gone. She would bury herself in her work for now and whatever happened, happened.

The early evening air was beginning to cool. Dana got up and shut the windows. She couldn't believe it was almost seven o'clock and she hadn't even unpacked yet. She turned on her laptop to check her e-mail. There was a message from her publisher asking if she made it to the apartment okay. Dana sent her a quick reply letting her know everything was fine, then she powered down the computer.

Even though it was past dinnertime, she wasn't really hungry, so she passed on eating. It was too late in the day to head over to the library to start her research. She'd start that the next day. Maybe it would take her mind off the other stuff that crowded her head.

Chapter Five

It had been two weeks since Tom's funeral. All the mourners and well-wishers had drifted away, returning to their lives. People who used to stop at the house every day now called periodically. Lindsay and Sara finished the school year without incident and were settling into their summer activities. Lindsay got rehired as a lifeguard at the city pool, and Sara helped coach pigtail softball.

It was time for Renee to go back to work. Mary, her supervisor, offered her full-time hours at the library, and Renee took it. She needed a steady income, especially since she was now the sole provider.

That numb period of grief, where she didn't feel anything, was wearing off. If she didn't do something, at least get out of the house for a few hours, she would lose her mind.

Returning to work at the library seemed more like a relief than a burden to her. Something about the quiet solitude there was comforting. Working in the library was challenging, and she had to adapt to change and unexpected events. She should be pretty good at handling unexpected events by now. After all, how much more unexpected can you get than having your husband die and leave you alone to raise two teenage daughters?

"Renee, how are you?" Mary stepped behind the mahogany circulation desk. Her voice, usually low and sweet, was even gentler, painfully gentle, as if she were afraid Renee was going to break into a million pieces.

"I'm good, Mary. Glad to be back," Renee said and meant it.

She shoved her purse into one of the wooden cubbyholes under the desk and perused the June calendar to see what events were coming up.

"Where would you like me to work today?" she asked.

"Do you feel like working the desk for a while? We've got a new shipment of books in the back that need checked in."

"Fine." Renee entered her account number and PIN into the computer system. Library patronage was light that day, not that unusual for the first part of June. Most people spent more time outside, enjoying the warm weather after enduring another harsh northeastern Ohio winter. That past winter had seemed especially long to Renee, being cooped up inside with Tom's illness and all. Yes, the winter had been harsh on everyone, some more so than others.

Dana had no problem finding the library. The largest building in Niles, it was a majestic edifice of gray marble with white marble columns out front. A statue of William McKinley stood in the center of a circular courtyard at the entrance.

The first thing she noticed upon entering was the strikingly attractive dark-haired woman behind the circulation desk. Her gaydar went off, and a long-forgotten but welcome twinge fluttered in her stomach.

As Dana approached the desk, she looked the woman over, noting how easy on the eyes she was in her floral skirt and navy blue top. The woman appeared to be having difficulty with the computer. She had a blue Bic pen tucked behind her ear as she tapped the keyboard, apparently unable to obtain the result she wanted. Dana couldn't help but smile.

"Excuse me," Dana said.

The woman looked up. Her frustration showed on her face. "Oh, hello."

"I'm visiting from out of town, and I need to get a library card." Dana found it hard to make eye contact, afraid the woman might read what was going through her mind.

"I can help you with that." The woman turned from the computer and rummaged through one of the desk drawers. She pulled out a pink application card and slid it across the polished wooden surface of the desk.

"I need to see some ID for verification," she said. "Something with your name and address on it."

Dana reached into her back pocket and produced a black leather wallet. She flipped it open, took out her Ohio driver's license, and laid it on the desk.

"Do you have a pen?" Dana asked. "I don't seem to have one on me." She patted her front and back pockets.

Renee handed her a pen. She noticed that the visitor's hands were lean yet strong and that she wore a simple gold wedding band on her right ring finger. How odd, wearing her wedding band on her right hand. Renee looked down at her own hand and realized that she still wore her wedding band. Wasn't this a lie? Now that Tom was dead, her wearing this ring meant nothing, right? Tears welled in her eyes.

"Are you okay?" Dana asked. Her ice blue eyes were soft with concern.

Renee nodded. "My first day back to work…" She fumbled under the desk for a Kleenex. The box was empty so she had to settle for a C-fold paper towel. She dabbed at her eyes with it.

"I see." Dana continued filling out the registration form.

As Renee watched her, she couldn't help thinking what a handsomely attractive woman this stranger was. She had a thin athletic build with salt and pepper hair—more salt than pepper—cut short, and piercing blue eyes. She reminded Renee of a softer version of Anderson Cooper, the guy from CNN whose mother was Gloria Vanderbilt.

The woman completed the form and pushed it and the pen over to Renee. Renee looked the form over for completeness and pulled a plastic library card from the file. "Dana Renato. That name sounds familiar. Are you related to any of the Renatos from Girard?"

Dana shook her head. "Afraid not."

"Hi anyway, Dana, and welcome to Niles. My name's Renee Del Fino." They shook hands.

"I see you've listed your permanent address as Cleveland. That seems like a long way to travel to go to the library."

"I'm renting a small apartment here for a few months. My publisher sent me down here to do some research on a new novel."

"A writer, how nice." Renee made an effort to hide her skepticism. Lots of people came into the library claiming to be writers but only worked on novels or books that never got published or even finished for that matter.

Renee handed Dana her new library card. "Here you go. What are you working on?"

Dana took the card and slid it into the back pocket of her jeans. "I'm working on my fourth book about organized crime. My publisher said this area has a fertile history of it. I couldn't pass up the opportunity to come here to do some research."

Then it came to Renee. "Dana Renato. Hey, you wrote *Omega, Alpha* and that other book, what was it called? Oh, yes, *Little Italy*. My husband's a big fan of your books, especially *Omega*."

Husband? Boy is my gaydar off. Figures the first woman I'm attracted to in years ends up being straight and married. Dana felt the heat of embarrassment slide up her face as she stood before Renee. "Thank you," she said. "I'm glad he enjoyed it. It's one of my favorites, as well."

"My husband isn't much of a book reader, either, reads the sports page mostly, but he really loves your books. He'd die if he knew…" Renee suddenly realized what she had said. She was talking about Tom in the present tense, like he was still here, still okay, not dead. She had fought to keep her grief contained behind an emotional firewall, but it started to spring a leak. Tears streamed down her face, and her lower lip trembled.

"Are you all right?" Dana reached out and touched Renee's hand. Dana's hand was cool, but the gesture was warm.

Renee looked up, finding it difficult to meet Dana's piercing gaze. "My husband just died. Two weeks ago," Renee blurted out, and now the tears came hard.

"Oh…Oh, my…I'm so sorry," Dana said. "I'm sorry for your loss."

Renee pulled two more C-fold paper towels out from under the desk. She wiped her eyes, smearing her mascara, and blew her nose. "Sorry," she said. "I guess I'm not ready to be out in public yet."

"No, don't apologize. That's a hard thing…losing your husband. Really, it's okay," Dana said.

Renee couldn't believe she was falling to pieces in front of this woman she hardly knew. Her face burned with embarrassment. Why now? Why here? She had been holding up so well at home.

"Really, I've got to get a grip." She tossed the paper towels into the wastebasket behind the desk.

"Grieving is a difficult thing," Dana said. She met Renee's gaze. Renee saw something there. Like she knew. Like she'd been there, too.

Renee took a deep breath and tried to pull herself together. She tried to conjure up professional Renee. The Renee who was efficient and levelheaded.

"Okay, now that we've got you signed up, is there anything else I can help you with?"

"Is there a way I can access old articles from some of the local papers?" Dana asked.

"There's a small desk over there, next to the microfiche reader. If you let me know what years you need, I can pull them from the archive."

"Thanks, I appreciate that." Dana slung her backpack over her shoulder and went to the desk Renee had pointed out. She unloaded her silver Dell laptop and several spiral notebooks. After booting up the laptop, she flipped through one of the notebooks while the computer warmed up.

She worked quietly for several hours, stopping only long enough to take a bathroom break.

Renee found that keeping her mind busy kept the overwhelming grief at bay, so she busied herself by reshelving the contents of the book-drop box and making phone calls to let patrons know their reserved books were in. She glanced over in Dana's direction, curious about what progress she was making. Curious about her in general.

Dana appeared at the desk again. "Do you have microfiche available for January 1923?"

"I'll check for you." Renee went downstairs to the archives.

The 1923 file box was covered with dust and smelled moldy. She spritzed it with an orange-scented antibacterial cleaner and wiped it off with a paper towel.

"Thanks." Dana took the box from her. "Can you show me how to load these? I've never done it on this type of machine."

Dana followed Renee to the microfiche reader. Renee sat at the small desk, loaded the first fiche into the slot, and turned on the bulb. Dana stood behind her and watched as Renee maneuvered the gears moving the fiche backward and forward.

"See, just turn this wheel. It will scroll front and back through the issues."

Dana was standing so close that Renee could smell her perfume. Although, it was more like a man's cologne, like Nautica or Hugo Boss. It smelled good.

"You should be all set." Renee stood so Dana could sit in the wooden chair at the small reader desk.

"Thanks so much," Dana said and continued with her research.

Close to closing time, Renee noticed that Dana was the only patron left in the library. She still hunkered over the microfiche reader, viewing slide after slide. Almost as though she sensed Renee looking at her, Dana looked up and smiled.

Renee smiled back. "We'll be closing in a few minutes," she said, trying to ignore the fluttering in the pit of her stomach.

"Oh, my, I lost track of time." Dana packed up her stuff, flipped the switch off on the microfiche reader, and returned the box of microfiche to the desk. "You doing better?"

Renee nodded. "Thanks, I'm fine."

"I know what it's like to lose a spouse," Dana said softly. "Three years ago, I lost my life partner, Risa, to breast cancer."

"I'm so sorry."

"So I know what you're going through," Dana said. "All I can say is that it does get better with time. The pain never really goes away, it just gets to the point where everyday life numbs it and makes it not hurt so much."

Renee looked at Dana. She seemed to come from a different place than Renee but had experienced the same feelings, the same loss Renee had experienced. She guessed grief wasn't prejudiced and no one was immune to its pain.

"If you'd like to talk sometime," Dana said, "maybe we can

go for coffee or something." She opened her wallet and took out a white linen business card. "You can catch me at this number." She scribbled her cell phone number on the back and handed the card to Renee. Renee took the card and read: Dana Renato, Writer, Author, and Journalist. "You're a journalist, too?"

"Used to be. I worked for *The Plain Dealer*. Got the job right out of college."

"Where did you go to college?"

"Cleveland State. That's where Risa and I met. I majored in journalism, and she majored in elementary education. She taught kindergarten."

"How long were you together?" Renee hoped she wasn't being too forward. After all, she hardly knew Dana and felt this was pretty intimate for two strangers to be discussing.

"Fifteen years. She was the love of my life." Dana glanced away, as though feeling uncomfortable being so candid.

She looked back at Renee and leaned an elbow on the desk. "How long were you married?"

"Tom and I were married for seventeen years."

"Any kids?"

"Two. Two girls. Lindsay's sixteen and Sara's fourteen."

Dana raised her eyebrows. "Teenagers? You don't look old enough to be the mom of two teenagers."

Renee felt her face flush. "Tom and I got married a year after we graduated from high school. Lindsay came along before our first anniversary, then Sara two years later."

"How are they doing with the loss of their dad?" Dana looked concerned. "That time in your life is difficult as it is. Losing a parent can make it devastating."

"They seem to be holding up pretty well. Better than me some days."

"Good. Kids are pretty resilient, Risa always used to say."

"I hope so." Renee stood and straightened her skirt.

"Oh, my gosh, it's past five thirty," Dana said. "Sorry to keep you past your quitting time."

"Don't apologize. I enjoyed talking to you. Are you having any luck with your research?"

"Yes. I'm finding a lot of great stuff here. I'll be back tomorrow."

"I'm working nine to three tomorrow," Renee said. "See you then."

Dana walked through the glass doors and disappeared into the early summer evening. Renee packed up her things, shut down the computer system, and flicked off the lights. She locked the front door and pulled on the safety bar to make sure it was secure. Then she headed home for another long empty evening and another lonely night.

Chapter Six

Renee pushed through the front door with her purse and book satchel slung over her shoulder and the day's mail tucked under her arm. Sara, Lindsay, and Justin sat on the couch watching *Dr. Phil.*

"Hi, kids, how was your day?" she asked as she walked through the room.

"Okay." Sara got up from the couch and followed Renee into the kitchen.

Renee deposited the load she was carrying on the kitchen table.

Sara opened the refrigerator and peered inside. "What's for dinner?"

Renee wasn't in the mood to cook. She wasn't in the mood to do anything except sit and vegetate, but she needed to buck up and take care of her family. The food left over from the funeral had run out, so she rummaged around in the freezer looking for a pack of frozen meat or something to throw together that somewhat resembled a home-cooked meal. She found a package of ground beef. Okay, that was a start.

"How about we have hamburgers on the grill?" She held up the block of frozen meat.

"Who's going to cook them?" Sara asked.

"I am."

"But you've never grilled before. Daddy always cooked on the grill."

"I know, but I can do it. It can't be that hard, can it?"

"I guess not." Sara opened the bread box on the counter. "We don't have any buns."

"So we'll eat them without the buns," Renee said. "Anyway, too much bread isn't good for you. Too many carbs, right?"

Sara shrugged, closed the lid on the breadbox, and walked back into the living room. Renee put the frozen meat in the microwave, closed the door, and pressed out five minutes. The microwave dinged just as Lindsay came into the kitchen.

"What's for dinner?"

"Hamburgers on the grill."

"Who's going to cook them?"

"I am!" Renee snapped.

"Can Justin stay for dinner?"

"Sure. Hope he likes hamburgers without the bun," Renee said.

"He's not picky. He'll eat anything," Lindsay said. "Do you have anything to go with the hamburgers? Like French fries or something?"

"I'm sure I can scare something up." Renee opened the freezer door and looked for a side dish. She found a frost-covered red bag of Ore-Ida steak fries lurking under a package of frozen venison. She pulled out the bag, sliced it open with a pair of kitchen scissors, and dumped the frozen potatoes on a cookie sheet. She took the defrosted package of ground beef outside and lifted the cover off the grill. Not surprisingly, the cover was dirty and dusty—after all, no one had used it since Labor Day of the previous year. The last person to use it was Tom.

She found a half-full bag of charcoal briquettes and dumped them into the bottom of the black Weber grill. She pulled the trigger on a long, fire-starter gadget Tom had used to light the grill. A blue and yellow flame emerged on the end of it, and she touched the flame to the charcoal, but it didn't light. What the hell? She stuffed strips of newspaper between the briquettes and lit them, but the charcoal still wouldn't catch. After twenty minutes of no success, she threw the fire starter into the grill and slammed the lid closed. She picked up the bloody, dripping package of hamburger, stomped back into the house, and tossed the meat into the garbage can.

"Come on, girls, we're going out for dinner," she yelled from the kitchen.

The cookie sheet with the frozen fries was still on the counter. She yanked it up and threw it into the sink. Frozen fries flew everywhere.

"Mom, are you okay?" Lindsay asked.

"Fine," Renee said through clenched teeth. "I can't even make a simple meal anymore, but I'm fine." She took a deep breath. "Where would you guys like to go for dinner?"

In unison, her daughters replied, "McDonald's."

"Wonderful," she said. "I could use a Happy Meal right about now."

"Can Justin come?" Lindsay asked. "He's starving."

"Sure, why not?" Renee snatched the car keys off the kitchen table.

They piled into the car. Sara sat up front with Renee, and Justin and Lindsay sat in the back. The kids chatted away as Sara changed stations on the radio looking for some hip-hop or head-banger station. Renee longed for the days when the girls were younger and listened to Radio Disney.

While they sat at a red light, Renee glanced into the rearview mirror and caught a glimpse of Justin and Lindsay in the backseat holding hands. Oh, my God, Renee thought as she pulled into the McDonald's parking lot. Apparently, there was more to Justin and Lindsay's friendship

Lindsay and Justin got out of the car and walked ahead of Sara and Renee. Renee pulled Sara aside.

"How long has this been going on?"

"What?" Sara said, looking confused.

"Lindsay and Justin…they were holding hands in the backseat. How long has that been going on?"

Sara shrugged. "I don't know. Awhile. Before Daddy died, I think. I'm not sure. Lindsay doesn't tell me much."

"Is that all they do when I'm not home…you know, just hold hands?" Renee asked.

"Mom!" Sara whined and ran inside the restaurant, leaving Renee behind.

She caught up to the kids at the counter. They had already placed their orders and were waiting for her. Renee got a Happy

Meal and a Diet Coke and paid for all of them. She watched Lindsay and Justin at the table, looking for signs of just how intimate their relationship actually was. Even with a polyurethane statue of the Hamburglar standing behind him, she saw Justin in an entirely different light. He was a lanky sixteen-year-old with sinewy muscled arms and fiery Italian looks that made even Renee's heart skip a beat. In the late afternoon sunlight, it appeared he shaved almost on a regular basis. If he was shaving regularly, then other things were happening on a regular basis, as well.

Renee suddenly felt the need to talk to Lindsay. Oh, they had had "the talk" when Lindsay was ten and Renee had to go to Lindsay's school to watch the film about why after a certain age, girls could only go swimming three weeks out of the month. But now she felt an urgent need to talk to her daughter again and to protect her before she got into something she wouldn't be able to get herself out of. She knew that kids Lindsay's and Justin's age didn't think twice when it came to having sex. They felt invincible, and who wouldn't with all those hormones coursing through their veins? Renee knew all too well because she had eagerly relinquished her virginity to Tom when they were sixteen.

Suddenly, she wasn't hungry anymore. The kids ate while she stared out the large window. In her mind, she saw visions of a very pregnant Lindsay waddling around in one of the row houses next to the school, with two little ones running around in diapers while her class graduated without her.

Lindsay broke her reverie. "Mom, if you're not going to eat your burger, can Justin have it?"

"No, I'm going to take it home." She wrapped up the burger in the paper and tucked it into her purse. She handed Lindsay a five-dollar bill. "Here, if he's still hungry, get him something else to eat." She hugged her purse to her stomach.

When they got home, Justin left and Lindsay went up to her room. Sara sat on the couch to watch TV, and Renee decided to clean up the kitchen. It would give her time to rehearse in her head what she would say to Lindsay.

Being in a relationship and having sex can be intense at any age, she reasoned. Although the experience can be one you'll never forget, the consequences can be devastating. Not only from the potential of STDs or an unwanted pregnancy, but also from the devastation that can occur when the relationship ends.

Kids Lindsay's age were under a lot of pressure to have sex. Those pressures could take a lot of forms. Some kids caved in hopes of being popular. Some kids did it to get their friends off their backs, to put a stop to the teasing about not having sex, or to prove to themselves and their friends that they were normal. This was the most difficult pressure of all.

The kitchen finally looked presentable again. Renee went into the living room to check on Sara and found her curled up sound asleep on the couch. She thought about picking her up and carrying her to bed, but then thought better of it. Sara was almost as tall as Renee and outweighed her by ten pounds. If Tom were here, he'd pick Sara up like she was a kitten, tuck her in his arm, and carry her off to bed without breaking a sweat. Renee clicked off the TV and covered Sara with the afghan her mother had crocheted when the girls were little. Then she headed upstairs to check on Lindsay.

A light shone under the crack of Lindsay's closed door. Renee took a deep cleansing breath and tapped on the wood surface just below the "Keep Out—This Means You!" sign. "Linz, are you awake?"

She turned the doorknob and let herself into the room. Lindsay lay on her bed reading a dog-eared copy of *A Tale of Two Cities*.

"Whatcha doin'?" Renee walked in and sat on the bed next to her daughter.

"Just reading. I have to finish this for Advanced Lit before summer school starts next week. I want to get it out of the way so I can take Honors English when regular classes start again."

"I'm proud of you, Linz. You and Sara have done so well with school, even going through all the stuff with your dad." Renee kissed her forehead.

She couldn't believe how much Lindsay had grown up. She was almost a head taller than Renee already, with long, thin, muscled legs and shiny, shoulder-length chestnut hair. Her hands that once resembled two tiny starfish were now long and slender with perfectly manicured nails.

"So…Justin…You guys have been spending a lot of time together," Renee said.

Lindsay looked up from her book.

"Anything you want to tell me?" Renee tried a tactic her mother had used on her when she was Lindsay's age whenever she wanted information that Renee could be hiding from her.

Lindsay shook her head and looked back down at her book.

"I saw you two holding hands in the car tonight. How long have you and Justin been more than just friends?"

Stains of scarlet appeared on Lindsay's cheeks, and Renee knew she had hit a sensitive area.

"Awhile," Lindsay said, never looking up from her book.

"So how long is 'awhile'?"

"Since April, I guess. Justin asked me to go to the spring fling dance. I told him I couldn't go because Daddy was so sick. So he asked me to be his girlfriend instead. I told him yes."

Renee's heart felt heavy for her daughter. She too had to put her life on hold during Tom's illness. She felt terrible that Lindsay missed the dance. She tried to think back to April and what was going on in their lives. Tom was in the hospital for a couple of weeks, she recalled. It was hard to remember; so much of it was a blur.

"So how serious is your relationship with Justin?"

"What do you mean by serious?"

"Have you and Justin…"

"Mom!" Lindsay screeched. "No."

"I had to ask. I want you to be okay," Renee said. "I want you to be safe."

Lindsay buried her head in her book.

"Lindsay, promise me that if your relationship with Justin gets to that point that you'll come to me first, okay?"

Lindsay nodded but didn't meet Renee's gaze.

"We can make an appointment with Dr. Michaels if you want. Do we need to make an appointment now?"

Lindsay shook her head. "No, Mom. I don't need to go on the pill." Renee's heart lightened a little with relief.

"Okay, but if you ever need to…"

"I know. I'll let you know." A muscle twitched in Lindsay's cheek.

"Thank you." Renee kissed her on top of her head. "You're a smart girl. I know you'll do the right thing."

Lindsay nodded.

Renee left the room and closed the door behind her, feeling a little better about Lindsay and her relationship with Justin.

Back downstairs, Sara was still sound asleep on the couch. Renee looked at her and couldn't help wondering when she would be having the same conversation about boys and sex with her that she'd just had with Lindsay.

Renee went into the kitchen and reached into the cupboard above the refrigerator for the bottle of Amaretto. She poured herself a drink, hung her head, and silently cursed Tom for leaving her here to deal with all this alone. She tossed back the shot and poured herself a double.

Chapter Seven

Since school let out, Lindsay and Sara had kept busy. They went swimming at the pool where Lindsay worked as a lifeguard, played soccer, and took part in other summer activities with their friends. It was good to see them getting on with their lives. It proved they were resilient, just like Dana had said. Renee, on the other hand, not so much.

While Lindsay and Sara thrived on being out and about with their friends, Renee wanted to curl up in a ball and disappear. Just getting up in the morning was an effort, let alone socializing. She was never much of a social butterfly; it took a while for her to feel comfortable around strangers. Now with the added baggage of being the grieving widow, it seemed even more difficult.

Her married friends, the couples she and Tom used to hang out with, seemed to shy away from her. As silly as it might sound, Renee almost felt like they considered her a threat to their marriages. She would occasionally go out for coffee with one of the wives, but she was never invited to go out with the group, like she did when Tom was alive.

Tom was her social outlet. He loved being around people and was usually the life of the party. But now that was over. Two weeks after Tom died, she attended a few graduation parties that she had received invitations to. She thought being around her friends would be a comfort, but it wasn't. She felt so terribly out of place. She wasn't part of Tom and Renee anymore; she was just Renee alone. It was awful.

Work had helped. At least it seemed to occupy her mind for a while. It was a more controlled social environment, like there was a thin wall still up, still there for protection but not too thick so as to isolate. Yes, work was what she needed. If anything, it gave her a reason to get out of bed every day. It also gave her a chance to see Dana.

Although Renee wasn't one to make friends quickly, she and Dana got on pretty well, pretty fast. Dana was easy to talk to and didn't feel threatened by Renee's widowhood. Dana came to the library practically every day, including Saturday and Sunday afternoons, and stayed until closing each evening. Renee enjoyed seeing her and was intrigued by the work she was doing.

When things were slow at the library, Renee would pour two coffees, and she and Dana would sit and talk about anything and everything. Dana's easy way was comforting to Renee. She liked to look over at the microfiche desk and watch Dana work. At times, she seemed so totally engrossed in what she was doing, Renee would have to remind her that the library would be closing soon. That day was no exception.

"Dana, closing time in fifteen minutes," Renee said as she reshelved a couple of books in the pre-teen section.

Dana looked up and smiled. "Thanks for the heads-up," she said as she powered down her computer and slid her notebooks into her backpack.

Renee checked out the last patron and put the backup tape into the library's server. Dana appeared at the desk, packed up and ready to go.

"So what kind of plans do you have for the Fourth?" Dana asked.

"Nothing special, really. My daughters are going out to the lake with their friends and their families."

"What about you? Aren't you going out to the lake, too? It's supposed to be a great day for it."

"Don't feel much like…you know." Renee wrinkled her nose in distaste.

Dana nodded. Her intelligent blue eyes shimmered.

"Anyway," Renee said, "I was just planning on staying home and catching up on some things around the house. There's a ton of work outside that has needed done for a long time. With Tom's illness, we never got around to it."

"Sometimes that mindless work is very therapeutic," Dana said. "After Risa died, I spent a lot of time outside doing manual labor. I painted our deck, cleaned out the garage, and redid the landscape all in about a month's time."

Renee grabbed her purse from the bottom shelf of the reference desk and searched for her keys. "Sounds like you got a lot accomplished." She pulled the key ring free of her purse. "I don't think I'll be so productive. I hate those types of chores, and I'm not very handy."

Dana laughed. "I love working outside." She slung her backpack over her shoulder. "I kind of miss it. I'm living in a cramped little apartment while I'm here."

Renee paused for a moment. "I don't want to impose on you, but if you don't have plans for the Fourth, would you be interested in coming over and giving me a hand?" Renee and Dana walked toward double glass doors. "When it comes to outside work, I'm clueless. I could use all the help I can get."

"Sure, I'd love to," Dana said. "Anyway, I could use a break from all this paperwork. I think if I look at another microfiche, I'm going to go blind." A broad smile broke across her face.

"Great." Renee pulled out a crumpled piece of paper, an old shopping list, from her purse and jotted down her address and phone number on the back. "Here's my address. Why don't you come by around eleven before it gets too hot out, so we're not working in the sweltering heat?"

"Eleven sounds fine. See you tomorrow." Dana slipped Renee's address into the pocket of her oxford shirt. They said their goodbyes as Renee locked the doors. As she watched Dana walk to her car, Renee thought she had never met anyone like her. She knew from their conversations that Dana was a lesbian, but she wasn't what Renee had been taught a lesbian was. Dana wasn't scary or perverse or strange. Yes, she wore her hair short and no makeup, but to be honest, she didn't need makeup. Dana had beautiful skin. Her short gray hair and the shadow of crow's feet at the corners of her ice blue eyes gave her a distinguished look.

She was easy to talk to, and they seemed to have a lot in

common, actually more in common than not. So what was this uneasiness that stirred deep inside her? Probably nothing. She stuck the key in the ignition, the car rumbled to life, and she headed home.

When she got there, she was greeted by a note on the kitchen table from Lindsay. It said that she and Sara went to a friend's house for a swim party and that they would be home at nine o'clock. Renee vaguely remembered Linz asking her about the party and if she and Sara could go. She must have said it was okay.

When the girls weren't home, the house was hauntingly quiet. All the fears and uncertainties she had pushed down throughout the day came bubbling to the surface again, where she would have to deal with them. She wished she could call somebody. Somebody who could take her away from all this loneliness. But there was no one.

She thought of Annie again, but Renee knew that would never happen. She hadn't seen nor heard from Annie in almost twenty years. Even after all this time, she still missed her. She missed how Annie could always make her laugh and her levelheadedness. If Annie were here, she would calmly tell Renee, yes, this is a bad thing that happened to you, but you are strong and will get through it. She would also have told her she would be there for her. Because Annie always was there for her—until Renee turned her away.

Renee laid her purse and book satchel on the table. She sat at the kitchen table and closed her eyes, feeling utterly miserable. What if she had gone with Annie when she asked? What if she hadn't stayed and married Tom? Her life would be totally different now. Renee shook her head as if that would make all the regrets in her life go away. Searching for comfort, she got up and reached into the cupboard above the refrigerator for the bottle of Amaretto and poured herself some dinner.

Chapter Eight

Fourth of July morning arrived sunny, warm, and bright. Lindsay and Sara came down for breakfast, both of them fresh-faced, hair tied in ponytails, and backpacks ready for their trip to the lake.

"Do you guys have enough sunscreen packed?" Renee asked as Lindsay reached into the cupboard for the box of Special K.

"Yes, Mom."

"How about a sweatshirt for later? You know it cools down at the lake after the sun goes down."

"We got them," Sara said. "Don't worry, we'll be okay."

"Yeah," Lindsay said, "it's not like we're going away for a month or anything."

"I know," Renee said. "I know you'll be fine."

The girls finished their breakfast and went upstairs to brush their teeth. A few minutes later, there was a knock at the back door.

"Hi, Mrs. Del Fino," Justin said. "Are Lindsay and Sara ready to go?"

"Come on in, Justin," Renee said coolly and stepped to the side to let him enter. She couldn't help wondering just how far this boy had gotten with her daughter. First base? Second base? Even though Renee had known this kid a short time, she couldn't get past the thought that he was now a threat to her daughter's virtue.

"Lindsay, Sara…Justin's here," she called out.

"Coming," Lindsay said. Seconds later, she bounded down the steps with Sara close behind her.

"Hi, Justin." Lindsay's smile was big and wide.

"Hey, Linz," Justin said shyly.

"Okay, you girls all set?" Renee asked.

They nodded. Renee went to her purse and pulled out two twenty-dollar bills and handed one to each girl.

"Thanks, Mom," they said.

She kissed each girl on the head. "Have a good time. I love you."

"Love you, too," they said.

Sara and Lindsay followed Justin out the back door and down the driveway to the awaiting car with a man Renee did not recognize behind the wheel. Justin opened the door, and Sara and Lindsay climbed into the backseat. Renee suddenly realized that she didn't know much about Justin and his family. She walked over to the driver's side door and introduced herself.

"Hi, I'm Renee, Lindsay and Sara's mom."

"Hi, I'm David, a friend of Justin and his mom." He smiled at Renee and extended his hand to her. Renee took it.

"I'll have them home by eleven. Is that okay?" David asked.

"That's fine. Thanks for inviting them," she said. David was a handsome man, about Renee's age or maybe even younger. He had the same dark brown hair and eyes as Justin, and Renee thought that maybe he was Justin's father. But no, that couldn't be right because he introduced himself as a friend. Renee finally came to the conclusion that Justin's parents must be divorced and that Justin's mom was dating this guy.

The car pulled away, and suddenly, Renee was all alone again. She busied herself by finishing up the breakfast dishes and made a list of all the things she needed to get done that day.

At eleven sharp, the front doorbell rang.

"Hello, Dana." Renee stepped aside, motioning for her to come in.

"Wow, Renee, you have a beautiful home," Dana said, looking around and taking in the view. The living room felt warm and cozy as the late morning sunlight filtered in through the large picture window.

"Thank you." They headed to the kitchen. "Would you like some coffee or something before we get started?"

"No, thanks. I already had two cups this morning. If I have any more caffeine, I'm afraid my heart will beat out of my chest."

They both laughed.

"So what needs done?" Dana asked. She was dressed in a navy blue Boston Marathon T-shirt and khaki cargo shorts that exposed lean muscular legs. She didn't look like she was anywhere near forty, and she had definitely come prepared to work. She even brought her own toolbox.

"I was going to start with the outside windows," Renee said. "There's an extension ladder in the garage. I might need your help getting it out. Tom used to—"

"No problem," Dana interrupted. "Just show me the way."

They walked out to the garage, which needed a good sweeping and hosing out. Renee showed Dana where the extension ladder was. Dana reached up and easily pulled it down from the two C-hooks Tom had it secured to. Renee was amazed at how strong Dana was, being such a slender woman.

"Where do you want it?" Dana swung the metal ladder around and tucked it under her arm.

"I'll start out front." Renee led her to the front porch. Dana released the latches on the ladder and had it set up in no time.

"That would have taken me half an hour to figure out," Renee said. "How'd you learn to do all this?"

"I have three brothers, all older. They taught me a lot about fixing things."

"That's great." Renee grabbed her bottle of Windex and a roll of paper towels.

"I can do these," Dana said, "if you'd like to get started on something else."

"Okay." Renee handed her the Windex and paper towels.

"I should be all right on the lower windows," Dana said, "but I might need you to hold the ladder while I do the ones on the second floor."

"Just holler when you need me." Renee went up onto the porch and swept out the leaves, dust, and dirt that had accumulated behind the wicker porch furniture over the winter and spring. After sweeping, she hosed off the porch.

"Renee, can you give me a hand?" Dana called from her perch.

Renee shut off the water and stood at the bottom of the ladder.

"Just hold it steady," Dana said, "until I get these top windows done." Renee held both sides of the metal ladder and placed one foot on the bottom rung as Dana climbed higher. "How're you doing down there?" Dana called out.

"Okay."

Dana was almost to the top. Her calf muscles strained as she stretched to wash the second-story windows. She shifted her weight and reached over to the right to get a stubborn area on one of the windows.

When Dana lifted her leg to keep her balance, Renee couldn't help but notice that she could see straight up Dana's cargo shorts. Renee felt her face flush, and she quickly averted her gaze.

"All done," Dana said as she descended the ladder. "What's next?"

"Some yard work, I think."

Dana returned the ladder to its storage place, and Renee got the electric trimmer. They headed to the backyard where Dana trimmed the boxwood and rose bushes while Renee raked up the trimmings and the old leaves, filling at least ten lawn and leaf bags. Renee swept and hosed out the garage, and Dana cleaned out the gutters, a job Renee knew Tom always hated and put off until it was winter again and too cold to do it.

The yard was looking great, she thought, as she hosed off the back patio and wiped down the patio furniture. By five o'clock, they had it all done. Dana even fixed the toilet in the guest bathroom that ran all the time unless you jiggled the handle.

"Whew, what a day." Renee sat next to Dana on the front porch step and handed her a glass of iced tea. Dana's face glowed from the heat and humidity. Droplets of sweat glistened in the sunlight as they clung to the short hair at the back of her neck. She took a big gulp of tea.

"Mmm...that's good." She took another big swallow.

"I can't tell you how much I appreciate you coming over here and doing all this," Renee said.

"No problem. I enjoy doing this kind of work. I sit in front of a computer all day, so any chance to get some fresh air is a break for me."

"I don't know about you, but I'm getting pretty hungry," Renee said. "I could make us something to eat if you'd like, but I'll need to run to the grocery store first. Got a hankering for anything?"

"Hankering?" Dana laughed.

"What's so funny?"

"I haven't heard that word in a long time. I never thought I'd hear it coming from someone as sophisticated as you."

"Sophisticated? Are you crazy? I'm about as sophisticated as a pig in mud."

"It just struck me as funny hearing you say that. Where did it come from?"

Renee thought for a moment. Then it came to her. "Tom used to say it. When we were going out to eat or deciding on what to make for dinner, he'd ask me what I had a hankering for. I guess it just stuck with me."

"I think it's great," Dana said. "So what do you have a hankering for? My car's behind yours, so I could do the grocery store run."

"You know, I haven't had a good steak in a while," Renee said. "But our grill seems to be on the fritz. I tried to cook the kids some burgers on it a few weeks ago but couldn't get the damn thing to light."

"Is it a gas grill?"

"No, charcoal."

"I can take a look at it if you like."

Renee took the lid off the grill. The fire starter thing and charcoal still lay where she had left them weeks before. She showed Dana that the charcoal had barely burned, even where she stuffed the newspaper. Nothing had seemed to work.

"Here, let me try." Dana looked around the patio. "Where's the lighter fluid?"

"Lighter fluid?"

"Yes, this is just plain charcoal. You need lighter fluid to get it to light," Dana said. A slow grin spread over her face.

"Oh, my God, I feel like such an idiot," Renee said.

They both burst out laughing.

"Let me wash my face and hands," Dana said, "and I'll run to the store and get what we need for dinner. I'll pick up some lighter fluid, too. That okay with you?"

"That's fine."

After Dana hit the bathroom and set out for the grocery store, Renee went upstairs to get cleaned up. Her muscles ached and she was grimy and sweaty. Twigs from the trimmed bushes stuck in her hair, but she hadn't felt this good in a long time. Dana was right about manual labor being therapeutic. She had to peel her sweat-soaked T-shirt off her back. She turned the shower on and stepped in. The pulsating warm water felt good on her sore shoulders and back. Her mind wandered as she luxuriated in the wonderfully soothing feeling, and suddenly, Annie came to mind again. Renee shook the thoughts from her head; they had no business cropping up now or ever. That was a part of her life she had tucked safely away.

After her shower, she slathered cocoa butter cream onto her sunburned arms and legs, dressed quickly in a clean T-shirt and pair of shorts, and headed downstairs. While waiting for Dana, she set the kitchen table with two places.

Dana returned with two armloads of groceries. She pulled out two Porterhouse steaks, two huge Idaho potatoes for baking, and lettuce and other fixings for a salad.

"You've brought us a feast." Renee helped Dana unload the bags. Also among the groceries was a small can of lighter fluid.

"I'll get the fire started." Dana picked up the container of lighter fluid.

"Great, I'll make the salad and get the potatoes ready."

Dana headed out back as Renee tore Boston lettuce leaves and put them in the glass salad bowl. This felt strangely familiar, but Renee couldn't ignore the feelings of guilt that hung over her. Guilty of what, she didn't know.

Dana had no trouble getting the fire started, and in less than half an hour, they sat down to a delicious meal. It was probably the most Renee had eaten in months. They cleaned up after dinner,

Renee made some more iced tea, and they sat on the back patio and enjoyed a cool drink. As the sun sank below the horizon, the evening air cooled. The light breeze felt good on Renee's sunburned skin.

"I bet you and your husband had a wonderful life here," Dana said, breaking the silence.

"Yes, we did." A lump formed in Renee's throat. "But I never thought I'd be a widow at thirty-six. I always assumed I would go before Tom. He was so strong and healthy."

"I know what you mean. Cancer's terrible. It ruins so many lives and wrecks so many dreams," Dana said.

"Yes, you're right. It sure did wreck our dreams. My dreams, my daughters' dreams…what an awful thing."

Crickets chirped and fireflies began to blink their tiny golden lights, adding to the peaceful summer evening.

"So tell me about you. About your life with Risa," Renee said.

Dana sat forward in her chair and looked out at the spacious backyard. She wondered just how much she should reveal. She'd never spoken about that part of her life to anyone who wasn't gay. She took a sip of iced tea and held her half-empty glass between both hands. "Risa was the best. I fell in love with her the minute I laid eyes on her."

"You said you were together for fifteen years. That's a long time." Renee sounded amazed. "I didn't think gay relationships lasted more than a few years."

"Why would you think that?"

"Oh, I don't know…I guess I just got that impression somewhere." Sensing that she had struck a nerve, Renee instantly regretted the comment.

Dana didn't know what to say. Did Renee think that because she was a lesbian her relationship with Risa was less real? Did she think that losing Risa meant less to her or was less painful than what Renee went through? Dana felt sad. In her gut, she knew opening up to Renee was a mistake. Why hadn't she listened to her gut?

Dana drank the rest of her iced tea and stood to leave. "It's getting late. I better be going."

"Wait, Dana. Don't leave," Renee blurted out. "I'm sorry if I said anything to offend you. I have to be honest with you. I don't know any gay people. So I don't know anything about your lifestyle." She raised a hand and beckoned toward a chair. "Please sit. Stay a little longer. Tell me about you and Risa. What was it like?"

Reluctant to be impolite, Dana sat back down in the webbed lawn chair. "Risa and I met in college and hit it off from the first day we met. She was a teacher. She taught kindergarten before she got sick."

"She had breast cancer, right?" Renee asked.

"Yes, inflammatory breast cancer."

"What's that? I thought breast cancer was breast cancer." Renee clasped her hands and leaned forward.

"Inflammatory's the worst kind. It's impossible to treat. Even with the expert care she got at University Hospital in Cleveland, she died twenty-two months after being diagnosed. Some days, I miss her so much…more than I could ever tell anybody. Risa was my lover, my life companion, and my best friend. When she died, a big part of me died with her."

"How long has she been gone?"

Dana's voice softened to almost a whisper. "Three years. Sometimes it feels like forever, and other times it feels like just yesterday."

"Dana, I'm so sorry. I got so bogged down in my own grief, it was hard to recognize someone else's."

Dana stared down at the concrete patio. "When I was going through it, I never thought the intense grief would go away, but it did."

"Does it ever go away totally?" Renee looked forlorn.

"Like I told you the day I met you and you were so upset, it never totally goes away but enough so you can function," Dana said. "Nighttime's the worst. Sometimes I'll dream that she's still here, then I wake up and reality sets in."

"Oh, my God, I've had that dream, too. Like Tom never died, and our life is like it was before."

"It seems so cruel, doesn't it? I did learn one thing."

"What's that?"

"I learned it's wrong to think someone else can fill the hole in your heart left by losing a loved one."

"You don't believe you'll ever find love again?"

"No, that's not it. I just don't think that hole ever heals." Dana felt a twinge even as she spoke.

"Have you dated since Risa died?"

"I went on one date, if you'd even want to call it that. Some friends of mine set me up. They said I was spending too much time holed up in the house alone."

"How was it?" Renee refilled Dana's glass with iced tea.

"It was a disaster," Dana said with a chuckle.

"Really? What happened?"

"It wasn't her...the woman they set me up with. It was me. I guess I wasn't ready. I couldn't stop comparing her to Risa. I remember watching the poor woman eat her dinner. She took a bite of meat, then a bite of potato, and all I remember thinking is that Risa never ate that way. Risa always finished her meat first, then went on to her vegetable, then the potato. She always saved the potato for last. Weird, huh?"

"No, I don't think it's weird. I can understand it. You get used to someone and how they do things. Sounds pretty normal to me."

"I guess we get so set in our ways that anything else seems foreign," Dana said.

"I know what you mean. Tom was my entire life. I can't remember a time when we weren't together. I don't think I'll ever date."

Dana waved a finger at her. "Never say never."

"What's that supposed to mean?"

"Renee, this is still a fresh, open wound for you. You're not going to feel this way forever. For crying out loud, you're thirty-six years old. You've got your entire life ahead of you. I'm betting you don't spend the rest of it alone."

Renee lifted her shoulder in a half shrug. "How can you be so sure?"

"Let's just say, I've got a feeling."

"Well, if you're so psychic about my life, what about you?"

"What about me?"

"You're further in the grieving process than I am. Why aren't you blissfully happy in a romantic relationship?"

"I'm not looking," Dana said. "Anyway, it's different for gay people."

"How so?"

"For straight folks, there's much more opportunity to find another life partner. Everything's right out there in the open for you. You have a bigger support group, more resources, even the bereavement counseling is geared toward you."

"Aren't there resources for gay people, too?"

"Some, but let's just say it's not so public a matter. Society almost feels obligated to find someone in your position another spouse. You're young, you have children, and it's not right for you to go through the rest of your life alone. For someone like me, society doesn't see it that way. Anyway, I feel lucky to have found Risa and spent the time we had together. That kind of love only happens once in a lifetime."

"It sounds like you had something very special with her."

"We did, but unfortunately, we couldn't celebrate it or share it with others. My family knew about Risa and me, but not much was said about it. I guess it was something they tolerated to keep me around. Risa's family was estranged. Her mother died when Risa was young, and her father hadn't spoken to Risa in years. The only time he visited was the day of her funeral."

"That's terrible. You must have felt so alone."

"We had a small group of close friends, but for the most part, our life together was invisible. Risa wasn't out at work, though I'm sure some of the people she worked with suspected we were a couple."

"But you were together for fifteen years. How do you keep fifteen years invisible?"

"We had each other and that's all we needed, so we kept to ourselves. But when Risa got sick, we found out how limited our resources were and how invisible our lives truly were."

"That's sad," Renee said. "I received an overwhelming

amount of help when Tom became ill. Medically, financially, and legally, it was all taken care of. It should be that way for everyone, no matter—"

"Who they love?" Dana said.

"Yes. There's no reason people should be penalized for who they love. In this day and age, especially with *Will & Grace* and Ellen DeGeneres on TV, you'd think people would be more understanding."

"See, you do know some gay people."

They both laughed.

"Those people are celebrities. I've never actually sat down with a gay person and got to know them like this. You're probably the first gay person I've ever met in real life."

Dana laughed again.

"Now what's so funny?" Renee asked.

"I'm sure I'm not the first gay person you've met."

"How can you be so sure? This is a small town. Everybody knows everybody's business."

"I'm just saying there had to have been a gay person in school or at the library or anywhere, really."

"Now that you mention it, in high school, we used to think Miss Fortunato, our gym teacher, was gay."

"Straight people always suspect the gym teacher."

Renee's face flushed with embarrassment. "Hey, give me a break. I'm trying here."

Dana reached over and touched her arm. "I know you are. Thank you for that."

The sun had gone down, and the breeze had cooled considerably. In the distance, flashes from the fireworks show at Waddell Park could be seen above the tall oak trees in Renee's backyard. Renee and Dana sat in silence as they watched the red, green, and silver starbursts accent the night sky.

Renee sighed and leaned back in her lawn chair. "Beautiful, isn't it?"

Dana nodded and felt a tiny squeeze on her heart as she remembered the last Fourth of July she and Risa spent together. "Yes, it is."

Once the fireworks show was over, Dana stretched her arms over her head and got out of the lawn chair with a groan. "I better get going. Your girls will be coming home soon and wonder what this strange woman is doing in their home."

"You're not strange." Renee stood next to Dana.

"Strange to them anyway. I'd like to meet them someday. Maybe we could take them out to lunch or something."

"Sure, I think they'd like that."

Renee walked Dana to her car. "Thank you so much for your help. And for the delicious dinner. Next one is on me."

"Dinner would be great." Dana unlocked her car with the tiny black remote she pulled out of her pocket. "Oh, I won't be at the library for a few days. I have some things I need to take care of up in Cleveland."

"Okay," Renee said. "Be careful, and have a good trip."

"I will. See you in a couple days." Dana's gaze caught Renee's, and suddenly, the moment felt awkward, like after a first date when you don't know whether to kiss the person good night. Dana wondered if Renee was thinking the same thing. Dana shook the thought from her head. What was she thinking? Renee was straight. Dana felt ashamed for even thinking such thoughts, but they kept popping up at the most inopportune times.

Renee looked into Dana's eyes. Dana's normally piercing blue eyes had paled to a soft gray. Renee got the feeling that there was a lot going on behind those eyes. She wondered, if things were different, what would happen at this moment? If Renee were a lesbian, too, would they be kissing right now? Why would she feel this way about a woman who was just her friend? Renee squelched the thought. She stuffed it deep inside her head like she did with most things she didn't want to think about.

Dana broke the heavy silence. "I better go."

"Thanks again for your help," Renee said. The temperature seemed to have dropped again, and she shivered. She crossed her arms tight across her chest to keep from shaking as Dana slid into the driver's seat. "Have a safe trip to Cleveland," Renee said as Dana started the engine and put the car into gear. She felt a tiny ping of disappointment in the pit of her stomach.

"See you in a few days," Dana called out through the car window.

Renee stood in the driveway and waved to Dana until just the taillights were the only reminder that Dana had been there. Renee pulled the neck of her T-shirt closer and went inside. It was close to eleven, so Lindsay and Sara should be home any minute. She sat on the couch and watched the end of some movie with Kevin Bacon in it.

She couldn't stop thinking about Dana and the feelings she stirred in her. Maybe it was because she was lonely. Maybe it was because she felt her friendship with Dana was safe. Whatever it was, for the first time in a long time, Renee didn't dread waking up in the morning. She already looked forward to the end of the week when Dana would be back.

At ten minutes after eleven, the back door swung open, and Lindsay and Sara burst in.

"Mom, the fireworks were so cool," Lindsay said.

"I guess you guys had a good time."

"Yep, it was great," Sara said.

Renee pulled them close and hugged them tight. "I missed you guys."

Sara broke away first and headed for the kitchen, undoubtedly for a midnight snack. Lindsay turned toward the stairs.

"Hey, where's my kiss good night?" Renee asked as Lindsay reached the bottom stair.

"Oh, I forgot." Lindsay came closer and gave Renee a peck on the cheek.

"Linz, what's that on your neck?" Renee pulled her close so she could get a better look at the red and purple blotch. "Is that a sucker bite?"

"Mom!" Lindsay cried. Her cheeks turned beet red. Lindsay covered the love bite on her neck with her hand and ran upstairs to her room.

Sara came out of the kitchen carrying a handful of chocolate chip cookies and a can of Diet Pepsi. "Did you see your sister's neck?" Renee asked.

Sara nodded, unable to speak because her mouth was

full of cookie. "I thought I told you to keep an eye on her and Justin," Renee said.

Sara washed down her cookie with a swig of Diet Pepsi. "I don't know what you're so upset about. They were only kissing, Mom. What was I supposed to do? Run over there and break them up like I'm the kissing police?"

"Kissing leads to…other things, Sara." Renee picked up one of Sara's cookies and took a bite.

Sara shrugged. "Lindsay's a big girl. She can take care of herself." She popped another cookie in her mouth and headed upstairs to bed.

Chapter Nine

Justin was now a permanent fixture at Renee's house. This was a curse and a blessing. He kept Lindsay and Sara occupied when Lindsay's summer school classes finished and she had more free time, but the threat that his and Lindsay's relationship would escalate to a higher level worried Renee. He got his driver's license shortly after the Fourth and had been chauffeuring Lindsay to the pool for guard duty and Sara to softball practice. This took a big burden off of Renee. And when she thought about it, other than the sucker bite, there was no real evidence that they were doing anything they shouldn't be. Justin's behavior, at least in her presence, was respectful and courteous. And how much trouble can two teenagers get into with little sister tagging along?

Renee knew she couldn't hold on to her girls forever. They would grow up and test their independence soon enough. That's what girls their age normally did.

Unlike them, Renee was stuck. Her only relationships were with the bottle of Amaretto, a bag of Chips Ahoy cookies, and Dana. After the Fourth of July, Dana was gone only two days, but Renee found herself looking for her every time the glass doors of the library would open. She missed talking to her, and she missed seeing her. She had felt safe having Dana stay at the library with her until she closed at night. It felt safe like it had felt with Tom. Dana seemed a lot like Tom: quiet, cool, and levelheaded.

Once Dana returned from Cleveland, she and Renee spent time together nearly every day. If the girls were off with Justin, Dana and Renee would go out for dinner or coffee and talk for hours. They often stayed at Starbucks until closing time. When they were together, the hours seemed to go by fast. They talked easily about everything and anything. They shared a deep love for books, baseball, and art galleries. Dana got tickets to an Indians game, and they took the girls, who seemed to enjoy it very much, especially Sara. It had been a long time since they had done anything like this as a family.

As summer waned, a new school year approached and the time came to get the girls ready.

"Linz, Sara and I are going out to the mall to do some school shopping. Do you want to come?" Renee asked.

Dressed in a faded softball T-shirt and cut-off jeans that were a little too short for her long brown legs, Lindsay looked different to Renee. Had she gotten taller over the summer?

"I've got some reading to do before my Honors English class starts next week." Lindsay opened the refrigerator and removed the carton of orange juice. She took a small tumbler out of the kitchen cabinet and poured herself a glass of juice.

"That's fine," Renee said. "If I see anything nice for you, I'll pick it up, okay?"

"Yeah, Mom." Lindsay headed back up to her room to study. Minutes later, Sara bounced down the stairs.

"Where's Lindsay?" Sara said. "Isn't she coming with us?"

"Not this time. She has some studying to do for English. I guess it's just you and me, kid."

A broad smile spread across Sara's face. "Cool. Can we go to Abercrombie first?" Sara had a twinkle in her eye.

"Sure." Renee grabbed her car keys and purse from the kitchen table. I'm sure we can blow through the entire clothing budget there, she thought, as they made their way out to the car.

As soon as Renee's car turned the corner, Justin ran across the eight backyards that linked their houses and let himself into the Del Fino house through the back door. His heart pounded in his chest, but he wasn't sure whether it was from the running or from what he hoped was about to happen in Lindsay's bedroom.

As soon as Lindsay heard the back door open, she cautiously came downstairs to see who it was. Her face split into a wide grin when she saw Justin leaning against the doorjamb in the kitchen.

"Is the coast clear?" he asked.

"Yep, they'll be gone for hours." Lindsay took Justin by the hand and led him upstairs to her room. She pulled down the window shade to give them privacy. With the room now bathed in muted sunlight, she and Justin held hands as they sat on the bed.

Renee had taught her daughters to be "good girls." She told them that having sex with only one man, preferably the one you intended to marry, was part of respecting yourself. Lindsay thought about this as she looked over at Justin sitting across from her. Something innate took over, and the longing and the hormones won out over everything Renee had preached to her.

Lindsay lay on her back, looking at the ceiling of her bedroom. Was that all there was to sex? What was all the fuss about? She looked over at the clock on her nightstand.

"Oh, my God, it's almost one thirty," she blurted out. "Mom will be home any minute." She startled Justin from his post-coital slumber. He stood and stumbled around the room collecting his clothes. Lindsay sat up and felt something hot and wet run out of her. She looked down between her legs and saw the bloodstain on her comforter.

"Shit!" She bolted up off the bed. "Mom's going to kill me when she sees this." She dabbed at the stain with a Kleenex, but it was no use. She ripped the comforter off the bed, balled it up in her arms, and ran naked downstairs. She stuffed the white eyelet comforter into the washing machine and dumped a cup of Cheer on top of it. She spun the dial for normal wash and pulled the knob to start the washer. The washer hummed to life, and Lindsay felt hopeful that maybe she could pull this off before her mom came home. Realizing she was still naked, she bolted back to her bedroom. Justin was still sitting on her bed. He watched as she dashed around the floor collecting her clothes.

"You look so hot right now," he said with a wide grin.

"Justin, you have to go home. Mom will be back soon, and I don't think it's a good idea for you to still be here when she comes in."

Lindsay dressed quickly and escorted Justin to the kitchen and out the back door.

"Can I call you later?" he asked before leaving.

"Sure." Lindsay tried to close the door. Justin pushed back through the kitchen door and kissed Lindsay on the cheek. "I love you, Linz," he said and took off running through the backyards to his house.

The mall was crowded with school shoppers—weary moms with kids in tow trying to get the best buys for their budget. Sara managed to spend over two hundred dollars in a matter of thirty minutes. Renee had to admit that the clothes she picked out looked great on her. Sara and Lindsay had very different tastes. Lindsay was a girly girl, who preferred skirts and dresses and frilly tops. Sara liked more tailored, almost masculine clothing with clean lines. Sara too had grown over the summer. All that running and playing softball had paid off, Renee thought. Sara's once plump little legs were longer now with a hint of calf muscles. She had gone from a children's chubby size fourteen to a svelte junior petite size eight.

After a morning of shopping, Sara and Renee stopped for lunch at the coffee shop. Renee enjoyed having lunch alone with her younger daughter. They rarely spent time, just the two of them, together. Renee looked across the table and saw Sara as if she were meeting her for the first time. In a matter of months, since Tom's death, she had changed so much. If he were alive, Renee thought he wouldn't recognize her. Her chestnut hair, which was usually an unruly nest, was now cut short into a layered cut that framed her tan face. Her lustrous skin glowed from all the time she had spent in the sun that summer.

Sara ordered a tuna melt and a Diet Pepsi, and Renee ordered a chef's salad with ranch dressing on the side and a Diet Pepsi. "So are you excited about going to high school this year?" Renee asked.

"Yep." Sara took a sip from her soda. "I signed up for the girls' basketball team. Tryouts start next week."

"That's great, Sara. Your dad would be really proud of you.

You know how much he loved watching you play sports."

"I know. I wish he was here to see me. I really miss him."

"I know you do, honey, we all do. We can only hope he can still see us and watch over us," Renee said. "I know he would be proud of you and Lindsay. You girls have been through a lot."

Sara's face clouded over. Renee knew she must be thinking of Tom and how much she missed him.

"It's been a while since you and Lindsay have been in the same school," Renee said, purposely changing the subject. "How do you feel about that?"

"I don't mind as long as Lindsay doesn't treat me like a moron."

"Lindsay wouldn't do that. Would she?" Renee took a bite of her salad.

"She might. She's different sometimes when she's with her friends."

"How do you mean different?"

"Like when she's with Justin. When she's around him, it's like she just wants me to disappear."

"Honey, your sister doesn't want you to disappear. What she's feeling right now has nothing to do with how she feels about you. Lindsay is experiencing her first crush," Renee said. "Someday you'll be going through the same thing. You'll see."

Sara took a bite of her sandwich and shook her head. "Not me."

"What do you mean not you? Don't you want to meet a boy and fall in love and get married someday?"

"Oh, no, that's not for me," Sara said. "I'm never getting married."

Sara's comment concerned Renee. Did she feel this way because of where she was in her life, stuck between childhood and adulthood where neither one felt right? Or did she not want to get married and have a family because she saw what could happen even when things seem to be going just great and all of a sudden someone dies and your perfect world gets ripped out from under you?

"Okay, talk to me in a couple of years, babe," Renee said. "I'm sure your feelings will change."

Renee hoped this was true. She didn't want her daughter to be afraid to fall in love. Love was a wonderful thing. She felt her own heart ache, just for a moment, as she remembered all the love she had shared in her life. Now that Tom was gone, was it over for her? Would she spend the rest of her life alone? Beginning to date again terrified her. She quickly banished the thought.

She and Sara finished their lunch and headed home. "Do you think Lindsay will like the sweater I got her at The Gap?" Renee asked Sara as they pulled into the driveway. Sara got out and followed Renee to the back of the car to retrieve her purchases.

"I think so. It's a nice sweater," Sara said. "But who knows what Lindsay thinks? She's been in her own world lately." Sara lifted two shopping bags out of the trunk and went into the house, clutching her purchases. Renee trailed along with the remaining packages.

The house was quiet. Lindsay must still be in her room studying, Renee thought as she laid the packages on the kitchen table. She searched through the bags to find the sweater she bought Linz. This would be a nice reward for her hard work trying to get ahead in her studies.

Renee tapped on Lindsay's door. "Linz, you in here?"

She opened the door and found Lindsay just where she left her, on her bed reading a textbook. She noticed that Lindsay's eyelet comforter was missing.

"Hi, Mom, how was shopping?" Lindsay asked, never looking up from her book.

Renee sat on the bed. "Pretty good. Sara made out well. I saw this and thought you'd like it." Renee held up the pale yellow sweater.

Lindsay looked up and smiled with approval. "It's great, Mom, thanks," she said and went back to her reading.

"Linz, where's your comforter?" Renee slid her hand over the percale bed sheet.

Lindsay's gaze flickered toward the empty juice glass on her nightstand.

"I spilled orange juice on it. Sorry, Mom...what a klutz." Lindsay's smile looked forced. "I put it in the washer. I hope it doesn't stain."

Renee stood, walked over to Lindsay's desk, and grabbed the pair of scissors that stuck out of a plastic pencil cup on top of the desk. She snipped the price tags from the sweater. As she tossed the tags into the wastebasket, something shiny and black at the bottom of the wastebasket caught her eye. She reached in and pulled out the familiar shiny black wrapper. With a feeling of horror, she realized the other piece of trash in the wastebasket was a used condom.

Her mouth went dry, and she felt like she was going to pass out. She turned toward Lindsay.

"Linz, what's this?" She showed Lindsay the used condom wrapper in her hand. Renee and Tom had used the same brand. They were still tucked in the back of her nightstand in their bedroom.

Lindsay looked up. All the color drained from her face. "Oh, God," she muttered.

"Where did this come from?" Renee asked more forcefully.

"Your room," Lindsay said quietly.

Renee fought to control herself. "Lindsay, what have you done?"

"I'm sorry, Mom." Tears streamed down Lindsay's flushed cheeks. "Justin said it would be all right if we used protection."

"Justin? No..." was all Renee could say through her tight throat. She had dreaded this moment.

"I'm sorry. You weren't supposed to find out. Justin said it was our secret."

"Justin. We'll see about Justin. He's not to set foot in this house unless I'm here, Lindsay, do you understand?" Renee shouted.

"Mom!" Lindsay shrieked. "That's not fair."

"What's not fair is you doing this behind my back. Not that I would give you permission. Why didn't you come to me? We talked about this."

Lindsay looked down at her trembling hands. "Because you seem so overwhelmed about everything since Dad died. I knew you'd flip out and get all angry and stuff."

"You bet I'm angry. I've asked you before to come to me with this so I could protect you."

"Your idea of protecting me would be to talk me out of it."

"Sex is an adult issue. You're a kid."

"Since Dad got sick, me and Sara had to grow up pretty fast. Isn't having to deal with your father's death an adult issue?" Lindsay said. "One minute you expect me to be an adult and the next you expect me to be a kid. Which is it?"

"Having sex can be very dangerous. You can get an STD, something incurable that you will carry with you for the rest of your life. Or you can get your heart broken when you realize that sex for you means something totally different than it does for Justin. Girls equate sex with love, with being in love, where boys see it as satisfying a need, something to accomplish."

"Justin's not like that," Lindsay said. "He loves me. He cares about me."

"That may be so, but you're still too young to be doing this. What if you get pregnant? Then what?"

"We used protection. At least give me some credit."

"Condoms are not one hundred percent effective." Renee held up the wrapper. "These things can break."

Lindsay shrugged.

"I don't want you to make the same mistake I made…" Renee's words slipped out before she could stop them. Her head pounded from the adrenaline rushing through her brain.

"What mistake?"

Feeling exposed, Renee sat on Lindsay's bed. She had hoped she would never have the conversation she was about to have with Lindsay.

"I never told you girls…your dad didn't see the point in telling you. Before we got married, I got pregnant with you."

Lindsay was silent. Probably in shock.

"I was older than you are now. And even though we had planned to get married eventually, it still wasn't easy. It changed our lives in ways we never dreamed of." Lindsay's expression made Renee hesitate.

"I just want to protect you. I want you and Sara to have the best opportunities in life. Getting pregnant before you're ready changes everything. All your plans and hopes and dreams come to a screeching halt because that new life you create needs all your time and energy."

Tears streamed down Lindsay's face.

Renee reached up and wiped her tears away. She pulled Lindsay close and held her tight. "Are you okay?" Renee stroked Lindsay's hair.

"It was just one time. I didn't even like it. It hurt."

Renee felt a lump expand in her throat. Lindsay started to cry heavy, uncontrollable sobs. Renee blinked back her own tears as she held her tight.

"I want you to know there isn't anything you can't tell me. I want you to be safe. That's my job, to keep you safe. If you're going to be sexually active, you have to be responsible. So I think we need to make an appointment with Dr. Michaels and see about some better birth control for you. Don't you think?"

Lindsay nodded against Renee's chest.

Renee held her daughter for a long time, afraid to let go—just like when she told herself that if she didn't let Tom go he wouldn't be gone. That didn't work with Tom, and it wasn't going to work with Lindsay, either. When they broke their embrace, Lindsay would be a different person. She wouldn't be gone forever like Tom, but she'd be changed.

Lindsay sat up and wiped her remaining tears with the back of her hand.

Renee stood to go downstairs. She needed a glass of Amaretto more than ever.

"Mom, can I ask you something?" Lindsay said before Renee left the room.

"Sure, honey. What is it?"

"Do you regret having me?"

"Oh, no, Linz, no, I don't regret having you, not for one minute. All I'm saying is that when you're young, you think you're invincible, but one slip, one mistake, can change your life forever. I'd hate for you to toss your dreams away because of one moment of indiscretion."

Renee recognized that they both had been presented with new challenges. She would have to deal with the fact that Lindsay was now sexually active, and Lindsay would have to go on for the rest of her life knowing she was the result of an unplanned pregnancy. Unplanned, maybe, but not unwanted.

Chapter Ten

Renee took Lindsay to Dr. Michaels's office as promised. After speaking to Lindsay and Renee together, Dr. Michaels asked Renee to step out of the exam room so he could speak to Lindsay privately. Renee returned to the waiting room.

In her talk with Dr. Michaels, Lindsay confessed that she and Justin did "other things," too, but only had intercourse one time.

A few minutes later, Dr. Michaels went to the waiting room to get Renee.

"You can join us in the exam room if you like." Dr. Michaels motioned for Renee. "I'm ready to do the exam, and I think Lindsay will feel more comfortable if you're close by."

When Renee opened the door, she found Lindsay sitting on the exam table dressed only in a blue paper gown and her socks.

"How ya doin'?" Renee touched Lindsay's shoulder.

"Okay, I guess. He's going to do the exam now."

"Yes, Dr. Michaels thought you'd feel more comfortable if I were here. Do you want me to stay?"

"Yes. Please."

Before Dr. Michaels performed the exam, he counseled Lindsay on sexual responsibility. Then he performed Lindsay's first pelvic exam and Pap test.

Lindsay watched over the tops of her knees while Dr. Michaels applied K-Y Jelly to the clear plastic speculum.

Dr. Michaels was gentle with her. "I'm going to put my hand on your thigh so I can examine your external genitalia," he said as Lindsay lay back on the table and stared at the ceiling. "How are you doing, Lindsay?" he asked before proceeding.

"Okay." Lindsay's voice was quiet.

"I'm going to insert the speculum now."

Lindsay gripped the side of the table. She looked over at Renee, feeling extremely uncomfortable. Her mom looked sad, but she stroked Lindsay's arm and Lindsay felt a little better.

First Lindsay felt the coldness of the K-Y, then she felt pressure. She cringed and squeezed her eyes tight when she felt Dr. Michaels scraping the inside of her cervix with the little paddle that looked like one of those flat wooden spoons she ate ice cream off of when she was little. As she lay there with her eyes still closed tight, she wondered how other women went through this all the time. This was something she surely didn't want to repeat for a while.

When finished with the exam, Dr. Michaels removed his latex gloves and extended his hand to help Lindsay sit up. He had been her doctor since she was a baby. She wondered if he thought differently of her now that he knew she was sexually active.

"Okay, Lindsay, all finished. Any questions?"

"No, I don't think so."

"Okay, kiddo. You can get dressed now. I'll give you a call when the test results come back. Probably in a week or two."

"Thanks." Lindsay forced a polite smile.

"Any questions, Renee?"

"No, Doc. Thanks."

Dr. Michaels excused himself from the exam room, giving Lindsay privacy to get dressed.

"I'll go out to the desk and get you checked out," Renee said.

"Okay, Mom."

Lindsay hopped off the exam table and removed the blue paper gown. She balled it up and before tossing it away, wiped the slimy cold K-Y Jelly from her private parts. Yuck. She balled up the gown even tighter and stuffed it into the trash bin next to the exam table.

Two weeks later, the test results came back negative. Lindsay was finally awarded a clean bill of health. Dr. Michaels prescribed a low-dose birth control pill and instructed her on the proper use of the medication, including abstinence or another means of birth control during the first month she was on the pill. They made another appointment for Lindsay to return in a year for a checkup.

Knowing that Lindsay was better protected, Renee breathed a little easier. They had made it through Thanksgiving, their first real family holiday without Tom, and Renee finally felt like she was getting a grip on things. Christmas was just around the corner, and although she wasn't looking forward to it, she would make the best of it, at least for her girls.

She looked out the library window as a light snow fell, covering the parking lot with a blanket of crystal white. The Ohio weather, as if on cue, decorated the landscape for the upcoming Christmas holiday. That afternoon, the girls stopped by the library for a visit.

"Mom, can we have some money to go Christmas shopping?" Lindsay asked. "Justin said he would take us to the mall. Can we go?"

Renee looked at her watch. It was only three thirty, and she didn't get off work until six. "Dana's supposed to stop by this afternoon. How about if she and I meet you there after work for dinner?"

"Sure, that would be great," Lindsay said.

Renee gave Sara and Lindsay money and walked to the door with them. Justin was waiting in the car, probably afraid of being around Renee now that she knew about his and Lindsay's shenanigans.

"Let's meet at Ruby Tuesdays around six thirty. Justin can eat with us, too, if he'd like," Renee said, more of a peace offering than a dinner invitation.

Lindsay's face beamed. "Thanks, Mom."

Sara and Lindsay kissed Renee goodbye and left through the glass double doors. Renee watched them get into Justin's car. Both girls seemed happy, got good grades in school, and even seemed to be coping well while getting through the holidays without their father. Renee was feeling more secure in her role as a single parent. This gave her new hope. But unfortunately, it could be false hope, and hanging on to false hope was like hanging on to cotton candy in the rain; it was bound to end up messy.

After the kids had been gone awhile, Mary came upstairs to the nonfiction area where Renee was reshelving books by Louis Dyer, Wayne Dyer, and Brian D'Ambrosia. "Phone for you," Mary whispered in her librarian's voice.

Renee's knees popped as she stood and headed downstairs to the reference desk to take the call. "Hello?"

"Mrs. Del Fino? This is Sergeant Hollenbach of the city police department."

An icy dread washed over her. The girls and Justin must have been in an accident, she thought. Oh, my God, I hope no one's hurt.

"Mrs. Del Fino, we have your daughter here. She was caught shoplifting. I need you to come down to the security office at the mall so I can release her into your custody," the officer said.

"Shoplifting? Are you sure?"

"Yes, ma'am. We were able to recover the items. She had them tucked under her sweatshirt. I can release her into your custody if you can come here. If not, I have to take her to the police station and hold her there."

"No, don't. I'll be right there." The phone receiver shook in her hand. Mixed emotions swirled in her head. She was relieved no one was hurt, but she wanted to kill Lindsay for doing something so stupid.

"Everything okay?" Dana walked up to the reference desk. Wet crystal snowflakes glistened in her hair and on the shoulders of her navy peacoat. "You look like you've seen a ghost."

Renee's voice trembled. "It's Lindsay. She's been arrested for shoplifting. I have to go to the mall and get her."

"Oh, Renee, I'm so sorry." Dana covered Renee's hand with hers. "What can I do to help? Do you want me to drive you?"

Renee felt numb as she handed Dana her car keys. Lindsay stealing? First the sex, now this? Renee tried to make sense of it all, but she couldn't. Lindsay had everything she needed. Renee had given both girls money before they went to the mall. Neither of them wanted for anything, so why this?

Dana reached over the desk, grabbed Renee's coat, and draped it over her shoulders. She took Renee by the arm, and they walked out to Renee's car. They drove in silence. Once inside the mall, a woman selling lottery tickets and renting strollers at the customer service area directed them to the security desk.

Renee's high heels clicked on the linoleum as she scurried past Santa Claus, who sat in his candy-cane throne with a toddler in a red and white snowsuit on his lap. At first, the security desk seemed abandoned, but as soon as they approached, an officer carrying a clipboard stepped through a door behind the desk.

"Mrs. Del Fino?" the officer asked.

"Yes."

"I'm Sergeant Hollenbach."

"Where's Lindsay?" Renee asked.

"Lindsay? Your daughter told me her name was Sara."

Renee felt as though her legs would buckle right out from underneath her. Dana steadied her with a hand under her elbow. "Sara?" Renee said. "Sara's the one you caught shoplifting?"

He looked at the clipboard. "She gave her name as Sara Del Fino, fourteen years old, of 125 Highland Street." He looked up at Renee for confirmation.

"Yes, that's her." Renee's voice was barely a whisper.

"She's in our holding room." Sergeant Hollenbach directed Renee into the back office. "I need you to sign some paperwork before I can release her."

He pushed some pink forms in front of Renee and handed her a pen from his shirt pocket. She scribbled her signature across the bottom of each form and handed them and the pen back. Even though the sergeant was formidable in handling the situation, something in his eyes told Renee that he understood what she was going through.

"The court will notify you when she needs to appear." He straightened the forms on his desk.

"Court appearance?"

"Yes. She stole merchandise that totaled over one hundred dollars. The store's pressing charges, so she'll have to appear in court. The offense is a misdemeanor, and she'll probably go in front of the judge within the next month or two. If she pleads guilty or no contest, they'll probably give her a fine and put her on probation."

"Probation? Oh, my God, she's going to have a record." Renee felt the stinging reality of the situation.

"Yes, ma'am, but she's only fourteen, so she's still a juvenile. Once she's eighteen, her record will be sealed. If she keeps her nose clean, she should have no problem getting a job or applying to colleges, that sort of thing." Sergeant Hollenbach tucked the papers into a manila envelope. "Any questions?"

"No." Renee was so upset, she felt as though she would jump out of her skin. But she knew she had to pull herself together.

"You can see her now."

"I can wait out here if you like," Dana said.

"Okay," Renee said. "Thanks."

Sergeant Hollenbach pushed open the gray metal door and led Renee into the holding area to collect her wayward daughter. Sara was curled up in the fetal position on one of the orange Samsonite chairs in the corner of the stark white room. "Sara," Renee said as she walked over and sat beside her, "what's going on?"

Sara didn't meet Renee's gaze. "I'm so sorry, Mom. I know what I did was wrong."

"You bet it's wrong. It's not only wrong, it's a crime. You weren't raised like this…and where's your sister?" Justin and Lindsay were supposed to be here with Sara, Christmas shopping.

"I don't know. She told me she and Justin were going to The Gap. I haven't seen her since."

"Sara, why?" Renee snapped at her. "It's not like we can't afford this stuff." She looked at the evidence: a pair of jeans, a Tommy Hilfiger T-shirt, and some costume jewelry.

"I did it on a dare. I met Dakota here after school. She's on the basketball team. She said it would be cool. You know, give me some street cred if I did it. She said she's done it a million times and never got caught. Anyway, all the kids do it," Sara said. "It's like a game."

"A game!" Renee yelled. "Don't be stupid. You know stealing's wrong." She could feel her rage reach the boiling point. "Sara, I'm so disappointed in you."

"I know, Mom, it was stupid."

"You bet it was stupid. And if your father were alive, he'd—" The words stuck in Renee's throat. "Where's Dakota? I want to talk to her. I think she has some explaining to do about this, too."

"She left. When she saw the security officer coming toward me, she took off."

"When we get home, I'll be calling her mother. This is ridiculous."

"Don't, Mom. Please don't call Dakota's mother. She'll kill her. This isn't her fault. I did this. It's my fault."

The security door opened, and Lindsay stepped into the room.

"And where were you when your sister was turning into a felon?" Renee asked.

"I was at the food court with Justin," Lindsay said. "He was hungry."

"Is that all you can think about? Justin and eating? I thought you were supposed to be shopping with your sister."

"I didn't know I was supposed to babysit her."

"Maybe if you were with her, this wouldn't have happened." Renee could feel her anger rise in her face.

Lindsay looked at the floor.

Renee's voice trembled. "I'm so disappointed in you. You both know better."

She apologized to Sergeant Hollenbach and assured him this would never happen again. She gathered her daughters and left the security office. Dana had been sitting on a plastic bench outside the office. She stood when Renee emerged with Lindsay and Sara. Justin was nowhere to be found.

The drive home from the mall was deathly quiet. Renee stared out the passenger's side window while Sara and Lindsay sulked in the backseat. Guilt and disappointment hung heavily in the air. Most of those emotions issued from Renee. She cursed Tom again for leaving her with all this. He was always the strong one, the disciplinarian. She was beginning to believe that now he was gone, their daughters felt they could just run amok because she was so weak. She had no clue what the right thing to do was. Taking care of the girls was easy when they were younger. Their problems were benign back then. Now that they were growing up, their problems were getting bigger. Renee didn't know if she had it in herself to deal with it.

The car barely came to a stop before Sara and Lindsay leapt out. They were upstairs and in their rooms, doors slamming behind them, by the time Renee and Dana walked into the kitchen.

"I hope they stay up there until they're twenty-one," Renee said, anger and frustration steeped in her voice.

"Renee, take it easy," Dana said.

"I'm sorry you had to see this." Renee set her purse on the table. "I didn't raise my kids to be criminals."

"Don't apologize. This is a hard thing to go through. Sara seems like a good kid. She just made a mistake."

Renee's head pounded. She felt drained, but her insides still trembled in anger. Instinctively, she reached above the refrigerator and pulled down the bottle of Amaretto. It was now less than half full. "You want some?" she asked Dana.

"No, thanks."

Renee poured herself a drink and tossed it back before the ice even began to melt. She leaned against the kitchen counter for support and poured another one.

"First it was Lindsay stealing condoms out of my nightstand and now this."

"Wait, Lindsay was stealing condoms?"

"Yes. I didn't tell you about it. I was too embarrassed." Renee waved her hand in front of her face in dismissal.

"There's nothing to be embarrassed about," Dana said. "When did that happen?"

"Labor Day weekend. I took Sara school shopping on Saturday. Lindsay said she had some studying to do for her upcoming English class, so just Sara and I went. We were gone for a couple of hours, and when we got back, I went upstairs to

Lindsay's room to show her the sweater I'd bought for her. When I went to throw the tags into her wastebasket, I found the empty condom wrapper and a used rubber."

"What did you do?"

"I became totally unglued. Not only from finding a condom in Lindsay's room, but because I knew she took it from my nightstand."

"How did you know where it came from?"

"It was the same brand Tom and I used." Renee's face flushed. Why was she telling Dana about this? Why would she care what brand of condoms she and Tom used? Renee felt as though she were coming unglued all over again.

"So what happened?"

"When I saw the condom, I snapped. I started yelling at her that she didn't know what she was doing and that she could be throwing her life away. Then I took her to the doctor to get checked."

"Is she okay?"

"Yes, thank God." Renee took another gulp of Amaretto.

"Renee, unfortunately, that's what kids her age do. At least give her some credit for trying to protect herself."

"But she's only sixteen. And condoms aren't all that safe. They can break, you know."

"I wouldn't know," Dana said. "I never had the need to use one."

Ice cubes clinked in Renee's glass as she finished her drink. "Never?" The question implied more than Dana's contraceptive use. Renee really wanted to know if Dana had ever been with a man.

"Never," Dana said. "In this day and age, I think there's more pressure than ever on kids to have sex. Lindsay at least tried to be responsible."

"But that's not how I raised her. I raised her to wait until she falls in love with someone. Not to just give herself away like it's nothing."

"But maybe she is in love. You said she and Justin spend a lot of time together. Don't you remember when you were sixteen? All those hormones circulating?"

"She's just a kid," Renee said. "Anyway, I didn't want her to make the same mistake I did." Renee voice was barely a whisper.

"I see."

Renee listened hard to hear any judgment in Dana's voice. She didn't hear any, so she continued. "I was already pregnant with Lindsay when Tom and I got married. Dealing with an unplanned pregnancy can be a stressful time in any woman's life. But if you're a teenager, the situation seems like a catastrophe. It was hard for us. And I didn't want her to have to deal with all those tough decisions. She's so young."

"She's growing up. She's not doing anything any different than a lot of other sixteen-year-olds."

"So you're saying I'm the one who's wrong?"

"No, you're not wrong. No one's wrong here. My God, Renee, you're so hard on yourself."

"But there has to be something I'm not doing right. Maybe I'm away from home too much. I only took the full-time position because we need some kind of income. We can't live on Tom's insurance money forever."

"Relax. Come with me." Dana took Renee by the hand and led her to the couch in the living room. "Sit."

Renee obeyed Dana's request, and Dana sat next to her.

"Renee, you're not doing anything wrong. Look at what you and the girls have gone through in the last year. Out of the blue, your husband gets sick and dies and your entire life is turned upside down in six months' time. He hasn't even been gone for a year yet, and you want everything to be back to the way it was. Do you know how ridiculous that sounds?" Dana's steel blue gaze pierced through Renee.

She looked down at her hands clenched together in her lap and nodded.

"Renee, look at me." Dana covered Renee's hands with her own. "Your life and the kids' lives will never be the way they were before Tom died. You have to take control and make a life for you and your girls from here on in. You can do that. I know you can. It's just going to take some time to work out the kinks.

Don't be so hard on yourself or on the girls, either. You know they lost someone close to them, too."

The red and gold lights of the Christmas tree twinkled like stars as Renee stared down at their hands locked together. She didn't know what to say. She knew Dana was right. But what she didn't know was whether she had it in her to do it alone. Renee had always relied on Tom to handle the tough stuff, and now it was up to her. Her life and her girls' lives depended on it.

"It's going to be okay," Dana said. "Things have a way of working themselves out, even in the most difficult of situations."

"How can you be so sure?"

"Because after I lost Risa, I thought my life was over. We had plans for our future, but her dying… What I'm trying to say is that even though we had plans, they weren't supposed to happen."

"I don't understand."

"I'm saying that when something bad happens, sometimes we think it's a kind of punishment when actually it's just a turn in our destiny."

"That's very philosophical, but I'm more of a common sense type of person. I can only deal in the here and now. And right now, things seem quite a mess."

Dana sighed heavily. She felt as if she would never get through to Renee. Part of her wanted to shake her, to wake her up to what was going on with her family, and part of her wanted to hold Renee and protect her from all the pain that seemed to swirl around her.

She tried another approach. "As far as this mess with Sara, I'll do some investigating, find out what's involved in the case, and we can take it from there. I have a friend who's an attorney in Cleveland who might be willing to help. I'll even go with you and Sara to court if you like. I just want you to know that you don't have to go through this alone."

That's when Renee's tears started. They came with such great force she couldn't even speak. She trembled as Dana drew her into her arms and held her close.

"You've been through so much." Dana stroked Renee's hair, soothing her, comforting her. Renee could hear Dana's heartbeat through her chest. It had been a long time since she had been this close to another human being. She liked how it felt in Dana's arms. She felt safe there.

Finally, she was able to pull herself together. She sat up straight, looked at Dana, and studied her face. Her facial bones were delicately carved; her lips were full and rounded over perfect white teeth. When she looked into Dana's clear blue eyes, she saw compassion there—compassion and caring and true concern for Renee and her daughters.

She had met Dana only a few months earlier but seemed closer to her than she did to friends she had known for twenty years. She felt something she thought she'd never feel again. Another secret from her past surfaced, one she thought she had stuffed down so deep it could never come back.

At that moment, Renee's heart swelled with emotion and longing. No one was more surprised than she was when she leaned in and kissed Dana full on the lips. The kiss was soft and sweet and stoked feelings in Renee that she never thought would be awakened again.

Dana pulled back first. "Renee, what—"

"Shush." Renee put her fingers to Dana's warm, soft lips.

Renee thought that if she didn't do this now, she would regret it for the rest of her life. She gently took Dana's face into her hands and kissed her again, this time more passionately. "I've wanted to do that for some time now," she whispered.

Dana looked down, her face flushed, as Renee looked up with a smile. "I have to say this is a pleasant surprise."

She pulled Renee close. Renee felt that she could melt away from the rest of the world and all its problems, here safe in Dana's arms.

She heard the upstairs toilet flush and suddenly remembered that her daughters could come down at any moment. Panic set in, and immediately, she broke their embrace. She got up off the couch as if it were on fire.

"Oh, my God, Dana, I forgot about Lindsay and Sara. You better go."

Dana looked bewildered. "Okay." She got up and Renee

walked her to the front door.

Before opening the door, Dana turned to Renee. "I have to admit I didn't see this coming."

"I didn't, either." Renee felt light-headed and leaned her head against the doorframe. Lust, confusion, and anxiety coursed through her. "I don't know what to say. I mean, I'm not...I mean...Oh, I don't know what I mean." Renee tried to stuff the forbidden feelings back into the dark place where they had been safely hidden.

The upstairs hallway light came on, and both women jumped.

"I better go." Dana opened the door. Cold air burst into the room.

Renee touched Dana's arm. "Are you all right?"

"I'm fine...a little stunned, but fine. I think we need to talk about this later, don't you?"

Renee nodded nervously.

"Call me tomorrow morning," Dana said. "I have some work to do at home, so I wasn't planning on going to the library. You can come by my apartment for lunch if you like, and we can talk then."

"Okay. We'll talk tomorrow." Renee felt sad and relieved all at the same time.

Dana left and Renee headed into the kitchen for another drink. Suddenly, there was a knock at the back door. It was Dana, looking sheepish.

"We drove your car here, and mine's still at the library. Can you give me a lift?"

"Sure." Renee set down the bottle of Amaretto. "Let me get my coat."

It started snowing again as Renee drove Dana to her car. They held hands during the entire trip. By the time they reached the library parking lot, the snow had become a blizzard.

"Go ahead and start your car," Renee said. "You can wait in here until it warms up."

Dana started her car and returned to the luxuriant warmth of Renee's car. Big fat snowflakes fell, covering the windows and concealing them from anyone who might pass by. There they were, two grown women alone in the library parking lot breathlessly making out in the front seat like two sixteen-year-old kids.

By the time Renee made it home, it was well past midnight. She closed the door tight and slid the deadbolt in place. Not bothering to turn on the kitchen light, she walked over to the refrigerator, reached into the cupboard above it, and pulled down the Amaretto. She sat at the kitchen table in the dark and poured herself a drink, this time emptying what was left in the bottle.

Chapter Eleven

The library was extremely busy that morning. Christmas vacation had begun for most of the kids, and many parents used the library as a babysitting service. Renee was having difficulty concentrating and had already made several mistakes filling out two new library cards. She couldn't get Dana and what happened between them out of her mind. Every time she thought about the night before, she got a tingling in the pit of her stomach.

"Are you doing okay?" Mary slipped in behind her at the reservation desk.

"Yes, fine. Why do you ask?"

"You seem a little distracted today. And you've dusted the same shelf twice since I've been here."

Renee looked down at the rag and the can of Endust she was using on the back shelves of the desk. "Sorry, Mary, I guess I've just got a lot on my mind." She put the cleaning supplies away.

"Don't apologize. This time of year can be difficult for anyone, especially for you now with Tom gone."

Mary reached out and touched Renee's arm. "I just want you to know if you need anything, I'm here."

"Thank you. That means a lot to me." Renee put her arms around Mary's doughy shoulders and hugged her tight. Mary was an old dear friend, but Renee couldn't help but notice the difference between hugging her and holding Dana.

Time seemed to click by slowly. She wanted to call Dana to set up a time for them to meet for lunch. She held out until ten thirty.

"Dana, it's Renee," she said nervously into the phone.

"Hi. How's your day going? Can you make it for lunch?"

96

"Yes, but I only have an hour."

"That's fine. I'll have everything ready when you come. See you around noon?"

"Yes, see you soon."

Now Renee's mind was truly reeling. It felt like she had just made a date with her secret lover. Was what happened the previous night real or was it a fluke? Was it just an emotional time, and she got caught up in it? Or was her past coming back to haunt her?

Dana rushed around the tiny apartment tossing out old newspapers and emptying the overflowing trashcan in the bathroom, as well as running the vacuum cleaner and wiping down the kitchen counters. It had been forever since she had company over, company that she actually looked forward to seeing. As much as she wanted to, she couldn't deny she was excited about this. In her mind, she wrestled with the thought of getting involved in a new relationship. And then there were her feelings for Risa.

Dana sat on the couch and rested her head in her hands. *What am I doing?* Her heart suddenly felt heavy at the thought of betraying Risa. When Risa died, she vowed she would never get involved in a relationship again. Her belief was that if she let someone else into her heart, there wouldn't be enough room for Risa. Yes, it had been three years, but her feelings never faded. They were as strong as the day they met. How could she square up her feelings for someone else and her feelings for Risa?

And anyway, Renee was a straight woman. What happened the previous night didn't mean anything. Renee was obviously upset over the events earlier that night, and she reacted to Dana's being there. Dana had to admit that she and Renee had become close friends, but they couldn't be more than that, could they? Dana knew the pitfalls of getting involved with straight women. She had done it in college before she met Risa. Back then, they called those girls LUGs—lesbian until graduation. Dana got her heart handed to her then, and she wasn't sure she wanted to go through that again.

She rubbed her hands over her face and sighed. She had made up her mind that she would discourage Renee from pursuing this any further. What happened between them could have been just a way for Renee to deal with her grief. Sometimes, grief could make people do strange things.

At twelve ten, Renee stood outside Dana's apartment complex. Her heart pounded and a wave of apprehension swept through her. What was she doing here? The feeling gnawed at her. It alternately frightened and thrilled her. She hesitated, torn by conflicting emotions. Finally, after taking a deep breath, she pushed the buzzer to Dana's unit. There was no verbal answer, but the door buzzer sounded and unlocked the door. Renee's legs trembled as she ascended each step to the third floor. The door was ajar when she reached Dana's apartment, and she let herself in.

"Hi, come on in," Dana said cheerfully. She had a white linen apron wrapped around her waist and exuded an air of efficiency that fascinated Renee. Her apartment was sparsely but tastefully decorated. A burgundy leather couch sat against one wall and an entertainment center took up another. The apartment smelled of fresh baked bread and tomato sauce.

"Mmm, it smells good in here. What are you making?"

"A little pasta. Cavatelli, to be exact."

"Are you baking bread, too?"

"Yes, but I must admit it's one of those frozen bread doughs you buy in the grocery store."

"It smells wonderful."

Renee walked over to the small dining table and was impressed with what she saw. A white linen tablecloth covered the table. Crisp white linen napkins rested next to shiny white plates and bright chrome silverware. A slim glass vase holding a single pink rose sat in the middle as a centerpiece.

"This looks beautiful." Renee bent to smell the rose.

"Thank you. I thought it would be nice…you know…for lunch." Dana gestured for her to sit.

Dana scooped out two heaping spoonfuls of pasta onto Renee's plate, then on her own. They ate a delicious lunch of cavatelli with marinara sauce, and roasted red pepper and mozzarella cheese bruschetta, made with fresh-out-of-the-oven Italian bread.

The afternoon sunlight filtered through the low-hanging snow clouds, giving the room a mysterious golden glow. Renee looked across the table at Dana and caught Dana looking at her. Renee's heart skipped a beat. "About last night," she started.

Dana set her fork down and gave Renee her full attention. Renee couldn't help getting lost in her eyes.

"What happened last night was something else." Renee nervously pushed the remaining pasta around her plate. "I don't think I've felt that way since I was in high school."

Dana cleared her throat. "You being straight and all, that was the last thing I thought would happen."

She picked up her fork and resumed eating. Renee watched her as she turned over in her mind whether this was the right time to reveal her secret.

"Dana, there's something I need to tell you."

"Okay."

Renee took a deep breath and began. "When I was in high school, I had a friend. Annie. We had been friends since kindergarten, and we were inseparable all through school. One night—I think we were fourteen or fifteen—we were at a slumber party and the subject of kissing boys came up. Since neither one of us knew any boys, let alone any boys that we thought would want to kiss us, Annie and I watched two girls do it, then we practiced on each other."

Renee nervously wound her napkin in her hands. She looked up at Dana, who seemed to be listening intently.

"I see." Dana paused for a moment. "But just because you've kissed a girl doesn't make you a lesbian."

"We kissed a lot," Renee said with a chuckle. "Almost every time we had a sleepover. And as time went on, things went a little further."

Renee looked across the table at Dana, waiting for her reaction. Dana sat very still. After a silence that seemed to last for eternity, she spoke.

"Lots of girls experiment like that when they're young, Renee. That doesn't mean they're all lesbians."

Dana's words stung a little. Was she trying to talk Renee out of her feelings? Was she trying to let her down easy?

"But how do you know if you're gay?"

"Like I said, kids experiment all the time. When I was a kid, I used to take one of my mom's good bath towels and tie it around my shoulders like a cape. Then I'd go outside, jump off our picnic table, and pretend I was Superman. That doesn't make me a superhero, now does it?"

Renee shook her head, frustrated that she wasn't getting her feelings across. Why was Dana being so cold? The night before, she felt that Dana wanted this as much as she did.

"I'm not talking about back then, I'm talking about now. How could what happened between us happen if—"

"This is an emotional time for you," Dana said. "You could have mistaken attraction for comfort."

"Comfort? I think there's more to it than comfort. With Annie, there was more to it."

"What do you mean?"

"I felt something for her. More than just friends. It scared me actually. I think it scared us both."

"I'm still not convinced that you're a lesbian. You were married for a long time. If your husband hadn't died, you'd still be married. Right?"

Renee didn't answer. She looked down at her hands in her lap. This certainly wasn't going how she intended.

"Renee, we've gotten to be good friends and you're pretty vulnerable right now."

"I have a lot of good friends, but I don't want to be with them the way I want to be with you," Renee blurted out. Her heart pounded in her chest.

Dana let out a sigh. She got up from her seat and knelt next to Renee. "What happened last night may just be a way for you to deal with your grief. I know none of this makes any sense, but don't mistake it for something it's not."

Renee's heart sank. "How could you think this was nothing? I don't know about you, but it's not every day that I go around kissing other women."

"I care about you a lot. And I have to admit that the first time

I saw you at the library, I was attracted to you."

Renee's face brightened. "Really?"

Dana nodded. "Last night caught me by surprise. I don't know where this is going, if it's going anywhere, but I do think we should take it slow. Don't you?"

"Absolutely."

"Okay then." Dana stood and her knees creaked. She glanced up at the clock.

"Hey, it's getting late and you need to get back to work." She took Renee's hands and pulled her straight up out of her chair.

As Renee stood, their gazes locked. Dana radiated a vitality that drew Renee in like a magnet.

"Would it be so bad if I kissed you goodbye?" Renee asked.

Before Dana could answer, Renee leaned in and kissed Dana on the mouth. Fireworks exploded in Renee's brain. Dana must have felt the same because she kissed Renee back.

Renee pulled Dana close and kissed her again. Dana's soft warm tongue sent shivers straight to Renee's groin. She grasped Dana by the shoulders and pressed herself against her, holding her against the wall. "What are you doing?" Dana asked, looking into Renee's eyes.

"Showing you that this has nothing to do with grief."

Renee slid her hands underneath Dana's shirt and cupped both breasts. She felt a familiar ache between her legs when Dana's nipples hardened in her palms. Her knees went weak when Dana reached down and slid her hand underneath Renee's skirt. Dana picked Renee up and laid her on the leather couch. That was all it took to make Renee an hour late getting back to work. She got lost in kissing and being kissed, caressing and being caressed.

Afterward, Renee stood and straightened her clothing. She carefully rebuttoned her blouse to make sure none was missed. She walked over to the table to get her purse and apply a fresh coat of pink coral lipstick.

Dana watched Renee cross the room. "So much for taking things slow," Dana said with a chuckle.

Renee smiled and came over to kiss Dana goodbye. Her lipstick left a pink imprint, and Dana licked her lips in obvious enjoyment of the taste.

"Can I call you tonight after work?" Renee asked as she slipped her shoes on.

"Sure, that would be great." Dana stood and walked Renee to the door.

Renee kissed her gently on the lips.

They said their goodbyes, and Dana softly closed the door behind Renee. As she listened to Renee's footfalls on the steps, she leaned against the closed door, fighting off the guilt that tried to overtake her heart. "My God, what am I doing?" she whispered.

When Renee got home after work that evening, the girls weren't there yet. Since Lindsay still wasn't allowed to be home alone with Justin, both girls were spending the day at Angie's making Christmas cookies and helping her wrap presents.

Renee picked up the phone and dialed Dana's number.

"Hello?"

"Dana, it's Renee. I called to see how you were doing and to thank you for a wonderful...lunch."

Just then, Sara and Lindsay walked through the back door. Suddenly, Renee felt as if she were doing something lewd. "Hi," she said to them, nervously covering the receiver. "I'll be off in a minute."

"Renee, are you there?"

"Yes, I'm here. Lindsay and Sara just walked in."

"I see."

"I just want to thank you."

"Thank who?" Sara walked past Renee to the refrigerator where she pulled out a can of Diet Pepsi.

"Nobody."

"What?" Dana said over the phone.

"I'm sorry, Dana. Can I call you later?" Renee asked, annoyed with Sara for listening in on her conversation.

"Sure. I'll be home working all evening. Talk to you later."

Renee hung up and playfully smacked Sara on the back of the head. "Since when do you listen in on my phone conversations?"

"I was just playing around. You seem to be in a good mood

today." Sara took a big gulp of her Diet Pepsi. "You've been so stressed out lately."

"And why do you think I'm stressed?"

"I know. I'm sorry, Mom."

"I know you are. I hope you've learned a big lesson from all this. It's still not over, you know. We have to go to court and appear before the judge." Tension seeped back into Renee's shoulders and neck.

Chapter Twelve

Christmas week had arrived. This was Renee and the girls' first Christmas without Tom, and a thick pall of sadness hung over the festivities. Even though filled with family, friends, food, and presents, the holiday felt empty. Renee seemed isolated from the group and wished Dana were there to distract her from the lonely ache deep inside her.

Lindsay and Sara spent time with their grandparents the evening before Christmas Eve, giving Renee a chance to share dinner out with Dana and exchange gifts. Dana bought Renee a pair of Italian gold earrings, and Renee bought Dana a gold serpentine bracelet.

After dinner, they went back to Dana's apartment where they curled up on the couch and, by candlelight, listened to soft rock on the Bose radio and sipped on coffee spiked with Baileys Irish Cream. Dana held Renee close, tucking Renee's shoulder under her arm as Renee rested her head on Dana's chest. The sound of Dana's heartbeat was comforting, but even though lying there together was cozy, nothing sexual happened between them. Actually nothing much had happened since their first encounter that afternoon a few weeks earlier at Dana's apartment. Granted, their time alone was limited, but when they were alone and things would heat up, Dana stopped before they got any farther than third base. Renee enjoyed the kissing and petting, but that night, she wanted more.

She wondered whether it was a lesbian thing. Since she and Dana had begun their friendship, she secretly read anything in the library she could get her hands on about the subject. One book she read mentioned lesbians who were called stone butches. A stone butch would make love to a woman but wouldn't let her partner reciprocate. Maybe Dana was a stone butch.

Whatever the problem was, they could surely work it out. Anyway, the anticipation was driving her crazy. She wanted to feel all of Dana next to her. She craved that contact so much that her body ached for it.

As they lay on the couch, Renee was determined that night would be the night and began kissing Dana's neck. Dana murmured as Renee's hands caressed her arms and chest. Dana stroked Renee's back as Renee climbed on top of her and kissed her way down Dana's neck and slowly began unbuttoning her white dress shirt. With each button she unfastened, she placed a kiss on Dana's newly exposed skin. After unbuttoning the last button, she nuzzled her face against Dana's soft warm breasts. Breathing in the heady scent of her clean skin and Nautica cologne was intoxicating.

Renee continued to kiss Dana as her hands slid down Dana's flat belly and lingered just above her jeans. Renee caressed the soft skin, moving her hand back and forth and dipping her fingers ever so slightly under the waistband. Finally, when she couldn't withstand the temptation anymore, she slid her hand beneath the waistband. As if by reflex, Dana grabbed Renee's wrist and stopped her.

"What's wrong?" Renee asked.

"Nothing's wrong." Dana lifted Renee's hand to her lips, kissed it, and placed it on her chest.

Frustrated, Renee got up. "I better get going."

Dana sat up. "So soon?"

"It's getting late." Renee stood and adjusted her clothes.

Dana stood, as well, and reached for Renee's hands. "What's wrong?"

"Don't you find me attractive?" Renee blurted out, tears threatening her eyes.

"Of course I do. Why would you say that?"

"Because we don't get much time alone, and here we are alone, and nothing's happening."

"What do you mean nothing's happening? We were doing

pretty well there, I thought."

"I need more, Dana. I want to be with you, really be with you."

"Oh, I see. I'm sorry."

Renee's voice was shaky. "So what does that mean?"

"I find you very attractive. It's just the timing."

"Timing? Are you on your period or something?"

Dana laughed. "No. And for your information, I had a hysterectomy five years ago, so that's not a problem for me anymore, thank you very much."

Renee flushed with embarrassment. "Oh."

Dana sat and pulled her back down on the couch. "What's your hurry? We have all the time in the world."

"I guess so, but…" Renee was teary-eyed.

"We both," Dana said, "have a lot going on in our lives. When we get together, I want us both to be there fully and completely."

"But I'm here now." Renee wiped her eyes with the cuff of her sleeve. "I'm here and I'm ready. Don't you want me?"

Dana reached up and wiped the tears from Renee's cheek. "Of course I do."

Dana felt bad. How was she going to explain to Renee what she was feeling inside when she didn't even know herself?

She took Renee's hands and placed them in her lap. "I know this may sound strange, but for some reason, I'm having trouble letting go."

"Letting go of what?"

Dana paused for a moment. She wanted to tell Renee the truth, but she didn't want to hurt her in the process. "Of Risa."

"Oh, I see." Renee lowered her gaze.

"It's not that I don't care for you, I really do. It's just that something's standing in the way."

"So what can we do?"

Dana was having trouble finding the right words. What she couldn't tell Renee was that she couldn't imagine ever making herself vulnerable again. Even though she had feelings for Renee, a committed relationship was still too risky and too painful. Dana felt safe in the way things were now. If their relationship ended that day, she would survive, but if she let her guard down and made love with Renee, that would open her up to that vulnerability all over again. Dana wasn't sure she would survive if she ever again lost a love like that.

"I don't know, Renee. I haven't done this in a long time."

"Well, I haven't, either. Hell, I can't begin to explain where any of these feelings are coming from. But I do know one thing. This feels good. It feels right." Renee paused. "Losing Tom as quickly as I did made me realize that life is much too short to not do things that can make you happy. Even though no one wants to admit it, nothing lasts forever. Your relationship with Risa ended. And what we have here may end, too. But shouldn't we enjoy what we have today instead of worrying about tomorrow?"

Even though Renee could be a basket case about some things, Dana had a feeling Renee was right about this. How much time had she wasted? Nothing could bring Risa back. If she didn't wake up and join the living, she might lose Renee, as well.

Dana looked over at Renee. She saw tenderness in her eyes, and suddenly, Dana's resolve to carry the torch for Risa melted away.

Dana unbuttoned Renee's blouse and pushed the silky fabric off her shoulders. Renee stood while Dana unzipped Renee's skirt and let it fall in a puddle at her feet. She held Renee's hand as she stepped out it.

Dana reached around Renee and with one hand, unfastened the hook on Renee's bra. Renee let the pink satin bra straps slide down her arms and onto the floor next to her other clothes.

Dana looked at Renee as she stood before her in only her pink silk panties and black high heels.

"My God, you're beautiful," Dana whispered.

Renee felt dizzy with desire. Her heart pounded and her breathing came in short gasps.

Renee reached for Dana and quickly pushed the cotton fabric of her dress shirt off Dana's muscular shoulders. Her hands slid down Dana's arms and came to rest at the button of Dana's slacks. Gingerly, Renee undid the button and slowly unzipped the zipper. She slid her hand inside Dana's slacks and was greeted by the warm wetness that made them both groan.

Dana's voice was strained. "See what you do to me."

She gently laid Renee down on the couch. She unfastened her own bra and tossed it aside. She slid her body on top of Renee's, and finally, they were bare breast to bare breast. Dana kissed Renee with such passion that Renee felt it in every cell of her body. Heat rippled underneath Dana's skin as she pressed her body to Renee's and finally allowed herself to fully feel the rush of sexual desire. They made love for the first time.

Chapter Thirteen

After their evening together, Renee crept into the house just before sunrise carrying a black suede pump in each hand as she tiptoed up the stairs to her bedroom and gently closed the door. She silently thanked God that the girls didn't wake up and hear her coming in at such an ungodly hour. How would she ever be able to discipline them when her own behavior reflected that of a juvenile delinquent?

She tossed her pumps into the bottom of the closet, quickly undressed down to her bra and panties, and lay on top of her bed. As first light shone through the window, she stared at the ceiling and replayed in her mind the events of the evening. She touched her fingers to her lips and was surprised to find them tender and sensitive. She smiled.

And then she thought of Annie.

She remembered the summer before their senior year that was a scorcher: record highs into the nineties every day and not a drop of rain for weeks. Renee and Annie had summer jobs working the afternoon shift at the Dairy Queen downtown, and because of the heat and the Little League Baseball season, the lines were relentless.

"If I have to make one more Peanut Buster Parfait, I'm going to scream." Annie filled a tall plastic glass with too much hot fudge, then hit the lever on the ice cream machine to fill the cup the rest of the way with vanilla soft serve.

That summer, Annie's parents left her on her own for two weeks while they drove Annie's older sister, Marissa, to Massachusetts to get her settled in at Boston College. Gianna asked Angie if it was all right if Renee stayed with Annie at night during those two weeks so her daughter wasn't home alone. Angie gave her blessing.

"And a no boys over, you hear a me, Anna Maria," Mrs. Castrovinci warned Annie in her broken English.

"Yes, Mama. No boys." Annie rolled her eyes.

The Castrovinci home was a big old house. Its floors creaked at night, even when no one was walking on them, and the plumbing rattled when anyone turned on the kitchen or bathroom faucet. Actually getting hot water for a bath or shower felt like winning the lottery. One big disadvantage was that the house had no air conditioning, and Annie's room was in the attic. Granted she had the entire third floor to herself, but in the summer, it was stifling hot. In an attempt to keep cool, Annie would sleep nude with the windows open, relying on a single box fan to circulate the warm air.

The Dairy Queen stayed open until eleven during the summer, and it took almost an hour to clean up and close the place, so Annie and Renee got home after midnight. Annie kicked off her chocolate-and-cherry-syrup-stained clinic shoes, which were a requirement of her boss as part of the uniform, and headed for the bathroom.

"I'm going to take a shower." She pulled her polyester uniform off over her head and dropped it in the hallway. "I have to get the waffle cone smell out of my hair."

"I'll get in when you're done," Renee said. "My uniform's sticking to my back. It's gross."

When Renee heard the shower turn on, she went into the kitchen to look for a snack. Annie's mom had left them some lemon cookies and biscotti in a Tupperware container on the counter. Renee popped open the lid and took out two cookies. She looked through the cupboards for a glass for milk and came across a bottle of Amaretto liqueur. She picked up the bottle and unscrewed the square cap. She sniffed at the opening. It smelled like almonds. She heard the shower shut off and quickly tried to put the cap back on the bottle.

"Shower's free." Annie stood in the doorway, wrapped in a pink towel that barely covered her breasts and thighs. Her long brown hair was wrapped in another pink towel that was piled on top of her head like a turban.

"Thanks," Renee said, still fumbling with the square cap of the Amaretto bottle.

"What are you doing?"

"Nothing. I was looking for a glass and found this. I've seen your dad drink it with ice...'on the rocks,' as he says. Did you ever try it?"

"Yes, it's pretty good." Annie giggled. "You want some?"

"Sure."

Annie stretched up on tiptoes to reach the highball glasses her father kept on the third shelf of the cabinet. She grabbed two glasses and filled them with ice and a generous amount of Amaretto. She handed Renee a glass.

"To friendship," Annie said. They clinked their glasses together, and each took a healthy sip.

"Mmm...this is good." The warm fluid heated Renee's throat.

"I know. I like to sneak some every once in a while. It helps me sleep when I've had a rough day."

Renee looked over at Annie. Her skin was still damp and glistened in the moonlight. Renee took another swig of her drink, hoping it would quell the fluttery feeling in the pit of her stomach.

"Aren't you going to shower?" Annie asked, breaking Renee's reverie.

"Yeah, sure." Renee was grateful that Annie couldn't read her mind.

After Renee showered, both girls headed upstairs to Annie's room in the attic. Annie still hadn't gotten dressed. It was fun to watch her maneuver the stairs as she held on to the Amaretto bottle and her half-empty glass while trying to keep her towel from falling off.

"Are you drunk?" Renee giggled. She herself was feeling pretty good.

"No, just a little tipsy." Annie leaned into Renee in the stairwell.

111

Both girls broke into fits of laughter. Renee slid her arm around Annie's waist, trying to steady herself as they climbed to Annie's room.

Once upstairs, Annie propped open the windows, letting in the warm night breeze. The window closest to her bed held the box fan. Annie turned the regulator knob, and the fan hummed to life. She removed the towel from her head and let the other drop to the floor. "Mmm, that feels so good," she said as the cool breeze washed over her naked body.

Renee couldn't take her eyes off her. It wasn't just a physical attraction, although there was that, too. Something much more intense took over Renee's entire being.

Renee stood next to the bed as Annie turned down the covers and climbed in. Annie lay on her back, spread-eagle, with her eyes closed. Renee looked down at Annie and watched as the breeze from the window fan combed through the silky dark triangle of hair between Annie's long tan legs. Renee's insides warmed.

She let her own towel fall to the floor and lay next to Annie. She lay on her back, as well, with her eyes shut tight, listening to Annie breathing. Renee was highly aware of where Annie's arm brushed against hers. The alcohol made her head buzz, while Annie's nearness made her heart race. Silently, Annie reached for Renee's hand.

This was the signal that "the game" was about to begin. The game had taken place every night since Annie's parents left for Massachusetts. It started out innocently enough a year earlier as a kissing game but then progressed to more. This was a game only she and Annie were privy to, and God help them if their boyfriends found out.

Renee's heart pounded as Annie lifted Renee's hand and placed it on her small firm breast. Renee let out a soft moan as she felt Annie's nipple tighten beneath her palm. Renee turned on her side and stared at her hand as it caressed Annie's supple breast.

"Mmm, that feels so good," Annie whispered.

The sight of Annie lying naked in the moonlight, her damp dark hair splayed across her pillow, and the sensation as she fondled Annie's breast, thrilled Renee like nothing else on earth.

Even with Tom, it wasn't like this. She got excited with Tom, but this was different. The world stopped when she and Annie were together like this.

Renee was afraid to breathe for fear that this would end or that she would wake up like this was only a dream. But this was no dream. Soft low moans escaped from Annie's parted lips as Renee bent down and kissed Annie's swollen breast. Renee bravely slid her hand across Annie's chest and caressed her other breast. It too swelled, and the nipple hardened into a plump little berry.

Renee's insides melted and warm wetness seeped onto her thighs. Annie squirmed on the bed, slowly gyrating her hips as Renee kissed and sucked her tight swollen breasts. Desperate for relief, Annie took Renee's hand and plunged it between her legs. Both girls moaned from the pleasure of it.

"Please, Renee. Please make me come," Annie whispered, her breath sweet from the liqueur.

Renee felt light-headed and her groin tingled as she touched the warm wetness between Annie's legs. Annie moaned softly, sending Renee's desire for her skyrocketing. Renee crawled on top of Annie and slid her thigh between Annie's legs. Renee held Annie's hands above her head as they rocked their bodies together, grinding themselves into each other until relief washed over both of them.

The next morning, they lay on opposite ends of the bed. The Amaretto bottle sat half empty on the floor, and the fan still hummed in the window, but now the air felt cold. Renee opened her eyes and had to reacquaint herself with where she was. She looked over at Annie, who was wrapped in a sheet, her hair a tangled mess cascading over her pillow.

The bright sunlight hurt her eyes, but not as much as her head hurt from the alcohol. Renee felt a twinge of sadness wash over her as she watched Annie sleep. She knew once the sun came up, they went back to being Renee and Annie, best friends. Best friends, with boyfriends, whom they should be doing these things with. Whom they did do these things with, but rarely got the same result.

Tired of torturing herself with scenes from long ago, Renee sat up on her bed. She drove her hands in her hair and tried to shake the thoughts from her head. When she and Annie had been together, they were just kids. What did they know? She wanted to move on with her life, but it seemed she was right back where she started so many years ago.

She went into the bathroom. The girls would be up soon. They had a busy two days ahead of them. Christmas was the one holiday that Renee had dreaded the most since Tom's death. But she would get through it like she got through the past seven months, one painful step at a time.

Looking at her reflection in the bathroom mirror, she wondered, *Is this who I really am? A lesbian?* Her face was thin, but her cheeks showed remnants of the healthy afterglow of satisfying sex. With her finger, she wiped smeared mascara from under one eye.

She washed her face and brushed her teeth, postponing her shower. Traces of Dana's cologne remained on her skin, a delightful reminder of the previous night. She wanted to hold on to those memories a little while longer before she had to turn back into old Renee: mother, widow, and dutiful daughter.

Chapter Fourteen

On Christmas morning, Renee and the girls visited Tom's grave. With runny noses and teary eyes, the Del Fino girls placed a pine wreath next to their father's black marble headstone. As they stood in front of Tom's snow-covered grave, Renee wondered what Tom would think if he saw what was happening to his family. Her life before Tom died seemed like a distant memory. How could so much change in so little time? If Tom hadn't died, would she have had the same feelings for Dana?

While Renee and the girls spent Christmas Day at Renee's parents, Dana drove to Cleveland. She visited Risa's grave with a large bouquet of pink roses, Risa's favorite. The pale winter sun bathed the cemetery in melancholy light. She brushed the snow away from the bronze urn she had placed there so she would have a permanent place to put fresh flowers when she brought them to Risa's grave. Risa had loved fresh flowers, and Dana brought them every week. She tossed the old bouquet of frozen carnations aside and wiped dirt and snow off the urn with her mittens. She dumped a bottle of Evian water into the urn and one by one, inserted the long-stemmed pink roses into it.

As she arranged the flowers, she couldn't ignore the ache in her heart she felt when she thought about what had happened with Renee. She couldn't shake the feeling that she betrayed Risa by being with Renee, and she felt guilty that her life seemed to be moving on without her. Dana and Risa had so many plans for their future: a trip to Italy, an Olivia cruise to the Greek Islands, and they even talked about having a baby. Dana always thought Risa would be a good mother. Nowhere in those plans was Risa getting cancer and dying at age thirty-eight. Deep down, Dana believed that things did happen for a reason, but for the life of her, she couldn't figure out any good reason for Risa's life to have ended so soon.

"Risa, I miss you so much." Tears filled Dana's eyes, blurring her vision. She squatted next to the headstone and brushed off more snow. She ran her wet red wool mitten across Risa's engraved name. "What I wouldn't give to have one more day, one more moment with you," Dana whispered as hot tears tumbled down her cold cheeks.

Suddenly, Dana sensed a presence behind her and jumped up. She looked all around, but no one was there. She looked back at Risa's headstone and saw her reflection in the shiny black marble, but it wasn't only her reflection she saw. Risa's was there, too.

Dana's heart raced and her legs felt weak as she backed away. She looked at the headstone again, but Risa's reflection was gone. "Great, now I'm hallucinating."

She crouched down in front of the headstone with her head in her hands.

"Reese, how did things get so messed up? We were supposed to be together for the rest of our lives. Why was that taken away?" Dana's words came out in a frosty puff of breath.

"You know you're the love of my life. I'd never want to do anything that would hurt you, but there's something I need to tell you." She looked around to see if anyone was in earshot and might overhear what she was saying. There wasn't, so she continued. "Reese, I've met someone. I've tried to ignore my feelings for this woman. Hell, I've even tried to talk her out of pursuing a relationship, but to be honest, I really like her. She's funny, she's smart…but, oh, God, I'm afraid if I let her into my heart, I'll lose you in the process. I don't want to lose you again."

Dana looked around again, positive that if anyone heard her they would surely think she was crazy. After all, she was talking to her dead partner's headstone.

"I don't know why I'm doing this. Maybe it's to relieve some of the guilt. Maybe I just need to tell you that, no matter what, you'll always have a place in my heart."

Dana stood. She kissed her two fingers and laid the kiss on top of Risa's headstone.

"I love you, babe. I always will." Dana voice was choked with sadness.

Suddenly, as if the sky had opened up, a large snow squall developed. Thousands of snowflakes the size of walnuts fell from the sky. A snowflake landed on Dana's lips as gentle as a kiss. Risa's kiss.

Dana tasted the cool snowflake on her tongue. It reminded her of frozen tears. She stood with her face to the sky as the cool snowflakes covered her skin. Then as quickly as the snow squall appeared, it disappeared, and along with it went Dana's anxiety over her relationship with Renee.

In her heart, she believed that this was a message from Risa, telling her that even though Risa wasn't there to share it with her, Dana deserved to be happy and live her life. Dana finally realized she was right.

On the drive back to Niles, she dialed Renee's number. Renee answered on the third ring.

"Hello?"

"Renee, it's Dana. I was wondering if you were free this evening to meet for coffee or something."

"Or something?" Renee giggled into the phone, hoping Dana meant the same thing Renee did.

"I'm on my way back from Cleveland. I can pick you up in thirty minutes. Is that okay?"

"Thirty minutes sounds great. See you then." Renee hung up and ran past Lindsay and Sara, who were in the living room watching TV. They watched from the couch as their mother ran up the stairs like a teenager who just got asked to the senior prom.

"What's gotten into her?" Lindsay asked Sara.

Sara shrugged. "Who knows?"

Twenty minutes later, Renee emerged freshly showered and dressed in a new pair of Calvin Klein jeans and a forest green cable-knit sweater, both Christmas presents from her daughters.

"Where are you going?" Lindsay asked.

"Dana's coming to get me. We're going out for a cup of

coffee. I'll have my cell phone with me. Will you two be all right alone here for a while?"

"Can we order a pizza?" Sara asked.

"Well, honey, it's Christmas night. I don't know if any pizza places are open."

"Jimmy's is open," Sara said. "But they don't have delivery."

"Justin could pick it up." Lindsay gave Renee a hopeful look.

"Lindsay, you know the rules. No boys in the house when I'm not home," Renee said.

Lindsay frowned and took the money from her mother. "It's not fair, Mom. Sara got caught shoplifting, and you still let her go to the store."

"Very funny," Renee said.

"Yeah, real funny, Linz," Sara chirped in.

"But I haven't seen Justin for two days. Even if I promise you that nothing will happen? We'll just watch TV. And Sara's here. Nothing's going to happen with Sara here."

"I don't know," Renee said, feeling her resolve soften. She had to start trusting Lindsay at some point, she thought. "What do you think, Sara? Can we trust Lindsay and Justin to behave themselves?"

Sara smiled, seemingly delighted to be included in deciding Lindsay's fate. "I don't know, Mom."

Renee handed Lindsay a twenty-dollar bill to pay for the pizza. "How about if she lets you keep the change from the pizza?"

"Okay." Sara reached over and snatched the twenty-dollar bill out of Lindsay's hand.

"Okay, Linz. Justin can come over, but you two must stay downstairs and he has to leave by eleven thirty. Do we understand each other?"

Lindsay's face brightened. "Yes, Mom."

The front doorbell rang.

"That's Dana." Renee reached into the closet for her coat. "Lindsay, I'm trusting you to do the right thing. And, Sara, any shenanigans between those two, you call me on my cell, okay?"

Both girls nodded.

Renee kissed Lindsay and Sara on the forehead. "I won't be late. We're just going to Starbucks for a cup of coffee." Renee opened the front door, letting in a gust of frigid air. Dana was standing on the porch.

"Ready?" she asked.

Renee's face broke into a wide grin. "Yep, ready."

They hurried down the front steps to the car. Dana had left the motor running and the heater on so it would be warm and toasty inside. She held the door as Renee slid into the passenger's seat, then ran around to the driver's side and got in.

"My goodness, it wasn't this bitter cold earlier." Dana rubbed her hands together over the heater vent to warm them.

Renee reached for Dana's hands, cupped them in hers, and rubbed them. She brushed her cheek against them. "My God, you're freezing."

Dana smiled at Renee's tenderness. She stroked Renee's cheek, then put the car into gear and backed out of the driveway.

"How was your day?" she asked.

"I guess okay. We stayed at my parents' most of the day. The girls seemed to do okay. Except for the cemetery, that was rough, but I guess it's what should be expected. How about you? How was your trip to Cleveland?"

"Enlightening."

"Enlightening? How do you mean?"

"I visited Risa's grave. I told her about us."

"Oh."

"I know it sounds crazy, but it was something I felt I had to do. And you know what?"

"What?"

"The strangest thing happened. When I was by her grave, I felt something behind me, like someone was standing there, but when I turned around, no one was there. I turned back and saw my reflection in her headstone. Then for a split second, I saw Risa's reflection, as well."

"You actually saw her reflection?"

"Yes."

"Oh, my," Renee said. Dana's story sent chills through her body.

"At first, I thought I was losing my mind. I panicked. And then I felt sad. I kept looking into the headstone to see if I could see her reflection again. But it never reappeared. I know she was there, Renee. I could feel it."

Dana paused, not sure she wanted to tell Renee the rest of the story. "But that's not all that happened."

"What? Was someone really there? Did someone try to hurt you?" Renee asked, now worried.

"No, nothing like that. It started to snow really hard. And as fast as it started, it stopped, and the sky became a brilliant blue. That's when I had this overwhelming feeling of peace. Like everything was going to be all right. That you and I were going to be all right." Dana glanced at Renee.

Renee took Dana's hand into hers and kissed it softly.

A few moments of silence passed as Dana drove on, holding Renee's hand.

"So where do you want to go?" Dana asked.

Renee looked out the car window. "Your place. I've really missed you today."

Chapter Fifteen

After the holidays, Dana made several trips to Cleveland, one being an overnighter. Dana explained to Renee that she had some things to take care of regarding the renovations at her house, which seemed to have stalled over the past few weeks. Renee thought Dana enjoyed the trips to Cleveland, but lately when she returned, she seemed distant.

January arrived with its cold bleakness and so did Sara's court date. On one of the trips to Cleveland, Dana met with her friend Allison, who was an attorney, and asked her if she would meet with Renee and Sara to see how they could best handle Sara's case.

Allison Winters was a college friend of Dana and Risa's. She used to work at the prosecutor's office in Cleveland before going into private practice at a small firm in Chagrin Falls.

Allison came down to Niles and met with Renee and Sara in Renee's kitchen over coffee and biscotti. Allison explained to them that because the value of the clothing Sara stole didn't exceed two hundred fifty dollars, she was charged with a misdemeanor and that was a good thing.

"The best way to proceed is to have Sara plead no contest." Allison scribbled down a few notes on her yellow legal pad.

"Why's that?" Renee asked.

"By pleading no contest, she's not exactly admitting guilt. A plea of no contest means she simply doesn't wish to contest the charges against her."

"So then what happens?"

"After Sara pleas, the judge will talk to her about what she did. The judge will tell her what a stupid mistake she made and warn her to never show up in his or her courtroom again." Allison directed her comment at Sara.

Sara's face flushed. "I know it was stupid. I didn't think it was a big deal. A lot of kids at school do it. It's like a game."

"Do you know how many times I've heard that explanation? It's not a game, Sara. This is serious. It could really affect your future. You want to go to college, don't you?" Allison asked.

Sara nodded.

"Well, if you would have picked up one more item, say another pair of jeans or some jewelry, you might have pushed the amount you stole over two hundred fifty dollars. If that were the case, you'd be looking at felony charges. And instead of being able to go home with your mom that day, the police officer would have taken you downtown and booked you into the jail. Do you have any idea what being arrested and processed is like?"

Sara shook her head.

"If you had stolen one more thing, they would have handcuffed you right there in the store, put you in the back of a police cruiser, and taken you to jail. There they would have taken your possessions, including your clothes, your really nice clothes, and handed you an orange jumpsuit. Before you changed clothes, in the presence of a female police officer by the way, you would be strip-searched, instructed to take a shower in one of the grossest facilities you can imagine, then be deloused."

Horror crept across Sara's face.

"After that, you'd have been fingerprinted, your mug shot would be taken, and you'd be led into a cell with no windows that's probably no bigger than your downstairs bathroom and not nearly as clean. There you would sit with one or two of your cellmates until your lawyer or your mom posted bond for you. If they couldn't post bond, then you would have sat there until your arraignment before the judge, which could be anywhere from two days to two months, depending on the court docket. Does that sound like something you'd want to be involved in?"

Sara shook her head. There were tears in her eyes.

"Good," Allison said. "Make sure this is the last time you do anything like this, okay?"

Sara nodded, then ran upstairs to her room.

"My God," Renee said. "I don't know about Sara, but you sure scared the crap out of me."

Allison smiled. "Sorry, I just wanted to make sure I got through to her. You know how kids her age are. They think they're invincible."

"You got that right. You seem to know a lot about kids. Do you have any of your own?"

"Yes, my partner and I have a daughter." Allison reached into her briefcase and retrieved her daughter's picture. "We adopted Lilly from China. She'll be three years old in May."

Partner? She adopted a child with her law partner? "Oh, she's beautiful," Renee said, holding the photo. The Asian girl's porcelain skin and shiny dark hair were well in contrast to her mother's blond California looks.

Renee was impressed. She thought Lilly was very lucky to have been chosen by such a wonderful woman. She handed the photo back to Allison.

"So getting back to Sara," Allison said. "Do you have any more questions about what to expect during her court appearance?"

"No, I think I can handle it. Basically, what you're saying is Sara got pretty lucky. I mean, this isn't as bad as I thought it was going to be, right?"

"Right, and to be truthful, you don't need an attorney to be present when she has her court date. I can be there if you like, but it isn't necessary. Like I said, this is a misdemeanor case, almost like a traffic ticket. With this being her first offense, she'll probably receive probation and community service at worse or a verbal warning from the judge at best. Because she's a juvenile, her record will be sealed, and if she keeps her nose clean, it will be expunged once she turns eighteen. So, no, it's not as devastating as you thought, but she needs to look at it as a hard-learned lesson. If she gets in trouble again, the judge won't be so easy on her. You really need to drill that into her head."

"Oh, I will."

Allison gathered her things. She closed and locked her Coach briefcase.

"Thank you so much for your help." Renee walked Allison to the back door. "I can't tell you how much you've eased my mind with all this. I really appreciate it."

"You're welcome."

"How much do I owe you for the consultation?" Renee asked, reaching for her purse. "I'd like to pay you for your time."

"No, please. This one's on me. Anyway, I'm happy to help. I'd do anything for Dana. She's been through a lot." Allison put her hand on the doorknob. "Let me know how things turn out. Tell Dana goodbye for me and that I'll catch up with her later in the week."

"I sure will and thanks." Renee closed the door and had tucked Allison's business card into her wallet for safekeeping when Dana came into the kitchen.

"Did Allison leave?" she asked.

"Yes, just a few minutes ago. She said to tell you goodbye and that she would catch up with you later. She's a great person. And she really explained everything."

"Good," Dana said. "Yes, Al is great. She helped me out a lot with Risa's legal stuff. I can't thank her enough."

"She showed me a picture of her daughter. Beautiful girl."

"Yes, Lilly is a cutie. I'll have to stop over and see her next time I'm up in Chagrin."

"Why would Allison adopt a baby with her law partner?" Renee said. "She's such a pretty girl, I'd think she wouldn't have any trouble catching a husband and settling down."

"What are you talking about?"

"She said she and her partner adopted Lilly. Why didn't she just get married and have a child of her own?"

Dana laughed. "Renee, her partner isn't her law partner. She's her partner like Risa was my partner. You know, together."

"Allison is gay? No, sir! A pretty girl like her?"

"What's that supposed to mean? Because she's a lesbian, she can't be pretty?"

"She was wearing high heels."

"Renee!"

"I never would have known she was gay by looking at her."

"Well, most of us don't wear a sign around our necks announcing it to the entire world."

"She's just so blond and so pretty."

"And you're not half bad looking yourself."

"Oh, I'm not gay." The words slipped out before Renee knew it. She read the hurt in Dana's face and immediately tried to fix it. "Dana, I didn't mean that."

"What did you mean?" Dana voice was soft and low.

"I don't know. I guess I never considered myself to have that label."

Even though she understood where Renee was coming from and it probably wasn't that big a deal, Dana felt a tiny deadbolt locking down her heart. Was her relationship with Renee too good to be true? Was their relationship just something to get Renee through the night, so to speak? Dana hoped not. Though she hated to admit it, she was falling in love with Renee.

Chapter Sixteen

On the morning of her court appearance, Sara came downstairs wearing a tailored skirt and Renee's navy blue blazer. Allison had advised Sara that she needed to dress professionally when she appeared in court, like she was going on a job interview. Allison explained that doing so showed respect for the court, and the last thing she wanted was to come across as disrespectful.

Renee had to look twice to make sure this was the same kid who normally lounged around the house in grubby sweatpants and torn T-shirts.

"You look great," Renee said as she poured Sara a glass of orange juice.

"Thanks, Mom." Sara took the glass of juice. "I'm sorry you have to go through this."

"Honey, look. You made a mistake. A big mistake. But you know something? We all make mistakes. It's part of life."

"I just feel so bad."

"The most important thing is that we learn from our mistakes. Because if we don't learn from them, they become even bigger ones. Do you understand?"

Sara nodded. She sipped her juice as Renee bustled around the kitchen.

"You want some breakfast?" Renee asked.

"No, thanks. I'm not very hungry. Guess I'll go brush my teeth."

Dana arrived at eight thirty sharp to drive Renee and Sara to the courthouse.

"Good morning," Renee said as Dana let herself in through the back door.

"Morning." Dana stood in the doorway, hands folded in front of her, practically standing at attention. "Ready to go?"

"Sara will be down in a minute. Are you okay?"

"Uh-huh."

"You don't look okay. What's going on?" Renee stepped closer to Dana. She looked into her eyes searching for what Dana wouldn't tell her.

Dana dropped her gaze. "I'm fine, really."

Sara came into the kitchen.

"Gee, Sara, you could pass for an attorney dressed like that," Dana said.

Sara smiled weakly. "Thanks…I guess."

The lobby of the family court facility was standing room only. Sara, Renee, and Dana stood against a glass-block partition and waited to be called. Harried lawyers hurriedly flipped through paperwork while police officers stood guard over their orange jumpsuit-clad clients. The number of kids, some even younger than Sara, who were waiting for their cases to be heard frightened Renee. It was sad to think that Sara had something in common with them. This was surely a lesson in what one lapse of judgment could do to someone's life.

The bailiff, a sheriff's deputy, walked through the heavy wooden doors of the courtroom. "Sara Del Fino," he called out.

Sara looked as frightened as Renee felt.

"Good luck," Dana said.

"You're not coming?" Panic sounded in Renee's voice.

"You can do this." Dana patted her arm. "I'll be right here when you're done."

Renee took a deep breath. "Okay."

She and Sara followed the deputy into the courtroom. The heavy wooden door swung closed behind them.

The bailiff directed them to one of two tables at the front of the room. At the other table sat the representative for the store where Sara had stolen the clothing. The representative, a dowdy woman in her fifties, had the items spread out on the table in front of her.

"I need to see her paperwork," the bailiff said.

Renee pulled the papers out of her purse. Her hand visibly shook as she gave them to the deputy. He looked them over, strode up to the bench, and handed them to the judge.

The judge sat behind a huge mahogany desk. The great seal of Ohio, as well as the Ohio flag, were displayed behind her on the wall. There was no gavel banging or calling anything to order. The bailiff announced the next case to the courtroom. "State of Ohio versus Sara Del Fino. Will the defendant step forward please?"

Sara stood and looked at her mother. The bailiff came over and escorted her to a podium in front of the bench. Clasping the sides of the podium to stop her body from shaking, she felt like she was going to throw up.

Judge Katherine Jacobson, a blond woman in her late forties dressed in a conservative gray business suit, looked over Sara's documents through half-glasses. A stern expression clouded her face.

"Sara Del Fino," she said without looking up from the papers, "do you understand why you are here today?"

Sara nodded.

"Are you able to speak?"

"Yes…yes, ma'am." Sara's mouth was dry and her tongue felt like sandpaper.

"You've been charged with petty theft, shoplifting. How do you plea?" Judge Jacobson looked up from her paperwork directly at Sara.

Sara turned back toward her mother. Renee mouthed the words to her.

"No contest, Your Honor."

"I see. Do you understand the amount of damage these petty crimes inflict on our society? Not only the dollar amount of what you stole, but also the inconvenience that store owners must endure? They not only have to interrupt their day by coming here, but they also have to bear the increased costs of insurance to replace their losses and protect themselves and their businesses."

Sara looked down at the podium. "Yes, ma'am."

"Miss Del Fino, I see that this is your first offense. I also see by your school record that you're a good student. Those two things are encouraging to me. It means that all hope is not lost. It tells me that you committed this crime because of an error in judgment and that because you're a smart girl, you will not repeat this behavior ever again." Judge Jacobson looked over her half-glasses at Sara. "Am I right about that?"

"Yes, ma'am, I'll never do it again."

"I'm counting on that."

Judge Jacobson wrote something on Sara's papers and handed them to the bailiff. Sara could feel her heartbeat pound through her fingertips as she continued her death grip on the sides of the podium.

"Since you're taking responsibility for your actions, I'm going to let you off easy today. The store has advised me that the merchandise you took has been returned to them in good condition, so no monetary restitution needs to be paid. However, you'll need to pay your court costs. I'm going to sentence you to six months probation and ten hours of community service, which will be set up through the court and coordinated with your school. The terms of your probation are to meet with a counselor at your school every week who will then report your progress to the court. You will serve your community sentence each day after school until your service is complete."

Sara could feel her knees tremble as Judge Jacobson looked over her half-glasses at her. "Do you understand the terms of your sentence, Miss Del Fino?"

"Yes, ma'am."

"Fine. I hereby sentence you to ten hours of community service and one hundred fifty dollars in court costs to be paid today. And another thing, if I ever see you in my courtroom for another offense like this, you can be assured I won't be as easy on you as I was today. So I suggest that you concentrate your energy on your schoolwork and keep yourself out of trouble. Am I clear?"

Sara nodded nervously. "Yes, ma'am."

"Best of luck to you," Judge Jacobson said.

"Thank you, Your Honor." Sara lost the fight not to cry.

Renee stood and collected her at the podium. "You okay?"

Sara nodded with tears welling from her eyes.

"It's going to be okay." Renee gave her a tissue. She pulled her checkbook out of her purse, wrote a check to the court for one hundred fifty dollars, and handed it to the clerk.

"Let's go find Dana and get out of here." Renee put her arm around Sara's shoulders and walked her out of the room.

The waiting area had cleared out considerably. Dana was sitting in one of the brown plastic chairs reading a copy of *The Rise and Fall of the Cleveland Mafia*. She stood when she saw Renee and Sara.

"How'd it go?"

"Court costs and community service," Renee said, still holding on to Sara.

"That's not so bad."

"No, like Allison said, Sara was lucky. I can't thank you enough for getting in touch with her to help us. She certainly eased my mind."

"No problem."

"Let's get out of here," Renee said. "I think I've seen enough of the legal system for one day."

On the way home, Renee slid her hand across the seat to Dana, and their gazes met. "I'm sorry," Renee said.

"Sorry? For what?"

With Sara in the car, Renee had to be vague. "For what I said the other day." She opened her hand and Dana's slid into hers. Their fingers entwined, and Renee squeezed tight.

That evening after Sara and Lindsay left to go to the movies with Justin, Dana and Renee had a quiet dinner at Renee's. After dinner, they settled in with a big bowl of popcorn and a couple of DVDs they had rented. Dana put the first one in but couldn't concentrate on the plot. Even though Renee apologized for what she said about not being a lesbian, it still gnawed at Dana to the point where she could no longer let it go.

"Renee, I don't want you to pretend to be something you aren't," Dana said.

"Huh?" Renee looked over at Dana, not sure what she was talking about.

"I don't want you to pretend like you have feelings for me when you don't."

"I'm not pretending anything. What I feel for you is real. It's just hard for me to see myself as a lesbian."

"Why? Because you think it's demeaning?"

"No, that's not it."

"Then what is it?"

"I'm not the kind of person who walks around with a sign around my neck advertising my sexual preference. That's a private thing, and I want it to remain private. It has nothing to do with being ashamed of who I am. I just don't feel comfortable advertising it."

"That's it? That's the whole story?" Dana asked.

"Yep, that's the truth." Renee slid into Dana's arms. She laid her head against Dana's chest and almost fell asleep. It had been an exhausting day.

Chapter Seventeen

After Sara's court case, Dana made another trip to Cleveland to check on the building contractor's progress. A three-month job was turning into a nine-month project. The contractor said he was having difficulty getting supplies and blamed it on bad weather in the South. He said in order to get the home up to code, they had to replace a lot of the wiring and pipes and insulation before the finishing work could be done.

Before Dana headed back to Niles, she stopped off at her attorney's office to sign more papers regarding what now seemed like the longest lawsuit in history. She wondered whether it would ever be resolved. Petitions to determine heirship, asset reports, requalification of executor all seemed Greek to Dana and so unnecessary. She and Risa had their wills drawn up when they purchased the house in Cleveland Heights. Now some man she had only met once was trying to take it all away. Every time she thought of the circumstances, it turned her stomach. She just wanted to go on with her life, but it seemed as if someone or something always stood in her way.

On her way back from Cleveland, Dana stopped by the library to see Renee.

"How are things up north?" Renee asked.

"The same. Everything is more time and more money. I'm beginning to think I should sell that money pit. But let's not talk about it, okay?"

"Okay. The Martin Luther King holiday gives the girls a long weekend. I'm thinking of taking them skiing to upstate New York. You interested in joining us?"

Dana's face brightened. "You know, it's been a while since

I've skied." This might be just what she needed, to get out in the cold, fresh air and clear her head. "Yes, I'd love to go."

"Great, then it's a date. I'll make the arrangements. We can leave Saturday morning if that's okay."

"Sounds fine."

Dana returned to her apartment and found three messages on her answering machine. Two were hang-ups, and one was from her publisher, wondering when she would be sending the first draft of the new novel. Dana cleared the messages, punched on her laptop, and made a pot of coffee. She had a long night ahead of her since she only had three good chapters ready to turn in. She had been neglecting the book she had been sent here to write in the first place.

The problem was, she couldn't think straight when Renee was around. Her presence made her think of other things instead of bootleg murder rates and Prohibition-era gang wars. Dana couldn't stop thinking about loving Renee. She also felt powerless to stop her feelings.

The holiday weekend rolled around and not a moment too soon. Dana was eye weary from two solid days of writing but was able to finish six more chapters of the book. She e-mailed them to her publisher that morning.

Four inches of fresh snow had fallen overnight, making the conditions perfect for skiing. As they headed from Ohio to Pennsylvania and into New York, more snow fell, giving the normally dull gray landscape the appearance of a winter wonderland. Driving was a little dicey, but Dana got them there safe and sound.

The ski lodge was a series of three multi-tiered buildings. The main building housed the restaurant, as well as a huge lobby with a stone-front, floor-to-ceiling fireplace. The lodge bustled with activity as it seemed many folks had the same idea about taking advantage of the long weekend. Renee checked them in while Dana and the girls brought in the luggage. A bellman met them at the door and loaded their suitcases onto a luggage cart, and they waited for Renee to return with the room keys.

"We're in rooms 203 and 205," Renee said as she approached the group. They followed the bellman down the hall, first stopping in room 203. There they had the bellman unload all the luggage except Dana's. Dana and Renee had decided before going on the trip that it would be awkward if they all stayed in one room since the girls hadn't known Dana very long. They also felt it would be awkward if the girls had a room and Renee and Dana bunked together. What explanation could they give to justify that? Anyway, Renee didn't feel safe leaving her daughters alone all night in a strange place.

After they unpacked, they met in the lobby to purchase their lift tickets and board the shuttle to take them to the slopes. In less than an hour, they were riding high on the chair lifts, headed up the mountain for their first run of the day.

Dana stood back and watched as Sara and Lindsay dashed down the slopes. Renee had told her both girls had their father's athletic ability. They were fearless and well-skilled skiers.

Renee skied up next to Dana. "You going down?"

"In a minute. I just want to admire the beauty of all this. I had forgotten what it was like being up here and feeling so carefree."

"It is beautiful." Renee looked out over the rugged, snow-covered landscape.

Dana turned to her. "Thank you for asking me to come along."

"You're welcome. Thank you for coming with us. It means a lot to me. It feels like a new beginning."

Dana smiled.

"Last one to the bottom is a rotten egg!" Renee slid her goggles over her eyes and took off down the hill. Dana followed fast behind her.

At six the next morning, the alarm clock radio blared Meatloaf's "I'd Do Anything for Love" next to Dana's head. She slapped at the clock to turn off the loud music. Apparently, the person who occupied this room before her was a heavy sleeper. She lay flat on her back, naked and buried under the thick down comforter. When she went to bed the previous night, every muscle in her body ached. Once she got undressed, she was too sore to get dressed for bed. That morning was no better. Not only did her muscles ache, she was stiff, as well. She gingerly got up to a sitting position, then hobbled into the bathroom.

She was sitting on the toilet with her head in her hands when she heard a knock on the door.

"Who is it?" she shouted from the bathroom.

"It's Renee."

"Just a minute."

Dana hoisted herself up by clutching onto the bathroom sink and the shower curtain. Once on her feet, she flushed the toilet, washed her hands, and grabbed for the complimentary fluffy white bathrobe the lodge provided every guest. Slowly, she made her way to the door.

"Geez, what took you so long?" Renee asked.

"I'm a little stiff from yesterday. Aren't you?"

"No, not really." Renee twisted and turned at the waist like she was ready to begin an aerobics class. "Nope, I feel pretty good actually."

Groaning with every step, Dana moved aside to let Renee in.

Dana noticed that Renee's face was pink from the sun and wind exposure the day before, giving her skin a healthy glow.

Renee watched Dana struggle to walk. "Here, let me help you." She slipped her arm around Dana's waist and helped her back to the bed.

Dana sat on the edge of the bed with a thump.

"Oh, my aching ass," she said, laughing.

Renee burst out laughing, too.

"Here, let me see if I can get some of the kinks out." She sat behind Dana and worked her hands expertly on Dana's tight shoulders.

"Oh, that feels good." Dana moaned, getting lost in the sensation of Renee's warm, supple hands on her aching muscles. The gentle massage sent currents of desire to other parts of her body, as well. She tried to fight it, thinking that this wasn't the most appropriate place for this. After all, Renee's daughters were in the next room.

Dana tried to think of other things to take her mind off what her body was telling her, but it was no use; it felt so good.

Renee moved closer on the bed. Her soft warm breath tickled the tiny hairs on the back of Dana's neck. Her touch was soothing, and she smelled fresh, like lavender and vanilla. Dana turned on the bed and faced her.

"What?"

Renee's hair was still damp from her shower. Dana reached up and tucked two loose strands of hair behind her ears. Slowly and seductively, Dana's gaze slid downward from Renee's eyes to her mouth. A chill raced through Renee's body. Her heart jolted and her pulse quickened as Dana leaned in close.

Their lips brushed, sending electrical charges through each of them. Hungry for each other, their kisses became urgent. Dana was surprised at her own eager response in spite of her aching body.

Renee pulled Dana close. She stroked her face, gazing into her jeweled blue eyes. Dana kissed the inside of her palm.

"I think I've wanted this from the first time I saw you," Renee said.

Dana smiled. "The first day I walked into the library and saw you there, it stirred something in me I thought was dead. I'm glad it's not."

Dana kissed Renee again, and her tongue sent shivers straight to Renee's groin. Dana slid her hands under Renee's sweater. Renee's skin was hot and Dana's hands were cool.

Dana pushed Renee's bra up with her sweater and lowered her mouth to Renee's warm breast. Renee moaned. Dana's tongue seared a path from Renee's ribs down to her belly, and Dana smoothed her face against the soft skin of Renee's flat stomach.

Renee reached down, unzipped her jeans, and lifted her hips. Dana tugged off Renee's jeans and tossed them onto the floor.

Renee pushed the heavy white robe off Dana's shoulders and down her arms where it puddled at her waist. Dana shook off the robe. They were both totally naked now, except for Renee's ski socks.

In one sleek motion, Dana laid Renee down. She slid down

Renee's body and rested her head against Renee's thigh. She ran her fingers through the silky dark hair between Renee's legs. Renee lay perfectly still, afraid to move, afraid Dana would stop. She could feel Dana's warm breath centimeters away from her aching sex. Finally, Dana dipped her head and fireworks exploded in Renee's brain.

This was heaven, Renee thought afterward as she lay in Dana's arms. She was drunk, but not from alcohol this time. She was drunk on Dana, drunk on love. Pale winter sunlight filled the hotel room as they lay entwined in the rumpled sheets, basking in the afterglow of their lovemaking. Suddenly, there was a knock at the door that ripped them from their tranquil place.

"Mom? Are you in there?"

"Oh, shit," Renee and Dana said in unison as they bolted up and turned to each other much like two characters in a sitcom.

Sara and Lindsay waited outside the door while Renee rummaged around Dana's room retrieving her clothing from the floor, the nightstand, and the windowsill. The girls apparently were losing patience; they knocked again.

"Mom, Justin's here," Lindsay shouted through the door. "Can Sara and I go and have breakfast with him and his mom?"

Renee stopped dead in her tracks. "Justin's here with his mom. Oh, my God," she whispered.

"Renee, what's wrong? You really hate the kid that much?" Dana pulled her robe on and tied the belt tight around her waist.

"I don't hate him. I just feel uncomfortable around him. Like there's something about him I should know. It's a very uneasy feeling."

Dana picked up Renee's bra from the nightstand and handed it to her.

Lindsay pounded on the door again. "Mom!"

Renee stuffed her bra in the back pocket of her jeans, then yanked the door open. "I'm right here."

"Oh." Lindsay looked at her mother. "What were you doing in there?"

"Talking." Renee prayed that Lindsay wouldn't notice the telltale pink flush that covered her neck and chest. "I was waiting for Dana to get ready, and we were trying to plan our day."

Lindsay peeked around the half-closed door. "Where is she?"

Renee turned around and looked across the room. Dana was nowhere to be seen. Her hand shook as she held on to the doorknob. Then she noticed the closed bathroom door.

"She's still in the bathroom getting dressed," Renee said, feeling a little more at ease.

"Can Sara and I go eat with Justin since Dana's not ready yet?"

"Okay, you and Sara go ahead. Dana and I will catch up. She's kind of sore from yesterday's skiing, so it's taking her a little while. But just breakfast, okay? I don't want you two intruding on Justin and his mom's plans, you hear me?"

"Okay," Lindsay said. The girls headed down the hall toward the restaurant.

"Whew, that was close." Renee plopped down in the fireside chair next to Dana's bed. Dana emerged from the bathroom fresh from the shower. She wore dark jeans and a sky blue polo shirt that made her eyes sparkle. Renee's heart turned over in response.

Dana came over and sat on the arm of the chair. She wrapped her arm around Renee's shoulder and pulled her close. "You okay?"

Renee nodded. Then she began to cry.

"Hey, it's okay," Dana whispered, now rocking Renee. She kissed the top of her head. "Tell me what's wrong."

"Everything," Renee said. "Look at me. I'm a mess."

"You're not a mess."

"What am I doing?" Renee asked. "I've got two teenage daughters to raise, and I'm falling in love with a woman." Renee started to cry harder.

Dana felt a warm glow flow through her. She stood, took Renee in her arms, and held her tight. "Renee, that's wonderful." She kissed Renee's tears away.

"Is it?" Renee asked through teary eyes.

"Of course it is. But why are you crying? Do you regret our getting together?" Dana asked; her joy at Renee's admission began to deflate.

"No, that's not it at all. I love being with you. You don't know how much. I'm just no good at this. I have little idea what it's like to be in a relationship with another woman, and I'm a terrible mother."

"You're not a terrible mother. The girls are fine. Yes, you've all hit a few rough patches, but things are starting to turn around. And as far as being in a relationship with a woman, this is territory that is very different than your experiences as a teenager. Just relax. It will all work out. You'll see."

Renee rested her head on Dana's shoulder. She could hear Dana's heartbeat. Renee thought Dana was wrong. Yes, Dana knew what it was like to be in a lesbian relationship, but what did she know about raising kids? There were certain appearances that had to be held up when you became a parent. Especially in a small town like Niles, where everyone knew everyone else's business. Also, Renee had been down this road once before, and it had ended badly. She didn't want her relationship with Dana to come to that same fate. But she didn't know how to make things right for her and her daughters and Dana, as well.

"Why don't we go down and get something to eat?" Dana said.

Renee moved her head up and down against Dana's chest. They broke their embrace. "How are your muscles?"

"I'm still a little stiff. But that massage you gave me this morning really helped."

Renee smiled. She kissed Dana on the cheek, and they headed down to the restaurant to meet up with Lindsay and Sara and Justin and his mom.

As Renee and Dana approached the dining room, they spotted Lindsay, Justin, and Sara at a big round table in front of the fireplace. Before them sat nearly empty dishes with remnants of pancakes, sausages, eggs, and toast.

"Good morning, Justin," Renee said cheerfully. "Are you here by yourself?"

"Hi, Mrs. Del Fino. No, my mom is here. She went back to our room to get her wallet. She should be back shortly. Oh, here she comes," Justin said.

Renee turned around, and a wave of panic shot through Renee's entire being. She couldn't believe her eyes and blinked several times because what she was seeing wasn't registering. The two women stared at each other, apparently neither knowing what to say.

Finally, Justin's mother spoke. "Renee, it's been a long time."

It took a minute for Renee to find her voice. "Yes, it has been a long time. How have you been, Annie?"

Chapter Eighteen

Renee was stunned, to say the least, to see Annie right before her eyes after all this time. If she was the least bit uncomfortable about being on this trip with Dana and her daughters, she was now in panic mode running into Annie, and finding out she was Justin's mother was too much to comprehend. She needed to pull herself together and handle this matter like an adult, even though she hadn't felt like one in a long time. She was so insecure about her life and the direction it was going that this might just put her over the edge.

Renee took a deep breath and tried to take control of the situation.

"Annie, this is my friend, Dana. Dana, this is Annie, Justin's mother."

Annie extended her hand to Dana.

"Nice to meet you." Dana took Annie's hand.

This was too much for Renee to handle. She just wanted to get the girls and get out of there. But Annie had different plans.

"Have a seat," Annie said. "The kids are almost done, and I was going to order another cup of coffee before Justin and I headed out to the slopes. That will give us some time to catch up."

"Thank you, Annie," Renee said as she and Dana sat at the table. Renee's knees were shaking under the table, and she felt as if she had stepped into a time warp. She'd look over at Annie, then at Dana, who shrugged and opened her menu.

Annie looked at Renee, then over at Dana. By the look on Annie's face, she didn't appear to be buying the "friend" thing. *Oh, My God!* Can she tell by just looking at them that Renee and

Dana were more than friends? Worse yet, could she tell that they just had sex? Renee shook her head; she had to keep her mind clear to deal with this.

One by one, the kids peeled away from the table. Sara left first to go back to the room and brush her teeth. Then Lindsay and Justin went onto the deck to watch skiers come down the mogul hill, leaving the three adults alone.

"The kids are sure growing up fast," Annie said as she watched Justin and Lindsay leave the dining room.

"Yes, they are." Renee looked over the menu.

"You know that from the first time Lindsay came over to see Justin, even before I knew her last name, I knew she was your daughter."

"Really?" Renee asked.

"Oh, sure, she looks so much like you. And Tom a little bit, too, but boy, Sara really takes after her dad."

Suddenly, Annie felt uncomfortable mentioning Tom. She knew Tom had died but didn't have the courage to go to the funeral home to pay her respects. She didn't know how Renee would feel seeing her again after all this time. She certainly didn't want to add to her grief, but she felt she needed to say something.

"Renee, I am sorry for you loss. Tom was a nice guy."

"Thank you. Yes he was." Renee couldn't believe the scenario that was playing out before her. Annie knew Lindsay was her daughter but never said anything? And she knew of Tom's passing? This was too much for Renee to comprehend.

Renee had so many questions for Annie—when and why she decided to come home, about Justin and his father, who seemed not to be around much or at all—but now wasn't the time for that. She just wanted to get through breakfast without having a nervous breakdown.

Annie glanced down at Dana's hand and saw the gold wedding band on her finger. "Do you have kids?"

"No, I don't," Dana said.

"You and your husband never wanted kids?"

Dana was taken aback by her comment. So was Renee.

"I don't have a husband."

"I'm sorry. I mean, I saw the ring…I didn't mean to offend you."

"That's okay. A lot of people assume that. It's not a problem."

Dana thought about telling Annie the truth, that she had a partner who had died, but that would make things even more complicated, and the tension in the air could already be cut with a chain saw. What was it about this woman that had Renee so freaked out?

The waitress approached the table and took their orders. Dana was ravenous and ordered a cheese omelet with hash brown potatoes and a side of link sausages. Renee was afraid she would upchuck anything she would try to eat, so she ordered dry wheat toast and black coffee.

"Is that all you're going to eat?" Dana asked.

"I'm not very hungry."

Renee and Annie talked superficially about the kids over coffee while Dana sat in silence observing the two. She could tell by Renee's actions that something was wrong—but what?

Dana added three packs of Splenda to her coffee and wondered what it was about Annie that made Renee so uncomfortable.

Dana didn't like the vibe she was getting from her, like she knew something secret about Renee.

The kids returned to the table just as Renee and Dana finished their breakfast.

"Mom, can we go with Justin to the snowboard area?" Lindsay asked.

"That's on the other side of the mountain, Linz, I don't know. And besides, I think Justin's mom would like to spend some time just the two of them. "

"Oh, I don't mind taking the girls for a couple of hours if it's all right with you," Annie said.

Renee was shocked at Annie's audacious suggestion. When she got her wits about her, she reluctantly agreed.

"Yeah!" the girls shouted, raising their hands in the air.

Renee reached into the front pocket of her jeans. "Here's money to pay for your rentals." She handed each girl a fifty-dollar bill.

Lindsay and Sara looked at the money in their hands. "Gee, Sara, maybe we should skip the snowboarding and go shopping instead," Lindsay said in a teasing tone.

"Lindsay…"

"Okay, okay, Mom, I'm just kidding."

The girls left the lodge with Justin and Annie and piled onto the shuttle bus that would take them to the snowboarding area. Renee watched through the window as the bus pulled away. She took a last sip of her coffee.

"Renee, can I ask you something?"

Renee turned to face Dana. "Sure."

"You seemed pretty freaked out around Justin's mother. What's going on there?"

Renee took a deep breath and let it out slowly. "Remember that afternoon at your apartment when you made me lunch? The day we first got together?"

"Yes."

"Remember I told you that when I was in high school, I became involved with a girl and that it was more than a friendship."

"Yes."

"Well, Annie is the girl I was involved with."

Dana's eyes flew open wide. "You're kidding!"

Renee shook her head. "Nope, I wouldn't kid about that."

"But she's Justin's mother. Did you know that before now?"

"Nope. I'm just as shocked as you are. I didn't know Annie had moved back to Niles, let alone that she had a son. She even knew who Lindsay was and about Tom's dying. That really surprised me. I mean, we hadn't spoken to each other in years, and what are the odds that our kids would be attracted to each other or that they would even find each other?"

"Geez, this is amazing," Dana said.

Renee didn't know what to say. Her mind was whirling trying to comprehend it all. She wondered what Annie thought about seeing her again and what she must have thought about seeing her with Dana.

Renee looked out the window. Snow started to come down, big puffy flakes that seemed to plop onto the ground. "I hope they'll be okay. Neither one of them has ever been snowboarding."

"They're pretty athletic girls," Dana said. "They'll be fine. I'm more concerned about you."

"Why me?

"Because you seem very upset about meeting up with this woman again."

"Well there's nothing to worry about. That was years ago. And we were kids then. So don't worry."

Dana nodded and took another sip of coffee.

"So…" Renee set down her coffee cup and let out a big sigh. "It appears we have some unsupervised time to ourselves. The girls and I have a Jacuzzi in our room. Can I interest you in a long soak in a hot tub, Ms. Renato?"

Chapter Nineteen

Dana took Renee up on her offer. They barely got the door shut behind them when clothes began flying off. Shirts, pants, undies, and socks littered the carpet around the bed in Renee's hotel room.

As the Jacuzzi filled, Dana and Renee lounged on the bed, amazed at how well their bodies fit together.

"Renee?"

"Hmm?"

"What is it about Justin's mother that has you so upset?"

"I don't want to talk about Justin's mother right now. Anyway, it's not important. We were friends a long time ago. It's been a while since we've seen each other, that's all." Renee rose to check the water's progress. Dana stood, as well, and pulled Renee to her.

"That's all?"

"That's all," Renee said, unable to meet Dana's gaze.

Renee kissed Dana hard. She reached down and parted the silky triangle of hair between Dana's legs.

Dana trembled at Renee's touch. "If you keep that up, we'll never get in the tub," she said with a sly smile. Dana gave a little laugh. "My butt's still sore. I don't know about you, but I'm going in."

With a groan, she climbed into the Jacuzzi. The warm circulating water felt so good on her aching muscles.

"Ah…this is heaven." She sank deep into the water.

Renee climbed in, straddled Dana's hips, and sat on her lap.

"Well, isn't this cozy?" Dana said. A wide grin covered her face.

Renee bent down and kissed her. The kiss was so deep, Dana could feel it clear down to her toes.

Suddenly, Renee heard the click of the access card in the door. Before she could do anything about it, Lindsay was standing in the doorway, staring in utter disbelief at the scene before her. Renee jumped up and wrapped herself in a towel. Dana slid down farther in the tub to conceal herself from Lindsay.

"Oh, my God, what are you doing?" Lindsay screamed. She covered her mouth with her hand, then ran down the hall. The door slammed behind her. Renee jumped out of the tub and threw on her clothes. She tore down the hall to find Lindsay.

Oh, God, Oh, God. I can't believe she walked in on us. Oh, my God, what am I going to say? Renee almost knocked over one of the maid carts in her path. She reached the lobby. No sign of Lindsay. She looked in the restaurant. No Lindsay. Finally, out on the deck, she found her curled up against the wooden railing.

"Lindsay." Renee put a hand on her shoulder.

"Don't touch me." Lindsay pulled away.

"Lindsay, we need to talk." Renee felt surprisingly calm considering that her daughter had just walked in on her and her lesbian lover. "What are you doing back so soon? You're supposed to be with Justin."

"Sara hurt her wrist. Justin's mom took her over to the urgent care place to have it looked at."

"Sara's hurt? What happened?"

"She was trying out Justin's new snowboard and fell. I think she broke her wrist. Justin's mom told me to come get you so you could sign for Sara to be treated."

Renee felt like all the life had been kicked out of her. Here was more proof that she was a terrible mother. And now she had to talk to her daughter about something she had never dreamed she would be talking to anyone about.

"I'm sorry about what you just saw. I'm terribly sorry, and once we make sure Sara's okay, you and I need to talk."

"I don't want to talk about anything." Lindsay turned away and clutched the wooden railing. "How could you, Mom? Ever since Daddy died, it's like you're someone else. Someone I don't know. Someone I don't want to know."

"I know you're upset."

"You don't know how I feel. How could you? Now that Daddy's dead, you've turned into a big lezzie? At least what Justin and I did was normal. You have no room to tell me what to do. What you do is disgusting."

Renee grabbed her daughter by the shoulders. She could barely see Lindsay's face through her hot tears. "No matter what has happened, I'm still your mother."

"Then start acting like it."

"Look, I'm sorry that you think I'm a terrible mother. I know it feels like your entire world is crashing in on you, but you know what? You're not the only one that the world is crashing in on. You're not the only one in this family who lost someone they loved. I loved your father, too, and it hurts me just as much as it hurts you." Renee's voice trembled. "I'm doing the best I can, Linz."

"Your marriage to Daddy was a lie."

"No, it wasn't. I loved your father very much. This has absolutely nothing to do with him. It's complicated. Even I don't understand it." Renee felt defeated. How could she make Lindsay understand where she was coming from if she didn't know herself?

"I wish Daddy never died."

"I know. I wish he never died, too. But he did, and now you're stuck with me. We can either move on from here and cope with what life has dealt us or we can give up and let life pass us by. I'm doing the best I can with what we have left. I'm not perfect, but no one is."

Renee remembered something she had heard on *Dr. Phil* about not expecting kids to deal with adult issues. She felt guilty for bringing this to Lindsay. It wasn't Lindsay's problem to deal with, it was hers. She needed to step up and take control of it.

"I'm sorry for putting you through this. This isn't your issue, it's mine. I don't want you to worry about it. I'll take care of it. You and Sara are more important to me than anything else in the world."

Lindsay's expression darkened with an unreadable emotion. "Do you regret marrying Daddy?"

"Oh, my, honey, no, not for one minute. If I hadn't married your father, I wouldn't have you or Sara. You're the greatest gifts we could have given each other."

"But you said I was an accident, a mistake," Lindsay said, tears now formed in her eyes.

"Lindsay, that's not true. You were unexpected, but you were always wanted."

"So what about now?"

"What do you mean, what about now?"

"Everything's different now."

"My love for you and Sara isn't different. It's still as strong as the day I gave birth to you. That kind of love never goes away."

"What about Dana? Do you love her?"

Renee thought about this for a moment. Did she really love Dana or was it the deceiving combination of intrigue and lust?

"I do care about her. We're just getting to know each other, so it's really too soon to tell where this is going. But my feelings for Dana have nothing to do with you. You and Sara are my number one priority, and I want you to know that I'm going to do my best to take care of you and love you because you're the world to me," Renee said. "Oh, my God, Sara's waiting…"

Renee grabbed Lindsay by the hand, and they rushed through the lobby and out into the snowy parking lot to their car. Fifteen minutes later, they arrived at the urgent care area. Sara was sitting in the waiting room with Justin and Annie, her right wrist wrapped in an ACE bandage.

"It's just a sprain," Annie said to Renee as she walked into the waiting area.

"Thank you so much, Annie, for taking care of her." Renee pulled Sara close. It had been an emotional afternoon, and she was exhausted.

"No problem," Annie said. "I'm glad it was just a sprain."

The group headed back to the lodge in separate cars. Sara rode with Renee while Lindsay rode with Justin and Annie. Renee wondered whether Lindsay would share with Justin what she had walked in on that afternoon. She shuddered to think if they would tell Annie and what her reaction would be.

If Annie figured out what had happened at the ski lodge, it would only make the relationship between the two women more strained. After all, it had been almost twenty years since Renee and Annie had spoken. Shouldn't two women who were once good friends be able to put their differences behind them, especially now that their children were dating?

Chapter Twenty

Three weeks after the ski trip, things were still strained in the Del Fino household. Lindsay found it hard to even look at Renee. She felt her mother was a stranger, someone she never knew, and she didn't know what to do with those feelings. She couldn't get the picture out of her mind of her mother with that woman. It made her sick to her stomach to think about it.

Instead of coming home after school each day, she went to Justin's house. The only thing that felt right to her was being with Justin. He was the only stable thing in her life now that her dad was gone and her mother was a lesbian. When she was with Justin, everything bad seemed to melt away. Plus she knew that her being with him drove her mother crazy worrying about what they were doing together.

For some reason, this gave Lindsay a sense of satisfaction. Her thinking was that her mother was no better than she was. After all, wasn't she also sneaking around having sex with someone she wasn't supposed to?

When the dust settled, Renee and Dana talked. They both felt guilty about the toll their relationship took on Renee's family. They decided that it would be better if they only spent time alone together at Dana's apartment. Everyone seemed to need a break, and this appeared to be the best answer for now. Although it was difficult for Renee to drag herself out of Dana's warm soft bed on the nights they were together, Renee made it a point to be home before her daughters woke up in the morning.

One morning just before the sun came up, Renee gingerly unlocked the back door and tiptoed into the kitchen. Instead of going upstairs to bed, she camped out on the couch until it was time to get ready for work. As she lay there, she heard the back door open. She bolted upright, and her heart pounded with fear. She got up and snatched the portable phone from its cradle on the end table to dial 911 if necessary. She hid behind the entryway wall between the kitchen and living room to get a glimpse of the intruder.

In the kitchen, she saw the outline of a petite figure with her hair tied in a ponytail. She immediately flipped on the kitchen light.

"Lindsay! Do you know what time it is? Have you been out all night?"

Lindsay jumped. Apparently, the bright light and Renee's voice had startled her. She held on to the kitchen counter to steady herself.

"What do you care? When I called here at ten thirty to ask if I could stay until eleven, Sara said you hadn't come home yet. She said she was going to bed, so I just stayed at Justin's."

"You know better than to stay out all night. What did Justin's mother say?"

"His mom ignores us. I don't think she likes me."

"Maybe if you'd come home at a decent hour, she might have more respect for you."

"But it's okay for you to stay out all night? You have the same clothes on that you wore to work yesterday. Maybe if you came home at a decent time, I'd have more respect for you."

"I'm the adult here, and you're the kid. Just because I'm not here 24/7 doesn't mean the rules change. You have a curfew, and I expect you to abide by that whether I'm here or not. You're old enough to know better."

"You know what, Mom? All those things you said at the ski lodge about how Sara and I are the most important thing in your life are a bunch of lies. I can see what's important to you."

Renee's anger simmered below the surface. It took every bit of restraint she had not to explode. She knew she shouldn't allow Lindsay to speak to her like this. But she felt guilty. She could say one thing to the girls, but her actions said a lot more.

"I'm sorry. I really thought you and Sara were okay while I was away. I made sure I was home before you got up for school. I thought that was enough. I guess I was wrong."

"What's going on?" Sara appeared in the kitchen doorway. She yawned, rubbed her eyes, and sat at the kitchen table.

"Nothing, honey," Renee said. "It seems Lindsay and I have both been out way past our bedtimes. But that won't happen again, will it, Linz? For either of us."

Lindsay and Sara went upstairs to get ready for school. Renee sat at the kitchen table and laid her head on top of her crossed arms. How did things get so messed up? Her life had changed so drastically that she didn't recognize it anymore.

Out of the corner of her eye, she saw the Amaretto bottle on top of the refrigerator. She fought the urge to reach for it.

Chapter Twenty-one

At the library, Renee poured two cups of coffee from the antique coffee urn in the break room and brought them over to Dana's table.

"Hi." Renee handed Dana a cup of coffee.

Dana looked at Renee and seemed to sense that something was wrong. She took the Styrofoam cup and took a sip. "You okay?"

"Uh-huh." Renee waited until Dana got settled in before she told her about what had happened with Lindsay that morning. She couldn't help but think that maybe she never should have brought Dana into Lindsay's and Sara's lives. Was she so naïve to think that her relationship with Dana would enhance the girls' lives, as well as her own? Maybe if she had talked to them first about her feelings for Dana, things would be better.

Renee sat across from Dana and stared into her cup.

"Are you going to tell me what's wrong, or am I going to have to guess?"

Renee looked up and forced a weak smile. "Lindsay stayed out all night last night."

"What? You're kidding."

"Nope. She said she called home around ten thirty to see if she could stay at Justin's until eleven, but when she found out I wasn't there, she took it upon herself to stay out all night."

"Oh, my. So what did you do?"

"I freaked out as usual. She knows better. It's like nothing I say to her matters."

"You know that's not true. She's just testing you. That's what kids her age do."

"I don't know, Dana. I think it's more than that. I feel like I'm losing control with her."

"Why do you think that?"

"Because when I reprimanded her for being out all night, she looked at me and commented on the fact that I was still wearing the same clothes I went to work in yesterday morning. She said I was no better than she is. And I'm afraid she's right."

Dana bowed her head. "I'm sorry, Renee. Maybe the overnight things aren't a good idea."

Renee tore at the edges of her cup. She swallowed hard, then spoke. "I was thinking the same thing."

"At least we have this place." Dana reached across the table and touched Renee's hand.

"Yes. At least we have this." Renee looked up and smiled.

The library seemed to be the only sanctuary left for Renee and Dana. It gave them time together that no one questioned. On the surface, they appeared to be two good friends. Renee was sure no one had any idea how deep their relationship had become.

Renee looked down at the shreds of Styrofoam that lay in front of her on the glossy oak table. She wished she and Dana could go on like they did last week and the week before that and the week before that. But she couldn't shake the sinking feeling in her heart.

She scooped up the Styrofoam shreds and went back to her duties at the reference desk.

Dana pulled several books from the reference shelf on James Munsene, an ambitious racketeer from Cleveland who moved to the Mahoning Valley in the late 1920s. He gained notoriety and an indictment when he was charged with bribing then-Sheriff J.H. "Jack" Smith in attempts to allow Munsene to operate a gambling room in Warren, Ohio.

Dana typed away on her laptop, not even bothering to break for lunch. Renee bought some cheese crackers from the vending machine and fixed Dana a fresh cup of coffee with cream and sugar, just as she knew she liked it.

"I thought you might be hungry." Renee set the crackers and

the coffee on the table next to Dana. "You seem to be getting a lot done today."

"My publisher called this morning. She's been pretty patient with me up to now, but she wants the finished manuscript on her desk in two weeks."

"Wow. I guess I never realized that your work here would be done someday."

"The research part will be done. I found a lot of great stuff here. For such a small area, it's rich in organized crime history. But actually, I found more here than I expected." A secretive smile softened Dana's lips. She opened the package of crackers and offered one to Renee.

Renee shook her head. "No, thanks." Renee felt a lump in her throat the size of New Jersey. "Will you be moving back to Cleveland once the manuscript is finished?"

"Yes. I have to. I have the house renovations to contend with."

"They're still not finished?"

"Not completely. The major stuff is done, and I can supposedly move back in within the next week or two." She took a bite of cracker and a sip of coffee.

Renee slid into the chair next to Dana. "I guess we need to talk about what happens next."

"Yes, I guess so. You know, Cleveland isn't that far away. It may be just the amount of distance from all this that will do everybody some good."

Renee felt like she was about to cry. "Are you breaking up with me?"

"Oh, no, Renee, I'm sorry. That's not what I meant. I just know things have been difficult lately, especially with all the stuff going on with Lindsay and Sara. I can't help but think my presence here has only complicated things."

"Don't say that. You've opened up so much in my life. If it wasn't for you, I don't know how I would have gotten through the last few months."

"That may be so, but our being together isn't helping Lindsay and Sara."

Renee wished it hadn't come to this. Would she have to choose between Lindsay and Sara and Dana?

"I was going to have my mother come over on Friday," she said, not willing to give in to their relationship's foreboding fate. "She can stay with the girls, and you and I can have some private time. Maybe we can talk about this then. Grab a bite to eat or something."

"Okay. Friday's good. I need to go to Cleveland for a few days to take care of some business that can't wait until I'm finished here, but I'll be back by Friday."

"Book business?" Renee asked.

"No, house business."

"Oh." Renee didn't push the matter.

A line was beginning to form at the reference desk. "I better get back to work." Renee returned to the desk. She glanced over occasionally and watched as Dana worked. It made her sad to even think about Dana not being there, but what could she do?

When it was closing time, Dana carried Renee's book satchel while she finished her tasks. Dana waited by her side until Renee got the place locked up tight. They walked near each other, their hands touching as they strolled along the marble walkway that led to the back parking lot, which was concealed in the shadows of the life-size statue of President McKinley.

Dana took Renee's keys and unlocked the car door. She set the satchel on the passenger's seat. "I'll see you Friday." Dana felt bad about being vague with Renee about the house business, but she didn't want to add more tension to their already strained situation. "I'll pick you up here, okay?"

"Yes, that's fine." Renee slid into the driver's seat.

Dana handed Renee her keys, bent down, and kissed her on the cheek. She closed the car door and waited until Renee started the car before getting into her own. As she sat in the dark and watched Renee pull away, her heart felt heavy.

Renee drove home with tears in her eyes. She had never been so torn between two things so much in her life as she was now. She wanted her girls to be happy, but she wanted to be happy, too.

Why couldn't those two things coexist in her world?

But her family was in trouble. Lindsay acted out more every day. She practically flaunted her sexual relationship with Justin in Renee's face. It wouldn't surprise her one bit if she came home and found them going at it on the kitchen table.

Sara, on the other hand, had become a hermit. Since her shoplifting experience, she'd broken her ties with Dakota. She would come home after school and spend the evenings holed up in her room, listening to Janis Joplin CDs.

At least Sara was keeping her weekly appointments with Mrs. Calderone, the school counselor. Mrs. Calderone sent written notice every week that she and Sara had met. Renee had hoped those meetings would help Sara, allow her to open up more about what was going on in her life, but they seemed to be doing the opposite.

Although Renee sensed Lindsay was angry with her, she felt that Sara wasn't so much angry as she was disappointed in her. After all, Renee wasn't like the other mothers anymore; she was dating another woman. That had to be a hard thing to accept at any age. Hell, who was she kidding? Renee had a hard time accepting it, so how could she expect her teenage daughters to?

Renee pushed through the back door and found Lindsay and Justin sitting at the kitchen table, not having sex like Renee imagined. Lindsay was making bologna sandwiches, a domestic chore Renee rarely saw her daughter perform.

"Wow, to what do we owe this honor?" Renee watched her daughter smear mustard on a slice of Wonder bread.

Lindsay slapped the slice of bread on top of a huge mound of bologna, lettuce, and tomato. She cut the sandwich in half, placed it on a white paper plate, and handed it to Justin.

"At least someone around here cooks," Lindsay said.

Renee took a deep breath, trying to calm down. "Lindsay, I know you're still upset over what happened this morning, and I'm sorry about that, but I'm still your mother. You have no right to talk to me this way."

Lindsay turned her back on Renee.

"Justin, would you mind taking your sandwich and eating in

the living room? I need to talk to Lindsay for a second."

Justin nodded. He picked up his sandwich and a can of Pepsi and lumbered into the living room.

"Where's Sara?"

"Upstairs in her room."

"I need to talk to both of you. Could you run up and get her?"

Lindsay wiped her hands on the dishtowel, then went to get Sara.

Both girls returned a few minutes later. Sara appeared to have just woken up. Her hair was plastered to her head and looked as if it hadn't been combed in days.

"Sara, what's wrong, honey? Are you sick?" Renee felt Sara's forehead with the back of her hand.

Sara shook her head. "No, Mom, I'm okay."

"Have a seat." Renee gestured to the chairs around the table.

Sara slid into her chair. Lindsay plopped down with a huff.

"Okay. We need to talk about my relationship with Dana." Renee paced around the kitchen trying to find the right words.

"What's to talk about?" Lindsay said. "It's over, isn't it? You're not going to hook up with her again, are you?"

"There's a little more to it than that," Renee said. "I like Dana a lot. And I thought you girls liked her, too."

"I like Dana. She's always been very nice to me," Sara said.

Lindsay shot a look of anger at her sister.

"I know this hasn't been easy for you," Renee said. "My relationship with Dana isn't what people are used to. But maybe if we talk about it, you'll understand it a little better and maybe help me understand what you're feeling."

Not in a million years did Renee think she would be having this conversation with her girls. By the looks on their faces, they wanted to talk about this about as much as she did, which was not at all.

"Because my relationship with Dana may be different doesn't mean I'm different. I'm still the same person I've always been."

"But you are different," Lindsay said. "It's like living with an imposter, like nothing we knew about you was true. So why should we believe what you say now?"

"Because I'm still your mom. And a mother's love for her children is unconditional. My love for you and Sara is unconditional, and that's the truth. No matter what happens or who might come into my life, nothing will ever change that."

"It's still not right." Lindsay folded her arms across her chest and stared down at the table.

Suddenly, Sara spoke up. "Mom, Mrs. Calderone told me that just because people that are the same sex love each other doesn't mean they're bad."

Renee was taken aback by Sara's comment. "You've talked to Mrs. Calderone about this? When?"

"Right after we got back from the ski trip. I couldn't stand how you and Lindsay were fighting all the time. And I missed having Dana around."

Renee plunked down in the chair, stunned at her daughter's straightforwardness. "What else did you tell Mrs. Calderone?"

"I told her everything. About Daddy dying. About how sad we all were. About how lonely you were until you met Dana. And that I thought you might be a lesbian."

"Oh, my God." Renee covered her mouth with her hand.

"You didn't!" Lindsay said, bursting into laughter.

"Shut up, Lindsay," Sara said. "I don't see you making things any better. All you care about is stupid Justin."

As if on cue, Justin came into the kitchen. "Any more Pepsi?"

Renee pulled open the refrigerator door and tossed Justin another can of Pepsi. He popped the top off and sucked on his fingers, trying to catch the cascade of foam that tumbled over the edge. He lumbered back into the living room, leaving the women alone again.

"So are you?" Sara asked.

"Am I what?"

"Are you a lesbian?"

Renee sighed deeply, feeling the weight of the question again. Was she gay or was she just trying it on to see how it fit?

"To be honest, honey, I'm not sure. I mean, I care about Dana very much." Renee lowered her head. She couldn't help thinking about what Lindsay had walked in on at the ski lodge, and she wondered what Lindsay was thinking now. Did she think Renee was a hypocrite? After all, what she saw in the hotel room would have left no doubt in anyone's mind that Renee was gay. She felt so vulnerable, so exposed; it made her feel ashamed.

"Anyway, Dana will be moving back to Cleveland in a few weeks. Her research is done here, and there's no need for her to stay any longer."

"Good." Lindsay looked up, her arms still tightly crossed across her chest. "Good riddance."

"Lindsay, please." Renee's patience was wearing thin.

"Does that mean you're breaking up with Dana?" Sara asked.

"No. Dana and I want to maintain our relationship. It would be long distance, but we think it's worth a try."

"Great." Lindsay slouched down in her chair and sulked.

"Are you planning on moving in with her someday?" Sara asked.

"No, honey. Not in the near future anyway. Why would you think that?"

"Because isn't that what people do when they like each other? Move in together?"

"Well, yes, sometimes they do."

Suddenly, Renee realized that she didn't want to move to Cleveland or anywhere else for that matter. There had been too much upheaval in their lives as it was. Having to move to a different city, a big city, would be too much for her and the girls. The decision she was reluctant to make would be made for her if she wanted to keep her family together.

"Well, if you're ever thinking of moving in with Dana, you can count me out," Lindsay piped in. "I'll go live with Grandma."

"No one is going anywhere, Lindsay." Renee was getting weary of this conversation. She couldn't change Lindsay's mind about her relationship with Dana.

Renee also learned something. At this point in their relationship, although she cared about Dana, she didn't love her enough to pull up stakes and make a life with her somewhere else. Was that what had happened with Annie? No, Renee admitted to herself, she had loved Annie deeply, but she had let her move away without going with her. She didn't have the courage or the heart back then to throw away her family and leave everything and everybody she knew, and she certainly didn't have it now.

She sometimes wondered what Annie thought now. Did she still hate Renee for not going with her? Although Renee was shocked to see Annie again after all these years, deep inside her lingered feelings for Annie she didn't want to deal with right now.

Chapter Twenty-two

Friday arrived and Renee was nervous. The thought of what she had to tell Dana tore at her heart. She rehearsed in her mind how she would tell Dana what a great person she was and what a wonderful time she'd had with her, but she had to be realistic. Renee didn't see any future for their relationship. She had her daughters to raise and didn't think it was in their best interest to openly live her life as a lesbian. She hoped and prayed that Dana would understand.

Dana arrived at the library twenty minutes after Renee finished work. "I was afraid you weren't coming." Renee gathered her things from behind the reference desk.

"I had some errands to run before we got together," Dana said. "Anyway, I planned a little surprise for you."

"A surprise? What kind of surprise?"

"You'll see." Dana took Renee's heavy book satchel from her and slung it over her shoulder.

"We'll take my car and pick yours up later," Dana said.

"How long are we going to be gone? I told my mom we were just getting dinner and wouldn't be late."

"Oh, we'll get dinner. And I'll make sure to have you home at a decent time."

Dana's shy smile brought a little lift to Renee's anxious mood. Dana took the rest of Renee's things and stowed them in the trunk of her car.

The early spring day was beautiful, unseasonably warm for the second week in April. "Where are we going?" Renee asked, reasonably curious. By the direction Dana was driving, they weren't going toward town to one of their usual dining spots.

"I thought we'd take a ride up north."

"To Cleveland?"

"Yep. That okay?"

"Sure." Renee was surprised. Dana always seemed a bit secretive about something in Cleveland.

The drive along Route 422 was lovely. The fields and farms seemed to be waking from their long winter sleep, ready to start life anew. After about a forty-minute drive, Dana pulled into a driveway with a closed iron gate. She pulled up to an intercom box and punched in a bunch of numbers on the keypad. Slowly, the gate slid open. Dana drove through it and down the paved asphalt road. After a while, the asphalt turned into a well-worn dirt road. At the end of the dirt road, Dana brought the car to a stop.

"Here we are." She got out of the car, ran around to the back, and opened the trunk. Renee watched from her seat in disbelief as Dana unloaded a card table, two chairs, a white linen tablecloth, some candles, an ice bucket and bottle of wine, three grocery bags of food, and a Hibachi grill.

Slowly, Renee got out of the car. "Where are we? And what is all this?" she asked, unable to keep the smile from her face.

"You said you wanted to go out for dinner. So here we are… out for dinner."

Dana poured charcoal into the grill and squirted lighter fluid on it from a small metal can. She held the can up to Renee as a reminder of the first time they cooked out together.

Renee laughed, remembering.

After lighting the grill, Dana unwrapped two thick steak filets and set them on the grill to cook. The sizzling meat smelled wonderful. Dana placed two skewers of shrimp on the grill rack next to the meat. She opened the bottle of wine and poured a glass for each of them.

"Dana, this place is beautiful," Renee said as she accepted the glass of wine.

"I haven't brought anyone here in a long time, but every time I come back, it feels like I'm coming home."

"You lived here?"

"This is where I grew up. My mother still lives up the road

a ways in the big house. When my father died, the property was sectioned off and deeded to me and my brothers. This section is property my father left me. A few years after Risa and I got together, we were going to build our dream house here, but then we found the house in Cleveland Heights. That house was closer to work for both of us, and we fell in love with it. So this lot has remained empty. We'd come out here once in a while on picnics or just to get away from the noise in the city."

Renee looked around at the budding trees and grass and foliage. "Thank you for bringing me here." Although Renee felt honored, her stomach tightened with guilt. Dana was finally opening up to her, and now she had to tell her that she needed to end their relationship.

Renee watched as Dana turned the steaks and shrimp skewers on the grill. A warm feeling spread inside of her as she thought of the first time she watched Dana barbecue on that day she helped her with the outside chores. How could she not want to spend her life with this wonderful woman?

"So how did your meeting go?" Renee asked, postponing the inevitable.

Dana was quiet for a moment. When she spoke, her voice held an undercurrent of anger. "Not so good. I found out today that I have to sell the house in Cleveland Heights."

"Why? Is there a problem with the contractor?"

"No. I lost half of it in a court settlement. Today was the last hearing, and I lost."

"Court settlement? I don't understand."

"Risa and I had wills drawn up leaving everything to each other. When Risa died, her father came here from Phoenix for her funeral. Up to then, I had never laid eyes on him, and Risa hadn't seen him since she graduated from high school. Her father got wind of the will and found out that his deceased daughter had some valuable assets. Risa and I owned the house in Cleveland Heights jointly, and he wanted Risa's half, so he contested her will."

"That's terrible. Is that the reason you made all those trips up here during the last few months?"

"Yes. Risa's father was relentless. He was bound and determined to take the house from me. I had to hire two estate lawyers, one an expert in gay and lesbian estate law."

"That doesn't seem fair. If you and Risa bought that house together and had legal documents drawn up stating your wishes, how can he just come out of the woodwork and have any right to take that away from you?"

"Because the state of Ohio said he has a right. The issue involves the constitutional amendment adopted in Ohio prohibiting gay marriage. Risa's will was a contract, so it was unenforceable. The beneficiary rights revert back to the next of kin, giving Risa's father the right to claim her half of our assets."

"Dana, I'm so sorry. How long has this been going on?"

"Almost three years. The case took forever to make its way through the legal system. Because it's so new and the language of the law is so vague, they didn't know how to interpret it. This law not only affects gay and lesbian rights, it also affects anyone who is in a domestic partner relationship or siblings who may own property together. Even if you wanted to give Lindsay or Sara, your children, power of attorney, it might no longer be valid to do so."

"It affects straight people, too? Who would be stupid enough to put that kind of law in place?"

"Our state government. Personally, I think the amendment was passed out of fear. Most things that don't make sense come from fear."

"I have to be honest with you. I've never given this legal thing much thought. When Tom died, I had more than enough help with his life insurance, our house deed, everything. All his assets flowed directly to me."

"Unfortunately, that's not the case for everyone. And not only is it the legal issues, this is a personal assault. I feel violated, misunderstood, misrepresented, and hated by people who are ignorant of who gays and lesbians truly are."

Renee didn't know what to say. She felt guilty because she was exempt from all this. "So what happens now?"

"Nothing. Today was the final hearing." Dana picked up a

knife and poked it into one of the steaks to check for doneness. The meat sizzled as she expertly flipped it onto its other side.

"There's nothing else they can do? What about an appeal?"

"My attorneys ran out of defense tactics. The law held up in court, and Risa's father is entitled to half of the house. I have to buy him out or sell it and send him her interest in the house within thirty days of the sale."

"Oh, Dana, I'm so sorry. I know how much that house meant to you. So what will you do in the meantime? Where will you live?"

"I haven't told my family yet, but I'm sure my mom will let me stay with her awhile. I've always loved this place and am seriously thinking of finally building here. That's why I wanted to bring you here to see it. Being with you has opened my eyes to a lot of things. One of those things is that you can't live in the past. At some point, you need to move on or you're just throwing away your life. So even though what happened today was devastating, it's liberating, as well."

"Why's that?"

"Because it gives me the chance to really start over."

"Well, that sounds like a good plan," Renee said, proud that Dana could turn such a terrible thing into something better.

Dana and Renee sat quietly as they looked out over the beautiful landscape. Renee's mind was reeling. Now that Dana told her about losing the house, this didn't feel like the best time to tell her that she needed to end their relationship for her family's sake.

Dana turned toward Renee. "You okay? You seem lost in thought."

Renee remained silent, not quite sure of what to say.

"Renee, I know now isn't the time. We both have a lot to work out, but what do you think about joining me here someday?"

Renee looked down. Dana's request was forcing the issue. She felt a touch of sadness. "Dana, my girls have had so much disruption this past year. I couldn't take them away from their home and friends. Besides, I don't know if this is right for me and the girls. You know, this lifestyle."

"Living in a nice home surrounded by all this beauty isn't a good way to live?"

"No, that's not what I mean. I mean, I don't know if I can ever live as a…"

"Dyke, lesbian, carpet muncher?"

"Carpet muncher? I've never heard that one before."

"No matter what you call it, those are just names, and didn't we learn in kindergarten that names will never hurt us?"

"Okay, I see your point. But—"

"But what? Renee, don't you get tired of hiding? Of pushing down your feelings about who you really are? Aren't you tired of being ashamed of it? There's nothing to be ashamed of."

"Okay, okay, I know what you're telling me is true, but what about Lindsay and Sara? What about my parents? Oh, my God, can you see me telling my mother that I'm gay? That would fix everything because she would just kill me. She'd have my kids taken away and kill me."

"When I told my mother I was gay, I was terrified. But you know what? After I told her, she said she already knew. She was just waiting for me to figure it out."

"That's all fine and good, but all I can hear is my mother wailing about what a selfish pervert I am."

"Renee, you're thirty-six years old. You've already lived one lifetime in someone else's shoes. Why not try the next thirty-six years in your own shoes?"

Renee didn't know what to say. Dana was right, but Renee couldn't risk losing her family.

"When I was on vacation in Provincetown a few years ago," Dana said, "a comedian named Georgia Ragsdale ended her show by saying, 'It's not how you love or who you love, it's that you love.' Just because we're the same sex doesn't make what we feel for each other less or wrong. Risa and I had a good life. And I thought that maybe someday you and I could have the same if we try. I know it won't be easy, but I can assure you it will be worth it."

Renee's voice lowered almost to a whisper. "I just can't put my own desires over those of my girls."

Dana removed the steaks and shrimp from the grill and set them on two plates. She refilled Renee's glass of wine and offered her some salad and crusty Italian dinner rolls. The two women sat and ate in silence as the sky turned from cobalt blue to yellow to pink.

Dana looked up from her plate of half-eaten food just as Renee looked at her. Tears filled Renee's eyes. She knew this would be their last dinner together as a couple. She reached across the white tablecloth for Dana's hand. "I am so sorry."

"I am too," Dana whispered.

"Dana, you're a wonderful person. You deserve someone who can give back all the amazing things you give to others. You have to believe that this has nothing to do with you. It's me and my family. I wouldn't feel comfortable living this lifestyle, how can I expect my daughters to live it?"

"I understand, Renee. I understand completely, but that doesn't mean it hurts any less." In spite of her words, Dana looked stunned. "When I met you, I felt like I had gotten a second chance in life to love again. I guess I was wrong."

Renee's heart felt like a lead balloon expanding in her chest. "I wish things could be different."

"Me too."

The breeze turned cold, and it was getting dark. Renee helped Dana pack up the grill and the remainder of their dinner. They drove back to Niles, holding hands in stony silence; tears streaked both their faces. When they reached the library parking lot, Dana helped Renee load her car with her bag of books.

"You better go." Dana unlocked Renee's car door for her.

Renee got into the driver's seat and rolled the window down. She reached through the open window and cupped Dana's face in her hand. "I guess this is goodbye." Dana kissed Renee's palm, then pulled away.

Renee sat in her car in the dark. She had difficulty moving because yet again she was faced with an agonizing loss. If she moved, the reality of it would set in and the pain would be unbearable, just like when she lost Tom.

But she had to move, had to pull herself together for her sake and for the girls' sake. She knew she made the right decision, but deep down inside, she couldn't silence the voice that quietly reprimanded her for letting Dana go. She had turned her back on love once more. Would she ever find it again?

Chapter Twenty-three

Renee got home just before ten o'clock and found Sara and Lindsay huddled close together on the couch crying.

"Hey, what's the matter?" Renee sat between her daughters and put her arms around them. She looked up as her mom walked into the living room.

Angie spoke up. "Justin's mother was in a car accident this afternoon."

"Oh, my God. Is she okay?"

Angie looked down and shook her head. "From what Justin said, she was hurt pretty badly."

Shock of the news that Annie was in a serious car accident shot through Renee like a lightning bolt.

"Mom? What's going to happen? Is Justin's mom going to die?"

"Oh, Lindsay, honey, I-I don't know." Renee wrapped her arms around her and held her close. Lindsay cried, rocking back and forth. Lindsay's grief seemed so acute, Renee's heart ached from the physical pain that burdened her.

After a few moments, Lindsay calmed down enough that Renee felt she could talk.

"Where's Justin? Have you spoken to him?"

"He's at the hospital. He doesn't say much. Just that his mom is in the emergency room and they might have to do surgery. He sounded scared," Lindsay said.

"Is someone there with him?"

"I don't think so."

"Do you want to go to the hospital? We can go and make sure he's all right."

Lindsay's face brightened. "Can we?"

"Of course we can. The best thing you can do for Justin right now is be there for him. You know, like he was for you when Daddy was sick."

Lindsay wiped her eyes with the sleeve of her sweatshirt.

Renee swallowed hard. She knew that taking Lindsay to the hospital would mean seeing Annie again. And if Annie was as badly hurt as they were saying, she didn't know how she would react seeing her like that. But Renee needed to put her feelings aside and think of Lindsay and Justin and Annie, for that matter, and although it might be difficult, she needed to do the right thing. After all, Annie was good to her daughters. She owed it to her.

"Okay, Linz, go wash your face and change your clothes. Sara, do you want to come?"

"Yes. I need to change, too." Sara nodded and followed Lindsay upstairs.

"When did this happen?" Renee asked Angie as they waited for the girls.

"This afternoon. Justin's mother was on a business trip in Boston. I don't know all the details, just what I could make out from Lindsay and Justin's conversation. Justin called around seven thirty. He was supposed to come over with pizza and some video games. "I feel bad for Justin, he must be scared." Angie pulled a Kleenex out of the pocket of her housedress and blew her nose.

"Mom, do you know who Justin's mother is?"

"Not really, why?"

"Justin's mother is Annie Castrovinci."

"Gianna Castrovinci's girl?"

"Yes."

"Poor Gianna, what she must be going through."

"Yes, this must be very hard for her."

"I thought Annie moved away from here after you and she graduated high school."

"She did, Ma. I think she moved back a year or so ago."

"So I guess you two have settled your differences?"

Renee was shocked that her mother even remembered what

had happened back then.

"We're working on it," Renee said hesitantly.

"That's a good thing. You were such close friends. You two wasted too much time over something so silly."

Renee turned toward her mother. "How do you know it was silly?"

"A mother knows."

"What's that supposed to mean?"

"All I'm saying is that when it was happening, Renee, you should have come to me. We could have talked about it. It's not like you're the first person in our family that has ever gone through that kind of thing before."

Shock waves shot through Renee. Her mouth went dry, and in that moment, Renee understood that her mother knew all along what had happened between Annie and her.

"Ma, do you remember when Annie left town?"

"Of course I remember. You cried for days. Nothing anyone could say or do could console you."

"We had a really big fight right before she left. She begged me to go away with her after graduation. But I was scared. I thought you and Dad would hate me and throw me out, like what happened to some kids."

"Why would you think that?"

"Because, Ma, I loved Annie, and…"

Angie reached out and touched her daughter's arm. "I know."

Renee looked at her mother. Her eyes were full of love and tenderness.

"Oh, we would never have thrown you out. I'm sorry you'd think that of us."

Renee had trouble getting her mind around that. Would her parents have accepted her and Annie as a couple? Would Annie's parents? Could a couple of teenagers have faced the world's contempt back then when an alternative lifestyle surely would never have been accepted? How different their lives would have been. But then, Lindsay and Sara and Justin wouldn't have been born. Surely, fate had played a hand in all of this. How much of life really happened through free choice? "If you knew, why didn't you say something?"

"Because you needed to work it out yourself. I couldn't do that for you. I have to admit when you married Tom, I was a little relieved that maybe it was just a phase you were going through. Marching to a different drummer can be a tough life. But your relationship with Annie was always in the back of my mind. And then after Tom died and you met Dana…"

"You know about Dana?"

"I may be getting older, but I'm not blind."

"Mom, I don't know what to say." Renee was trembling now.

"There's nothing to say." Angie looked at Renee and smiled. "All any mother wants is for her child to be happy. That's all I want for you."

Tears tumbled down Renee's cheeks. She brushed them away with the back of her trembling hand.

"Dana seems like a nice person," Angie said.

"She is. And she helped me a lot after Tom died when I really needed someone. But we're not together anymore."

"Why?"

"We ended our relationship. Actually, tonight. That's where I was while you were watching the girls. We decided to end things because of the toll it was taking on Lindsay and Sara. Besides, she moved back to Cleveland to stay, and I couldn't just pick up the kids and go with her. It's funny because I told Dana that if you ever found out about us, you'd probably have the kids taken away from me."

"Oh, don't be ridiculous. You know that's not true. I hope you know that now."

Renee nodded. Angie handed her a Kleenex from her pocket, and Renee blew her nose.

"So, Ma, you said I wasn't the only one in our family to go through this. Who else is gay?"

"Didn't you ever wonder why my sister Connie never got married?"

Renee was floored. "Aunt Connie, the pin-up girl from the

fifties, is gay? I never would have guessed."

"Well, honey, no one would ever guess that you were, either."

Renee's mind reeled with the fact that her mother knew all along that she was a lesbian—yes, she could say it now—and that it was no big deal. She felt like a huge weight had been lifted from her shoulders.

Before Renee could react to Angie's comments, Lindsay and Sara returned, wearing clean clothes and looking a little more fresh-faced, even though their eyes were still red-rimmed and puffy from crying.

"Ready, girls?" Renee handed them their coats, and they headed for the door.

"Mom," she said to Angie, "I can drop you off at home on our way to the hospital."

"Are you sure? I can call your father to come get me."

"No, he's probably asleep in his chair by now. I'll take you home."

Angie gathered her coat and purse and followed Renee and the girls out to the car.

Angie reached across the seat and touched Renee's arm. "Are you going to be okay?"

"Yeah, I'm okay," Renee said with a weak smile.

Heavy silence hung in the car on the ride to the hospital. The only sound came from Lindsay's and Sara's sniffling noses. Renee dropped Angie off in her driveway.

Before closing the passenger-side door, Angie leaned into the car. "I'll be up if you need to talk later."

"Thanks, I appreciate it."

Renee waited until her mother was safely in the house, then drove to the hospital. In spite of the late hour, the emergency room was bustling with activity. Renee's knees shook as she walked up to the receptionist window. Lindsay and Sara held on to her, but it was hard telling who was supporting whom. "We're here to see Annie Castrovinci, actually her son...my daughter is..."

A muted voice came through the thick glass window. "Step through the sliding doors to your left."

A nurse dressed in green scrubs met them on the other side of the doors. "Ms. Castrovinci is in room 10, they're almost ready for her in surgery, so you can only see her for a few minutes."

"Is she awake?" Renee asked.

"No, I'm afraid not." The nurse led the way to where Annie lay on a gurney.

"Where's her son, Justin?"

"He's been sitting at her bedside the entire time. He refuses to leave, even for a minute. Tough kid."

Renee's heart pounded in her chest as she and her daughters walked with the nurse down the beige-tiled hallway to a cubicle where Annie lay unconscious. The pungent smell of alcohol permeated the air.

Renee's breath caught in her throat when the nurse pulled back the curtain that surrounded the cubicle where Annie lay.

"Oh, Annie," Renee whispered.

Chapter Twenty-four

Annie lay on a gurney under a thin white sheet. Her thick dark hair was tangled and matted. Her forehead was bandaged with thick white gauze, and her right arm was in a sling. Her fingers were swollen and purple and looked like five fat link sausages. IV tubing and electrode wires were attached to every part of her body. Renee looked up at the heart monitor just above Annie's head. Renee had no idea what the wavy lines meant, but she was sure that their presence was a good thing. Justin sat in a chair at his mother's side when the girls walked in. His face lit up when he saw Lindsay and Sara.

"I'm so glad you guys are here." Justin stood and drew them both into a big bear hug

"Justin, are you okay?" Lindsay looked into his swollen, bloodshot eyes.

"I can't believe this happened. Is she going to be okay?" Lindsay pulled him close. He buried his face into her neck. His body trembled, and she could feel the sobs wracking him as he cried in her arms.

"Why don't you guys go take a break? I'll stay here with your mom, Justin." Renee reached into her purse and handed Justin a twenty-dollar bill. "Why don't you and the girls go down to the coffee shop and get something to eat?"

"Thank you, Mrs. Del Fino." Justin seemed relieved for the break and took the money and he and the girls left.

Renee was now alone with Annie. She stood next to the gurney and looked down at her.

Tears welled up in her eyes as she gently touched Annie's hand.

"You're gonna be okay, Annie. I know you will. Be tough. Hang in there for Justin. He needs you."

Suddenly, Annie's friend David appeared. "Renee, I was hoping you would come. I know Justin will appreciate having Lindsay here with him. He's a pretty tough kid, but this is really hard on him."

Renee tried to smile. "Lindsay said Annie was away on business. Is that when the accident happened?"

"Yes, she was in Boston at a drug rep convention for pharmacists. Her company sent her there to promote a new heart medication. Last Sunday, she flew into Logan to get ready for the convention that was scheduled for Thursday. She was supposed to fly home this morning, but a storm had blown in overnight, and her flight was canceled. The Boston Marathon was this coming weekend, and the airlines were packed. She wouldn't be able to get a flight home until Tuesday, so she rented a car and tried to drive back."

David paused. "The accident occurred on I-80 just outside of Newton Falls."

"She was practically home at that point. What happened?"

"The state highway patrolman said driver fatigue may have been a factor, and she probably never saw the tractor-trailer bearing down on her when she pulled into the passing lane."

"Oh, David." Sadness squeezed Renee's heart.

"The most difficult part was having to tell Justin his mom was in a bad accident." Tears formed in David's eyes. "She's a good mom, Renee. Always insisted on doing it all on her own."

"Yep, that sounds like Annie. And I'm sure you've been a good friend to her, David. I'm sure she appreciates everything you've done for her."

Renee reached over and touched David's arm, trying to comfort him. Whatever his relationship was with Annie, he obviously cared about her and Justin.

A few minutes later, a female doctor in a white lab coat entered the cubicle. The name embroidered above her breast pocket read *Mina Caselli, M.D. Chief of Emergency Medicine.* "We're ready to take Ms. Castrovinci up to surgery in a few minutes. You're welcome to wait in the family lounge on the second floor just outside of the surgery suites. Once they have an idea on how she's doing, the nurses will keep you updated on her progress."

Dr. Caselli examined Annie by lifting her eyelids and flashing a small light in them.

"Any change in her condition?" Renee asked.

"Not really. We have her pretty sedated right now to control her pain," Dr. Caselli said. "So it's really too early to tell. Her vital signs are stable, and that's always a good thing."

Dr. Caselli placed her stethoscope on Annie's chest and adjusted one of the clamps on the IV medications. Then she checked the arm that was in the sling.

"Is it broken?" Renee asked.

Dr. Caselli nodded. "Yes, she dislocated her shoulder, as well. We were able to reduce it here in the ER. We put an air cast on her arm. After her surgery, they'll put a permanent one on."

Renee nodded, trying to fathom everything Annie had gone through.

Dr. Caselli finished her exam. "The surgical nurses will be here shortly to take her upstairs."

"Thank you, Doctor," Renee said.

Dr. Caselli disappeared though the curtain. A few minutes later, two nurses in green scrubs wearing gauzy surgical caps arrived to take Annie to surgery.

The two nurses expertly transferred Annie from the emergency room's gurney to their gurney in one fell swoop, not even disturbing one IV line or electrode. "We are going to take her to the OR now. Her doctor will come to the surgical waiting room to talk to you as soon as the surgery is finished," one of the nurses said.

Renee felt her throat tighten, afraid things wouldn't go well and she may never get the chance to make things right with Annie again. Before they took Annie away, Renee bent down close to Annie's ear and whispered, "I'll be here when you wake up, Annie. Everything is going to be okay." Then Renee kissed Annie lightly on the cheek.

David reached over and touched Annie's hand. "Hang in

there, kid. It's gonna be all right."

Renee and David stood in the hall and watched as the nurses pushed Annie down the hall and onto the awaiting elevator up to surgery. Neither knowing when he or she would see her again.

Chapter Twenty-five

Renee and David sat in waiting room chairs drinking bitter coffee while the kids lay spread out on the three leather couches asleep. Annie's mother, Gianna, had joined them shortly after midnight. She sat in a chair between David and Renee, working black Rosary beads in her arthritic hands as she silently said the prayer. Gianna would have been there sooner, but she didn't drive anymore, and with Annie's sister still living out of town, she had to rely on a neighbor to bring her to the hospital.

Gianna's reaction when she saw Renee was cordial at best. Gianna was one of those stoic Italian ladies who were hard to read. God knows what she thought or knew of Renee's and Annie's previous relationship. Renee was afraid that being there would make things worse for Gianna, and she thought about leaving. But something stronger pulled at her and she had to stay. Had to see this through—for Annie.

Gianna Castrovinci had aged well over the years. Her once chestnut brown hair had matured to a silvery snow white, and not a line was visible on her plump, luminous face. She still wore her hair in a tight bun, the cinnamon bun Renee and Annie used to tease her about when they were teenagers.

The sun had just started to come up when Dr. Dobos, the neurosurgeon came into the waiting area. Renee and David stood as the doctor asked, "Castrovinci family?"

"Yes," David said. Renee nodded. She felt her insides tighten as she scanned the doctor's face for a clue to how Annie was and if she would be all right.

"This is Annie's mother, Gianna," David introduced Gianna to the doctor.

181

Dr. Dobos smiled. She walked over to where Gianna was sitting and sat next to her. "Your daughter is going to be fine," Dr. Dobos said. Relief was evident on Gianna's face. Renee felt her heart lighten, as well.

"We were able to relieve the pressure in her brain that her head injury caused. Fortunately, there was no permanent damage, and she should make a full recovery." Dr. Dobos said. "It was a good thing she was wearing her seat belt because it could have been a lot worse."

"Oh, thank God," Gianna said. She made the sign of the cross and started to cry.

"Thank you, Doctor. That's great news. When can we see her?" David asked.

"She'll be in recovery for a few hours, then we'll transfer her to the ICU. I suggest you all go home and get some sleep. Maybe by this afternoon, she'll start to wake up and you can visit for a short time."

"Sounds good." David shook the doctor's hand.

Renee helped David wake the kids. Justin cheered when he heard his mom was going to be okay.

"I can take Justin back to my place," Renee said. "Lindsay and Sara can keep him company until it's time to come back to the hospital."

"Okay, I'll take Gianna home," David said.

Renee said goodbye to David and Gianna. As she turned to get the kids, Gianna touched Renee's arm.

"Thank you for being here, Renee. I know it will mean a lot to Anna Marie that you were here."

Renee paused, amazed that this woman, whose daughter she had hurt so much in the past, would say such a thing. "You're welcome, Mrs. Castrovinci," Renee said, and to her dismay, her voice broke.

David helped Mrs. Castrovinci out while Renee led the three sleepy kids outside into the bright morning sunlight. She made sure each kid was buckled in before buckling herself in and starting the car. Her head hurt from lack of sleep and the fading adrenaline rush caused by her brain being in crisis mode. When they got back to Renee's, Lindsay made everyone a snack, then the kids spread out in the living room, watching the remainder of Saturday morning cartoons. Renee sat in the recliner and put her feet up. It had been a long twenty-four hours. Sleep hit her like a ton of bricks.

Chapter Twenty-six

Annie's recovery had been right on track, according to her doctors. Twenty-four hours after the surgery, she was up in a chair eating green Jell-O. If everything went as planned, Annie would be released from the hospital in a day or two.

Justin had been staying at Renee's since the accident. It was Monday morning and time to get back to the normal flow of life. Renee was scheduled to go back to work. Lindsay, Sara, and Justin would be able to fend for themselves. Even though they had school that day, Renee suggested that they do something fun afterward since the last few days had been stressful on everyone. With Justin able to drive and the fact that he had his own car, even though it was a beater, the possibilities were endless. Renee suggested the four o'clock matinee at the Regal Cinema by the mall. She gave them enough money to pay for the movie tickets and plenty of snacks.

Working at the library was always a welcomed distraction for Renee. It helped after she lost Tom, and she hoped it would help her sort out what to do with her life next.

When she awoke that morning, the first thing that came to her mind was Dana. She hadn't spoken to her since the night they had dinner, the night of Annie's accident. She hoped that she would see Dana one more time before she left for good. Had she already moved back to Cleveland? Was she packing up her house and facing the difficult memories of her life with Risa? Should Renee have offered to help her undertake that wrenching task? After all, look at all Dana had helped her get through. She felt sad that Dana wouldn't be in her life anymore.

On her way to work, Renee dialed Dana's number, and after

a few rings, the call went to voice mail. If Dana saw on the caller ID that is was Renee calling, she always picked up. It was becoming obvious to Renee that Dana wanted this to be a clean break. Feeling sad, she respected Dana's wishes and didn't leave a message.

As she drove to work, the events of the past thirty-six hours reeled through her mind. How fast life can change. Was she any better off today, a year later? She thought she found love again but chose to let that chance go to save her family. Did she know where her life was headed now? What about Annie? How much of a part of Annie's life would Renee be? Did she have any control in the matter? It certainly didn't seem like it. She pulled into the library parking lot and out of habit looked around for Dana's car. It was nowhere to be found.

Renee hung her head. Had she made the wrong choice? Did she prematurely let go of what she and Dana had? She missed her and was afraid of never seeing her again. Renee got out of the car when suddenly a wave of anxiety shot through her. Gasping for breath, she held on to the car door and steadied herself. She used to get these panic attacks after Tom was diagnosed with cancer but hadn't had one since. Her life felt out of control then, and it was beginning to feel that way again.

With Dana gone and Annie back in her life, nothing seemed normal. A few minutes later, the attack subsided, her breathing settled down, and she felt a little better. She gathered her book bag and purse and headed into work.

The library was abuzz with activity. Mary was at the circulation desk logging on to the server. She looked up as Renee walked in.

"Renee, are you okay?" Mary asked.

Renee trembled, still feeling the effects of the panic attack. "Yes, I'm fine. Rough weekend."

"Oh?"

"A friend of mine was in a serious car accident."

"Oh, Renee, I'm sorry to hear that. Is she all right?"

"She's doing well. She's still in the hospital but should be coming home soon. I'm taking care of her son while she's in the hospital."

"That's awfully nice of you. I'm sure she appreciates all you're doing for her."

Renee nodded. She stuffed her book bag and purse under the desk and got to work. Renee worked the circulation desk while Mary shelved books and helped at the reference desk. She was grateful that they were busy. Her work kept her mind off everything that was going on. Well, almost everything. Every time the front door opened, Renee's heart jumped, thinking any minute Dana would walk through. But she didn't.

Before she knew it, it was four o'clock. With her shift done, Renee left the library and headed to the hospital to visit Annie. When she got to Annie's room, Annie was sitting up in a chair. The bandage from her head had been removed and the only visible sign that she was in an accident was the pale blue sling that cradled her right arm.

"Hey, you look great." Renee walked into Annie's room.

Annie smiled when she saw Renee. "Thanks. I just got done with therapy. They said if I keep making progress, I can go home tomorrow."

"That's great!"

"Renee, I need to thank you for taking care of Justin."

"He's a great kid. And you should be proud of him. Justin is lucky to have you as his mom. And David seems nice, too. You're lucky to have found him. How did you meet?"

"David is an old friend from my days in Boston. We met at a reception for Merck. It's amazing how gaydar can work in any situation."

"Gaydar?"

"Mmm…The minute David and I were introduced by one of our colleagues, we knew the other one was gay."

"David's gay?

"Yes, of course, what did you think?"

"I thought he was Justin's father."

Annie laughed. "Oh, Renee. David came to Niles with me when I got transferred back here. His stay here is temporary as he is just here to help me get our Youngstown office up and operating. The company put him up at the Holiday Inn on Belmont, and he's flying back and forth from here to the regional office in Boston. Unfortunately, in two weeks, he'll be returning to Boston, where he lives with his partner, Ken, for good. He has been a great friend to me and Justin. I'm really going to miss him."

"Well, you can see how I would make that assumption. I just assumed when Lindsay said Justin's parents weren't married, you were too progressive to make any formal commitment."

"Are you saying I have trouble making commitments?"

"No, no, I'm not saying that at all. I just never thought of you as someone who wanted to settle down."

"I wanted to settle down with you." Annie's voice was barely a whisper.

An awkward silence filled the air. All of the sudden, Renee had so much to say to Annie but had difficulty saying it. When Renee looked up, she saw Annie studying her face.

"What?" Renee asked.

"Where were you just now? You looked so sad."

"I didn't come here to tell you my woes. I came here for you."

"And you have been here for me, but what's going on with you?

Renee paused and chose her words carefully. She struggled with the uncertainty that the answer to Annie's question would bring. "Well…uh—"

"How's your friend? Dana? Is that her name?" Annie interrupted.

Renee was floored by Annie's boldness. She wasted no time getting to the heart of the matter. But then again, that was Annie.

"Dana, yes, Dana. She's fine, I think." Renee's voice was weak and tremulous.

"Oh?" Annie's dark eyebrows rose in inquiry.

Renee knew she couldn't keep the details of her relationship with Dana from Annie any longer.

"Renee, can I ask you something?"

"Sure."

"Were you and Dana friends or more than friends?"

Renee sighed as she reflected on how she and Dana met and

where their friendship took them. She clasped her slender fingers together and stared at them. A heavy sadness centered in her chest when she thought of Dana now. She wondered if she should continue. She was afraid if she told her about her relationship with Dana, it would add to Annie's pain. She certainly didn't want to do that.

"More than friends," Renee finally said. "Annie, I'm sorry. Maybe we shouldn't be talking about this now. I know I've hurt you in the past, and I don't want to hurt you anymore."

Annie looked down. "Renee, we were kids then. When I look back now, knowing how important your family is to you, I understand why you couldn't go with me.

"Being at Mount Holyoke was great. But I had to admit, I was lonely. Being away made me homesick. My mom would write me letters telling me all the things that went on back home. She also told me that you and Tom were dating and that it looked like it was getting serious. Every time she would tell me how you and Tom were doing, it broke my heart. I really missed you, Reen."

"I know. I'm sorry. I just couldn't leave," Renee said, her voice was fragile and shaky.

"One night I was so upset I went out to one of the bars on campus. It was that night I was determined to find out what the big deal was about having a man in your life. About living a respectable life, even though what you have to do to get that respect goes against every fiber of your being."

"What happened?"

"I was sitting at the bar, and this guy comes over and asks if he can buy me a drink. I look him over. He's a nice enough looking guy, so I say yes, and he pulls up the stool next to me. He not only buys me a drink, he buys me several more. The next thing I know, it's five in the morning and I'm doing the walk of shame into my dorm. Nine months later, Justin was born."

"You're kidding! Annie…oh, my. How did you handle all that? My God, what did your parents think?"

"My parents were devastated. My dad especially. I felt like he was so disappointed in me. When they heard I was pregnant, they wanted me to come home. But I was determined that I wasn't ready to give up on all my dreams, even with a baby on the way."

"So what did you do?"

"I moved off campus and rented a small apartment. I went to class during the day and waitressed at night until Justin was born."

"Oh, my," Renee said, her head spinning with all the details of Annie's life. "And you never married Justin's father?"

"No. I didn't want to. I didn't want to marry someone I didn't want to spend the rest of my life with or barely knew."

Renee was amazed at everything Annie had gone through. She knew if she were in Annie's shoes, she couldn't have done it.

"How did you manage school and a baby being on your own?"

"It wasn't easy. Getting pregnant caused me to have to drop out of the pharmacy program. But I wasn't going to let anything stop me from getting my education and providing a good home for me and my son."

"I'm so sorry you had such a hard time."

"Reen, don't feel sorry for me. Justin and I have a good life. He's healthy and happy. And he loves living here. I was afraid that when I got transferred from Boston to here, he would have a hard time adjusting, but so far, he's been fine."

"Well, good for you. And good for Justin. He's so lucky to have you for his mom."

A heavy silence settled between them. Renee looked over at Annie. "I'm sorry so much time has passed between us. I missed you. I tried to see you, and I wanted to tell you how sorry I was but wasn't sure how to do it. Even when your dad passed away, I went to the funeral home to express my condolences to you and your family, but when I got to the receiving line, you disappeared."

"I know. When I saw you come in that day, my heart stopped. It meant a lot to me that you came for my family, but I just couldn't face you. It still hurt too much."

"I know. I was hurt, too." I still hurt sometimes, Renee realized. "Can we start over, as friends?"

"I'd like us to be friends again," Annie whispered. "But a lot of time has gone by and so much has changed."

"Just because time has gone by doesn't mean you stop caring about someone."

"I don't know what to say or how to feel. Right now, I just feel numb."

"I know what you mean. Let's just take one day at a time and see where that leads us."

Annie nodded. A few minutes later, Justin, Sara, and Lindsay appeared in the doorway of Annie's room.

"Hey, Mom, you look great," Justin said. He walked over to Annie and kissed her cheek.

"You too, kiddo. Hey, looks like I'm gonna get out of this place tomorrow. How's that sound?"

"Great! Are you going to stay at Mrs. Del Fino's, too?"

"No, honey. That would be nice, but no. We have imposed on Renee and her family too much already," Annie said.

"It's no problem having you and Justin for a few days. At least until you're stronger. You do have a broken arm, Annie."

"You don't mind?"

"Of course not. When they tell you you're released from the hospital, give me a call and I'll come get you."

"Thank you. That means a lot to me."

"It's my pleasure."

After their visit, Renee followed Justin and the girls home. She felt good about her talk with Annie and felt that they were no longer estranged friends holding a grudge, but two women brought back together by a common bond.

Renee knew there was more that needed to be said, but now was not the time. Annie needed to get through this. Maybe later, they would sort out their past and see where they would go from here.

Chapter Twenty-seven

On Annie's first night out of the hospital, David dropped Gianna off at Renee's so she could visit with her daughter. It was hard for her to get to the hospital, and Renee made sure she made Gianna feel welcome.

That evening, Angie Cardone delivered a pan of her famous lasagna to Renee's house. "Thanks Ma, this is great." Angie went into the living room to say hello to the kids and Gianna while Renee slid the pan of lasagna into the oven to heat it up.

When she turned around, Annie was leaning against the kitchen counter watching her. Renee's heart pounded. Annie walked across the room, closer to Renee. "Renee, I can't tell you how much it means to me that you've brought me here."

"I'm glad I could be here for you." Renee looked down. She felt her face flush under Annie's gaze.

Annie reached for Renee and hugged her with her good arm. Annie buried her face into Renee's neck. The scent of her skin brought back a flood of memories.

A few minutes later, Gianna came into the kitchen. "Mmm, that a smells a so good. Is that Angie's lasagna, Renee?" Mrs. Castrovinci asked.

Renee and Annie broke their embrace. Annie turned her back to her mother and looked out the window over the sink.

"Yes, it is." Renee's voice was shaky. "She brought it over along with a loaf of Italian bread."

"Your mama still a makes a the best lasagna this side of Briar Hill." Mrs. Castrovinci opened the oven door and inhaled deeply.

After everyone was fed, the kids and Annie and Gianna went

into the living room to watch TV. Angie helped Renee clean up the kitchen. Late afternoon sunlight shone through the kitchen window. Renee thought this was nice, she and her mother together like this. She couldn't help thinking back to their conversation a few days earlier and that her mother knew all along that what she and Annie shared was much more than friendship. While Renee finished the last of the dishes, she looked over at Angie and couldn't help but notice how much her mother had aged. She had always looked the same to Renee, but she seemed to move a little slower now. Her once strong, sometimes overbearing personality had softened, too.

"You feeling okay, Ma?"

"Yes, I'm fine. Some evenings my knees don't work as good as they used to. Just a touch of 'old Arthur,' I guess."

Renee smiled at her. Angie was the one constant in Renee's life. She had truly been there every time Renee needed her.

Renee folded the dishrag and hung it over the faucet. "Done?"

"Done." Angie folded her tea towel and laid it on the counter.

Angie and Renee stood in the doorway of the kitchen. Renee felt very content as she watched Lindsay and Sara and Justin on the floor playing a board game. Annie and Gianna sat on the couch next to each other watching the evening news.

"Annie looks like she's holding up well," Angie whispered.

"I think so, too. I'm sure she'll get better every day. She's been through a lot, so it's going to take some time to recover fully."

"You know, this is a good thing you're doing for Annie. I'm glad you and she got things straightened out."

Renee reached over and hugged Angie. "Thanks, Ma."

Angie looked at the kitchen clock. "Well, I better get going. It's getting late and your father will be wondering where I am."

Renee followed Angie into the foyer. She reached for Angie's coat that lay across the oak banister and helped her put it on.

Angie shrugged into her coat. "Call me if you need anything. Promise?"

"I will."

Angie hugged her daughter goodbye.

Just as Angie turned to leave, Renee touched her arm. She looked into Angie's dark brown eyes. "Thanks, Ma...for everything."

Angie smiled and covered Renee's hand with her own. "You're welcome, honey. Take care of yourself."

Chapter Twenty-eight

The glaring morning sunlight hurt Annie's eyes as she lay on top of her bed. She had finally returned home after spending nearly a week at Renee's. Although she appreciated everything Renee did for her, she did not want to be a burden, so it was time to move back home.

Annie was still wearing the same rumpled sweats with the arm cut out that she wore the past two days. She threw her good arm across her eyes to block out the intrusive light. Her body hurt as though someone had beaten her up, and the pain, although dulled by the pills, never seemed to go away. The last few days, it took everything Annie had to get up in the morning. Some days, she just couldn't get up at all. If it wasn't for Renee, she didn't know how she and Justin would have survived.

It seemed Renee had come back into her life just when she needed her most. On the days when Annie just couldn't do it, Renee took care of the kids, getting them fed and off to school. Justin, Lindsay, and Sara were pretty self-sufficient, which made things a lot easier

Each day, Justin drove Sara and Lindsay to school. After work, Renee would stop by Wendy's or Kentucky Fried Chicken to make sure they at least had a hot meal in the evening. She brought dinner to Annie's house almost every night, sometimes finding Annie in the same place she left her that morning.

Once Renee arrived, Annie would force herself to get up and be productive, even though it always seemed like a struggle.

"I don't know what I would do without you," Annie said as she helped Renee serve chicken from the red and white bucket. She scooped out dollops of mashed potatoes, plunked them onto paper plates, and dribbled brown gravy over them. The kids came into the kitchen and collected their plates, then retreated into the family room to eat, leaving Annie and Renee alone in the kitchen.

Renee took two chicken breasts and two biscuits from the bucket and laid them on plates for her and Annie. Annie poured two glasses of Diet Coke, then sat at the table across from Renee. She looked at the food in front of her and pushed the plate away.

"Not hungry?" Renee asked as she took a bite of chicken.

Annie wrinkled her nose and shook her head.

"You have to start eating, Annie. You're going to waste away to nothing." Renee set her chicken breast down and looked across the table at her friend. Her heart ached for her. She knew the pain she was going through, and she wanted to take it away, make everything all better. But she knew she couldn't, that Annie had to do this herself. She needed to get up and moving and get on with her life.

"Would it help to talk about it?"

"What's to talk about?

Renee reached across the table and took Annie's hand. "Honey, I know things seem difficult right now, but they're not hopeless. I know that with the therapy and medications, you'll feel better soon. You were in a bad accident, you can't expect to get better in a short time. Your body has to heal. Give it time."

"I just feel so lost. So worthless."

"You're not worthless. My God, look at everything you've been through. Don't you think it's normal to feel like you do?"

"I don't know. I just wish it would all go away. That things could be like they were before. I was working, I felt productive, for God's sake, we were skiing only a few months ago."

Renee stroked Annie's hand with her thumb. "You just have to do your best to get through it. You owe that to yourself and you owe that to Justin."

"I know you're right." Annie looked up and gave Renee a weak smile. This tiny show of affection made Renee's heart turn over in response. "Thank you for being here and for everything you've done for me and for Justin. I can't tell you how much I appreciate it. It's good having you back in my life again."

Renee felt her heart beat in her throat. If things had been different, she would have kissed Annie right there and then. But she knew that the last thing Annie needed was to deal with more of the painful past. After all, the past was the past and Annie was probably way over her feelings for Renee. Renee shook the thoughts from her head. Her friend needed her, and she needed to keep her head straight to be any good to her at all.

"At least try and eat something." Renee slid the paper plate back in front of Annie.

"Now you're starting to sound like my mother."

"That's not such a bad thing," Renee said. "We both love you."

"What?" Annie said. "What did you say?"

Renee's face flushed with embarrassment when she realized what she had said. She looked down, unable to meet Annie's steady gaze. "I'm sorry. It just slipped out."

"Are you saying what I think you're saying?"

Renee shrugged.

"Well, are you?" Annie reached across the table, lifted Renee's chin, and looked her in the eye.

"I guess I've been thinking about it a lot lately. I missed you, Annie. I was wondering if you missed me, too." Renee said the words tentatively as if testing the idea.

"Why would you even say such a thing?" Annie's heart beat wildly in her chest. She pushed the paper plate with the chicken breast away. "And even if I did, what makes you think I would take the chance that you wouldn't break my heart again?"

Immediately, Renee regretted the comment. Renee looked across the table at Annie. "I'm sorry. I never meant to bring this up. Especially not now." She picked up her plate with her half-eaten chicken breast and dumped it into the garbage.

She suddenly realized that her being here wasn't helping Annie, it was actually hurting her. That meant it was time to go. Renee grabbed her purse. "I better go. Do you think Justin can drop the girls off later? If not, have them call me when they're ready to come home."

"Wait a minute! I think we need to talk about this. Sit." Annie gestured to the kitchen chair.

Hesitantly, Renee sat. She looked over at Annie warily, not knowing what to expect.

Annie struggled with the uncertainty that Renee had aroused in her. How could she still think of them as they were so many years ago? "Reen, I thought you were over that...over us...a long time ago. You certainly seemed to have moved on with your life. First marrying Tom, then your relationship with that woman... Dana...right?"

"Yes. Dana."

"So what really happened with Dana? Did you end the relationship, or did she?"

"I did."

"Why? Did things get too serious and you ran away from her like you ran away from me? Or was it because she wasn't who you thought she was, or did it have something to do with you and who you think you should be?"

Renee flinched, feeling the sting of the truth.

"She wanted me to move away with her. I couldn't do that, not with Lindsay and Sara." Renee sighed wearily. "It just wouldn't have worked out."

"So what was she like?" Annie asked.

"Dana's a wonderful person. At the time we met, we seemed to be going through a lot of the same things. She had lost her life partner to breast cancer and felt she would never find love again. Well, it's not like she felt she wouldn't find love again, she felt like she didn't deserve to find love again. Then we met. We became friends at first, but I began to feel attracted to her. I struggled with that because I knew what the consequences would be if I gave in. Believe me, it was one of the most difficult things I had ever done. We both finally let our guards down, but we were still carrying too much baggage. She seemed to come to terms with hers, but in the end, I think it was my guilt that tore us apart."

"Why? What did you feel so guilty about?" Annie asked.

"She wanted me to come live with her, and I couldn't do it, live like that."

"What about Lindsay and Sara?"

"She wanted them to come, too. But I couldn't do that to them. They had their lives here, their schools, and their friends. And they had been through so much already. Besides, they found out about my relationship with Dana in a not so nice way."

"What happened?"

"Well, you remember the ski trip we took in January."

"Yes, I remember it quite well."

"Well, that was the first trip we took together, you know, me and Dana and the girls. Dana had her own room, of course, and I shared one with the girls. Our room had a Jacuzzi in it. That morning, we ran into you, then you took the kids to the snowboarding side of the mountain."

"Yes, go on."

"While you were gone, Dana and I took the opportunity to have some alone time in the Jacuzzi. What we didn't count on was Lindsay coming back to the room to get me because Sara had fallen and hurt her wrist. Unfortunately, she walked in on us in a…let's say a compromising position."

Annie laughed, then covered her mouth.

"What's so funny?" Renee glared across the table at Annie.

"I'm sorry. I mean, I know it had to have been horrible at the time. I bet you freaked out."

"Yes, I did. I didn't know what to do. Lindsay was so upset that she wouldn't talk to me. And when she did, she said the most hurtful things."

"Like what?"

"Like my marriage to her father was a lie. That I didn't really love him or her for that matter. It was horrible and I felt so ashamed. Then after the trip, I tried to explain to Lindsay and Sara what was going on between Dana and me. Sara seemed okay with it, but Lindsay wanted nothing to do with me or Dana. If you remember, that's when she was spending so much time here with Justin."

"I do remember that. I asked Justin if he knew what was going on, but he said he didn't know anything. Just that you and Lindsay weren't getting along. I assumed it was over their relationship. I asked him if he did anything he wasn't supposed to with Lindsay to cause you to be upset. That's when he told me what had happened that afternoon in Lindsay's room. He said they used protection and he didn't regret it because he loved her. He also said he didn't want to do anything that would hurt her."

"He's a very responsible kid," Renee said. "In spite of everything that happened, he was great with Lindsay and Sara after Tom died."

"Thanks," Annie said, feeling pride in her son.

Suddenly, all the tension in the air seemed to dissipate. Maybe talking this out was what they needed all along.

"Is that what ended your relationship with Dana? The incident with Lindsay?" Annie asked.

"Not exactly. After our little talk, things went from bad to worse. Dana and I decided that we should limit the time we spent together, so I would go over to her house at night when the girls went to bed. Sometimes I'd be so exhausted, I would fall asleep there and would make it home just before they got up for school. One morning, I snuck in around six and laid on the couch to wait until it was time to get the girls up for school. Around six thirty, I heard the back door open. Thinking it was an intruder, I almost called 911, only to find out it was Lindsay, who had taken it upon herself to stay all night with Justin. She pointed out that I apparently had stayed all night at Dana's. That's when everything really started to fall apart."

"I remember that night. Lindsay was curled up on the couch. Justin made her a big bowl of popcorn, and they sat up watching movies. She seemed so sad."

"I guess during that time, I wouldn't have won a prize for Mother of the Year."

Annie smiled. "People do some crazy things when they think they're in love. Were you in love with her?"

Renee thought a moment. She knew her feelings for Dana were more than just a friendship or a physical attraction, but was it love? "I cared a lot about her." Renee had trouble admitting to Annie how she truly felt about Dana.

"Do you miss her?"

"Sometimes I do. Dana's a great person. She was fun to be around and got me through one of the toughest times in my life. But when I look back, I still don't think it would have worked out. Not with the girls anyway. My main responsibility is to them."

It was getting late, and the next day was another school day. An air of calm seemed to surround them as they cleaned up the remnants of dinner together. When they were done, Annie walked Renee to the door. They stood on the porch while Lindsay and Sara got into the car.

"Thanks for bringing dinner tonight. How about if I cook for us tomorrow night?"

"That would be great." Renee smiled and turned to leave. Annie touched her arm, stopping her.

"About what you said earlier...about us. You know I can't make that kind of decision right now. Heck, I can barely decide what to wear each day. I need time to get my life back on track."

"I understand," Renee said. "You let me know when you're ready."

Chapter Twenty-nine

Eight months had passed since Annie's accident. It took a good six of those months for Annie to fully get her strength back. She returned to work soon after that. One good thing did come from all this: Reconnecting with Annie gave Renee the opportunity to be there for her like Dana had been for Renee.

Being close to Annie during those times was truly enlightening for Renee. She realized for the first time that she was over her own grief because Annie's struggle was more important than her own.

Renee's and Annie's families were becoming closer than ever. The kids seemed to benefit from the closeness of the blended family as their day-to-day activities resembled a more normal time. Renee and Annie's relationship remained platonic as they focused more on the children's needs than on their own. But there were times when Renee thought that Annie's old feelings for her might awaken and stir.

The holidays were approaching. Although Renee and the girls had already gone through a Christmas without Tom, Renee wanted this year to be different. After all, the past year had been rough on Annie and Justin, as well as Renee and the girls. Annie had been though a lot in the past year. Renee wanted to do something special for her. So instead of having a traditional Christmas at home, Renee suggested to Annie that they take the kids on vacation during Christmas break.

"Oh, I don't know, Reen. Wouldn't it be better if we just stayed home?" Annie asked.

"Where's your sense of adventure?"

"Don't you think we've had enough adventure for a while?"

"Aw come on, it'll be fun. Anyway, I think the change of

scenery will do everyone good."

Annie surrendered. "I guess you're right."

Renee wanted this to be stress-free for Annie so she made all the arrangements for their trip. On the night before they were leaving on vacation, Renee invited Annie out to dinner at Alberini's, one of the nicest restaurants in Niles. Just the two of them. Renee felt she and Annie deserved some time to themselves since they would be spending the next week in close quarters with their kids. Renee arrived at Annie's house just before six. She let herself in with the key Annie had given her months before.

"Annie, you ready to go?" Renee shouted when she didn't see anyone in the kitchen or family room.

A few minutes later, Annie came down the stairs, adjusting her pearl earring. She was dressed in a black pencil skirt and white silk blouse. Renee's breath caught in her throat when she saw her.

"Wow, you look great," Renee said.

Annie smiled warmly. "Thank you."

"Ready?"

"Yes, just let me get my coat."

Annie pulled her black dress coat out of the closet. Renee stepped forward and helped her put it on.

"Thank you," Annie said. Renee could see a faint pink blush color Annie's graceful neck.

As they walked to the car, it started to snow. Big fat, floppy snowflakes that landed in Renee's dark hair and glistened like diamonds as she held open the car door for Annie.

At the restaurant, they were escorted to a candlelit private area with a table for two next to a big stone fireplace. Annie's eyes gleamed in the firelight.

"This is beautiful, Renee. Thank you for bringing me here," Annie said over her black leather menu.

"You're welcome. You deserve nice things."

They ordered two glasses of chardonnay before dinner, which seemed to relax both of them. Renee couldn't help looking across the table at Annie and thinking things she hadn't thought about in a long time. Annie was so beautiful, inside and out. How could she be so careless to let her go so many years ago?

"What are you looking at?" Annie whispered.

Renee looked down at the linen-covered tablecloth. She was grateful that the semidarkness of the room hid the flush in her face. "You," she whispered.

Annie felt an eager affection for Renee and reached across the table and touched her hand. The spark from that touch seemed to ignite the smoldering flame of love and affection in both of them. Annie and Renee looked down and saw their fingers laced together.

"Renee, you have been so good to me and to Justin over this past year. I can't tell you how much that means to me."

"It means so much to me to have you back in my life."

Before they could say any more, the waiter brought their dinners. Between forkfuls of beef tenderloin medallions with bleu cheese sauce for Renee and baked orange roughy with asparagus risotto for Annie, the two eagerly talked about the present, the past, and what the future might bring. After dinner, they shared a square of tiramisu and coffee laced with Baileys Irish Cream.

During the ride home, Renee and Annie held hands. Renee's heart was reeling with happiness. As she pulled the car into Annie's driveway and shut off the motor, she went to get out of the car, but Annie stopped her. Their gazes met, and slowly, one by one, the bricks of the walls they had built up around their hearts crumpled. Annie leaned in and kissed Renee. The kiss was slow and thoughtful and as sweet as Renee remembered.

As soon as the kids got out of school the next day, they packed up Annie's new SUV and drove to Florida. They spent Christmas Eve and Christmas Day in Disney World, then headed down A1A to Fort Lauderdale, then on to Miami. The trip seemed to be what both families needed. Sara and Lindsay hadn't looked this happy since before Tom got sick. Justin seemed pretty happy, too.

After spending the day at the beach and having an early dinner, they dropped the kids off at the movie theater to see *The Golden Compass*.

"The show's over at nine o'clock. We'll be here at the entrance when you come out." Annie handed Justin two twenty-dollar bills to pay for the movie tickets. Renee gave Lindsay money to buy popcorn and soft drinks.

Annie and Renee watched as their kids filed into the movie theater entrance, suddenly leaving them alone for the first time since they left home.

Annie put the car into gear to head back toward their hotel.

"So…what do you want to do?" Renee asked.

Annie answered with a tremor in her voice, "I think we can figure out something." She reached across the front seat and covered Renee's hand with hers. "Together."

Renee's heart swelled. Passion radiated from the soft core of her body as uncontrollable joy spread through her entire being.

On a warm, balmy night in Miami Beach, Renee pulled Annie into her arms. Soft reggae music from a party below drifted up through the open balcony door of their hotel room, and they began to slow dance to the music. As they looked into each other's eyes, a warm breeze caressed their skin. Annie couldn't help but notice the tingle of excitement deep inside her.

Although it was awkward at first, after their first kiss, the longing and passion came flooding back.

Renee led Annie by the hand and gently laid her on the bed. Her instinctive response to Annie's nearness was overwhelming. Renee kissed her softly as she unbuttoned Annie's shirt with trembling fingers. She kissed each area of exposed skin that lay underneath. A delightful shiver ran through her as she pushed the cotton fabric to the side and gazed down at Annie.

Annie's cheeks colored under the heat of Renee's gaze. "This isn't the body of an eighteen-year-old anymore, especially after having a kid," Annie whispered.

Renee smiled. She bent down and kissed Annie deeply. "You're just as beautiful as I remember."

Reminiscent of their teenage "game," Annie reached for Renee's hand and placed it over her breast. Renee moaned softly as she caressed Annie's soft breasts, kissing them lovingly. Currents of desire surged through her.

With obvious eagerness, Annie pulled Renee's shirt over her head. Her hands explored the soft curves of Renee's body as her tongue teased Renee's swollen nipples through the lacy cups of her Victoria's Secret bra. They were able to take their time to explore, arouse, and give each other pleasure. It was no longer a game they played, but a reconnecting of souls that were separated so long ago.

"I've missed you so much," Annie said as she lay in Renee's arms afterward.

"Me too. I'm so glad we found each other again."

The ocean breeze blew in from the open sliding-glass door. Waves broke with swishing sounds onto the beach below.

"Annie, what made you decide that this was all right?"

"I couldn't deny the fact that I know after all this time, you still love me."

Renee gently kissed the top of Annie's head. "I do." Renee pulled Annie close.

"So, Reen, what made you decide that this was okay?"

"I had to stop pretending I was someone I wasn't."

"Wow, how did you come to that realization?"

"Although I loved Tom and we had a good life together, something just didn't feel right. Like something big was missing."

"Did you ever tell Tom about us?"

Renee shook her head. "I couldn't. He did ask me a long time ago what had happened between us. You know, why we weren't friends anymore."

"What did you say?"

"I made up some flimsy excuse. I think I blamed it on you being stubborn."

"Stubborn? Me?" Annie joked.

"I know. I couldn't tell him the real reason. It would have hurt him too much. My mother knows about us," Renee said.

"What?" Annie propped herself up on one elbow.

"Yep. I never said a word, but Angie knew all along."

"You mean even from before?"

"Yep."

"And she's okay with it?"

"Apparently. The night of your accident, when I told her you were Justin's mother, she told me she knew and that I should have come to her to talk about it. She said all she wanted was for me to be happy."

"And this makes you happy?" Annie's voice was soft with concern.

"Yes, it does. Very much. How about you?"

"Absolutely." Annie kissed Renee, reveling in the velvety softness of her lips.

When they got back from vacation, the two families seemed to merge, forming a sort of *Kate & Allie* scenario without the part of actually living under the same roof. Both women decided it was the best way. They didn't want to uproot their kids and cause stressful changes, but they wanted to be together and have the children be part of one another's lives.

Although Renee and Annie knew they loved each other, they remained secretive about their relationship. Even though Annie's family had known for years she was a lesbian, she was always very private about her life. When Renee and Annie wanted time alone, they would tell the kids they were going to the movies or to grab a bite to eat but would end up at the Comfort Inn out by the highway, locking themselves in the room, away from the world for a few precious hours.

That worked for a while until one morning Renee was sitting at the breakfast table sipping her second cup of coffee when Sara came into the kitchen. Renee had just gotten off the phone with Annie, their usual early morning phone call before they got their day started. Sara opened the fridge and grabbed the carton of orange juice.

"Mom, can I ask you something?"

"Sure, honey," Renee said without even looking up.

Sara sat at the table and poured a glass of juice for herself. "What's going on with you and Annie?"

Renee stirred uneasily in her chair, not knowing how to answer this question. She remembered the response she got when she told her girls how she felt about Dana. Her heart hurt when she recalled the disastrous outcome and was afraid if she were honest with Sara, the same thing would happen. She was happy with the way things were, everyone seemed to get along, and she didn't want to jeopardize that.

"Well, honey, as I'm sure you can see, Annie and I care a lot about each other."

"Do you care about her like you cared about Dana?"

Just then, Lindsay walked into the room. "What about Dana? She's not coming back, is she?" Lindsay asked.

"No, Lindsay," Renee said.

"So what are you talking about?"

"I asked Mom what was up with her and Justin's mom." Sara took a sip of juice.

"Yeah, what is going on? You two are like inseparable." Lindsay took the juice carton from Sara and poured herself a glass and leaned against the stove.

"Like I was telling Sara, Annie and I care about each other very much."

"Oh, no, not again!" Lindsay said.

Renee's stomach churned with anxiety and frustration, but she wasn't going to let Lindsay's reaction get the best of her. She took a deep breath and tried to calm down before she spoke.

"Lindsay, Sara, I never thought I would be saying this to the both of you, but I'm in love with Annie."

"Oh, Mother!" Lindsay pushed off the stove and tried to leave before Renee stopped her.

"Lindsay, sit down," Renee ordered.

Angrily, Lindsay pulled out one of the wooden kitchen chairs and plopped down into it like an angry child.

"Look, I know our lives have been difficult for the past two years, and I'm sorry for that. I know that my feelings for Annie are different, but you need to understand something. This is who I am. I love Annie with all my heart and soul. I've loved her for a long time, even before I met your dad."

"Really?" Sara asked.

"Yes, really."

"Then why did you marry Dad?"

"Because she was pregnant with me, stupid," Lindsay said.

"Lindsay, stop!" Renee shouted. Nervously, she ran her hands through her hair.

"Is that true?" Sara asked.

Renee's heart pounded in her throat. She hated having to have this conversation with her daughters, but now was the time to get everything out in the open.

"Yes, Sara, it is. I was pregnant with Lindsay when your dad and I got married. But that doesn't mean I didn't love your father. I did."

"So how could you love Annie and Dad at the same time?" Lindsay asked.

Renee's composure was a fragile shell around her. She looked across the table at her daughters. She knew she had to be honest with them even if it meant alienating them. "I married your dad and let Annie go because I thought it was the right thing to do. I was afraid of how I felt about Annie. I didn't understand it. I knew it wasn't what was expected of me, and I didn't want to hurt my family. But you have to understand something. I never stopped loving her, even after all this time."

The only sound in the kitchen was the ticking of the black kitty clock that hung above the sink. Both girls sat in silence while Renee brushed away her tears with the back of her hand.

"I'm sorry, girls. I'm sorry if you're disappointed in me, but this is what it is."

"So what are you going to do?" Lindsay asked.

"Well, I gave up on a chance at love once. I'm not going to let it happen again."

Lindsay stood. "Well, whatever you decide, there's nothing I can do about it." She pushed her chair in and walked away.

Renee looked over at her youngest daughter. "What about you, Sara? How do you feel about this?"

Sara looked up at her mother with tears in her eyes.

"I'm sorry to upset you." She reached over and took Sara's hand. "You know that I will always love you and Lindsay. Nothing can take that away."

Sara sniffled and nodded. Then her crying became more intense.

"Sara, what's wrong, honey? You can tell me."

Sara shook her head. She got up and wrapped her arms around Renee's shoulders, hugging her tight. Her voice was barely a whisper. "Nothing, I'm okay."

Renee was grateful that the fallout from her admission to her daughters was minimal. Neither Lindsay nor Sara treated Annie any differently than before Renee told them how she felt.

The highlight of the summer was celebrating Justin and Lindsay's high school graduation. Although it was a happy time, the fact that Tom wasn't there to see his daughter graduate loomed large over the festivities. Both kids visited the cemetery before the commencement ceremony, leaving rose bouquets wrapped with blue and red ribbons, Niles McKinley's school colors, at Tom's grave.

Now summer was winding down, and a new school year was about to begin. Sara completed her probation period without incident but still saw Mrs. Calderone from time to time.

The visits seemed to have helped Sara come out of her shell as she made several new friends, including her now proclaimed BFF, or Best Friend Forever, Calli, whom she met while trying out for the high school softball team. Something had changed for Sara over the summer. What it was, Renee couldn't quite put her finger on, but something was definitely different about her youngest daughter. Sara seemed happy and excited to be starting her junior year at Niles McKinley.

Justin and Lindsay would be attending Kent State University in September. Lindsay was accepted into the nursing program, while Justin would be taking classes in the criminal justice program.

Annie and Renee kept busy getting ready to send them off to college. The kids would be living in Verder Hall, the freshman dorm, which consisted of tiny rooms that you could barely turn around in. They were sparsely furnished with two desks, two beds, and two dressers. Annie was on a mission to turn the dismal living spaces into a college freshman's dream. She gave each of the kids a stocked hotel-size refrigerator, a fourteen-inch HDTV, and the tiniest microwave oven Renee had ever seen.

Renee made sure the kids had prepaid dining hall passes, prepaid bus fares, and two prepaid credit cards with two hundred-dollar limits for other expenses that might crop up. She was amazed at how much classes and books and living expenses cost to send your kid to college for one year. She was thankful that Tom had looked out for them and planned ahead.

Even though Renee's life was busy with the girls' activities and her relationship with Annie, she often thought of Dana. There seemed to be constant reminders all around her. Renee still felt a twinge of sadness when she would be at the library and look over at the table where Dana used to work or when she would stop at Starbucks for coffee in the morning and remember all the days they spent there talking, the hours slipping by without them noticing.

In her heart, she knew she owed Dana a lot. If not for Dana, there was no way Renee would have gotten through that first year after Tom died. It was also because of Dana that she was finally able to admit to herself who she really was and to have the courage to heal her relationship with Annie.

Renee wondered how Dana was doing, if she sold her house or was building a new one, and whether she finished the book. She also wondered if Dana was dating again. And even though she had no right to feel that way, that thought always tugged her heart.

Chapter Thirty

The leaves had just begun to change, and a crispness filled the morning air. Renee picked up the bundles of daily newspapers from the library steps and carried them over to the reference desk. Excitement surged through her as she recognized the face in the picture on the front page of the *Daily Times*. She cut the twine that held the papers together and read the announcement: "Cleveland author to appear at Borders Bookstore. *New York Times* best-selling author Dana Renato will appear October 14 at Borders for a reading and signing of her latest book, *Mahoning Valley Connection.*"

Renee pulled the paper from its bundle. Her hands shook a little as she folded the paper in half and stuck it in the cubby where she kept her purse.

After Dana left Niles and returned to Cleveland, they had spoken only a few times on the phone. Dana called Renee back a few weeks after returning to Cleveland. She apologized for not calling back sooner, explaining that she was busy with the final chapters of the book and hadn't checked her voice mail in weeks.

After that initial call, their sporadic conversations, always initiated by Renee, were superficial at best, up until the day she got the nerve to tell Dana about her reconciliation with Annie. Although Dana was shocked to hear that Renee was now dating Justin's mother, she told her she was happy for her but was unable to hide the trace of sadness that lingered in her voice, which told Renee otherwise.

The book signing was next Saturday afternoon. Although Renee had to work that morning, she knew she had the afternoon free because Annie was going to Kent to see Justin and Lindsay and deliver more living essentials like toilet paper, shampoo, soap, and so forth. That Saturday was also the high school homecoming dance at Sara's school.

Although two boys in her class asked Sara to the dance, she declined, opting instead to work on the decorating committee with Calli. Calli had been good for Sara. Since they met, Sara seemed to blossom. She no longer holed up in her room for hours on end. She even looked different: more confident.

Calli was a quiet down-to-earth girl. Renee had met her parents at the girls' first softball game. They seemed like nice people. Calli's dad was an engineer at the GM plant in Lordstown, and Calli's mom was a substitute teacher at Niles Middle School. Calli had an older brother, Steve, who was a year ahead of her in school.

Calli and Sara seemed to have a lot in common. They were into sports and were good students. Now that Lindsay was away at school, Calli spent many nights at the Del Fino house.

Saturday morning arrived, and Renee was up early. She read the paper and had already had three cups of coffee by the time Calli and Sara came downstairs for breakfast.

"Can I get you girls something to eat? Juice? Toast?"

Sara opened the refrigerator. "I got it, Mom, thanks." Sara poured a glass of milk for Calli and one for herself. She grabbed the bag of Oreos from the counter and brought them to the table.

Both girls sat at the kitchen table munching Oreos and flipping through the newspaper. Renee liked the feeling of contentment she felt as she watched the girls together. She was happy that Sara had found such a good friend.

The phone rang. Renee knew it was Annie. "Good morning."

"Good morning. How'd you sleep?" Annie asked.

"Okay. And you?"

"Not bad. Are you still going to the book signing?"

"Yes. Are you okay with that?"

"Of course I am. Are you?"

"Why wouldn't I be?"

"It's been a while since you've seen her."

"I know. I'm nervous, but I feel like I need to go. You know, for some kind of closure. Does that sound weird?"

"No, it doesn't sound weird. It'll be fine." There was a pregnant pause at the end of the receiver. "I should be back in town around dinner time. Call me later?"

"I sure will. Drive careful."

"I love you."

"You too," Renee said and hung up.

"Mom, can you drop us off at school on your way to work? Mrs. Calderone wants us there by nine o'clock to decorate the gym."

"Sure, honey. I'll be ready to leave in a few minutes."

Renee drove Sara and Calli to the school and dropped them off at the gymnasium entrance.

"What time do you want me to pick you up?" Renee asked.

"Oh, you don't have to. Steve said he would bring us home after the dance. Anyway, I was just going to stay at Calli's tonight. Is that okay?" Sara slid across the backseat with her backpack in hand.

"Okay, honey, have fun." Sara closed the door and Renee waited until both girls were safely inside the school, then drove to work. Her palms were sweaty on the steering wheel as she thought about meeting up with Dana that afternoon.

The library was always a busy place on Saturday mornings. Two craft programs for kids were going on in the children's room. Although Renee only had to put in three hours, it seemed like the morning would never end. At eleven thirty, she was grateful to see Mary, who was her relief for the day.

When she got home, she took a nice, long, hot shower, reveling in the warm water, relieving the tension in her shoulders and neck. She had thought about asking Annie to go with her to the book signing but decided against it. She wanted this to be just her and Dana. Actually, she wasn't sure how Dana would react to seeing her again, which made her a little uneasy.

After her shower, Renee tried on ten different outfits before deciding on a pair of brown corduroy slacks and a cream fisherman's cable-knit sweater. She blew dry her hair twice and elected to wear it down, the way Dana used to like it.

It was one forty-five when Renee pulled into the Borders parking lot. The place was packed, and she had to park in the adjoining Chuck E. Cheese lot because all the Borders spaces were taken. Two large posters with Dana's picture and a picture of Dana's new book graced the front entrance of the bookstore, announcing the signing.

Nervously, Renee got out of her car and walked up the sidewalk to the store entrance. The signing would be held next to the coffee shop. Several rows of wooden folding chairs had been set up with a lectern placed in front of the chairs.

The hair on the back of Renee's neck prickled. She saw Dana from across the room, speaking to a woman whose expression seemed animated as they spoke. Almost as if she sensed Renee's presence, Dana looked up and smiled.

Dana ended her conversation with the woman and made her way over to Renee.

"I was hoping I'd see you here." Dana drew Renee into a tight warm hug. "How have you been?"

"I'm good, Dana. Things are good." Heat flushed Renee's face. She wasn't sure whether it was from embarrassment or remnants of desire.

Dana looked great. Renee couldn't take her eyes off her. "So how are you? You look wonderful."

"I'm doing fine. Thanks."

"How's the book doing?"

"Better than expected. Who knew there was such an interest in the crime world in this little part of the universe? The reviews are doing well, too. I'm very pleased." Dana studied Renee thoughtfully.

"What?" Renee stood back, nervous under Dana's appraising gaze.

"You look great, Renee."

The bookstore manager came over to Dana. "Excuse me, Ms. Renato, we're ready to begin now."

"Thanks," Dana said. "Can you stick around after the signing?"

she asked Renee.

"Sure. I'd love to." Renee took a seat in the back row.

There was standing room only as Dana took her place at the lectern. Renee couldn't help but feel a sense of pride as she watched Dana speak about her research and about the book. She wondered if Dana still thought about her as she went through her day doing research or working in the yard, like Renee thought of her sometimes.

Renee was startled out of her reverie when she heard her name. Dana had introduced Renee and praised her and the McKinley Memorial Library for her help in Dana's research. Renee wondered what these people would think if they knew the real basis of their relationship.

After the signing, Renee and Dana grabbed a table in the corner of the coffee shop and talked while they had coffee and scones.

"So how have you been? You look well." Renee added sweetener to her coffee and stirred it.

"I've been good. Busy with the book tour. How are Lindsay and Sara?"

"They're getting along pretty well. Sara's a junior and is the starting catcher on the girls' fast-pitch team. Lindsay started her first year at Kent State in September. She's going into nursing. Justin's there, too. I think that helps her not feel so homesick. I think having each other there is good for both of them."

"That's great. They seem to have turned out to be great kids. I remember how worried you were when their relationship began."

"Yes, you're right. It turned out to be the best thing for both of them. For two young kids, they seem pretty devoted to each other."

"And how are you and Annie doing?"

Renee swallowed and stared into her coffee cup. She felt guilty about the way things ended with Dana and even guiltier for picking up with Annie where they left off almost twenty years before.

"Things are going well." To Renee's dismay, her voice broke.

"There's been a lot of adjusting to do with the kids and all, but for the most part, we're doing just fine."

"Wonderful." Dana took a sip of coffee and a bite of scone.

Renee fiddled with her coffee cup. "Dana, I need to apologize to you."

"For what?"

"I feel bad. It's almost like I used you."

"Used me? How?"

"I think I was in love with Annie all along. I just couldn't admit it to myself. You helped me realize who I am...and to be okay with who I am."

"Renee, it's never wrong to find out who you really are."

"But you have to understand, I never wanted to hurt you."

"I know that. We're both adults. I can't speak for you, but I went into our relationship with my eyes wide open. After Risa died, I never thought I'd feel anything for anybody ever again. You changed that for me, and I thank you." Dana smiled.

Now Renee really felt bad. She lowered her eyes before Dana's steady gaze. Renee knew how hard it had been for Dana to let go of her feelings for Risa and take a chance at finding love again. She couldn't help but feel responsible for causing more pain in Dana's life. Pain that she didn't deserve.

Suddenly, a woman Renee didn't know came over to their table and sat down. "There you are. How did the signing go?" the woman asked. She was very attractive, with silky, dark hair, cut in a stylish bob. Jeans and a cashmere sweater clung to her athletically trim body.

"Great. I think they want me to come back at Christmas time for another signing."

"That's great, babe."

Babe? The connotation of the endearment wasn't lost on Renee. Oh, my God, Renee thought. When she realized who this woman was to Dana, she felt a gamut of perplexing emotions.

"Renee, I'd like you to meet my partner, Brooklyn Sanders."

Renee smiled and extended her hand to Brooklyn. "Pleased to meet you."

"So you're Renee. Dana has told me a lot about you."

Renee smiled awkwardly and flicked her gaze to Dana, then back to Brooklyn.

"Don't worry, it was all good things." Brooklyn stood. "I'm going to get a cup of coffee. Anybody need a refill?"

"Thanks, hon." Dana handed Brooklyn her mug.

"No, thanks, I'm good," Renee said, unable to take her gaze from the beautiful woman who walked away.

"So how did you guys meet?" Renee asked.

"She's my Realtor. We met when I sold the house in Cleveland Heights. Allison hooked me up with her. Brooklyn owns her own agency. She did an excellent job and got me top dollar for the house. She and Allison helped me through all the legal stuff of paying Risa's father what he had coming to him. She made a very tough situation pretty painless."

"She's beautiful," Renee said, embarrassed the words slipped out before she could stop them.

Dana smiled. "Yes, she is. And a wonderful person, too."

Brooklyn came back to the table with two steaming mugs of coffee.

"So are you two getting caught up?"

"Yes, it's amazing how much can change over time." Dana took the mug and took a sip.

Renee looked over at Dana. Her eyes sent her a private message. The message was that she was happy for her. Her guilt over ending their relationship dissolved immediately.

The three women sat and talked for a long time. They made plans to get together, the four of them, for dinner sometime.

On the way home from the book signing, Renee called Annie on her cell phone to tell her the events of the day.

"Sounds like it went really well," Annie said. "How're you doing?"

"I'm doing just fine. Hey, how far away are you?"

"About ten minutes, why?"

"Sara's at the high school with Calli to work the homecoming dance. She's planning on spending the night at Calli's afterward, so the house is empty for the rest of the evening. I'm going home to draw a bath, light some candles, and add some music." Renee finished in a sultry whisper, "Meet me there as soon as you can."

"I'll be there."

When Annie arrived, she let herself in and went upstairs. Renee stood naked in the steamy bathroom, lighting a candle.

"Hey." Annie looked Renee over seductively as she entered. Lavender and vanilla permeated the air, and Howie Day's song "Collide" arose from the CD player that sat on the counter between the two sinks.

Renee reached for Annie and drew her close. She buried her face in Annie's soft hair and breathed in her scent. "I missed you today," she whispered.

Annie's hands moved gently down Renee's back, then cupped her bare bottom, pulling Renee closer.

Renee pressed herself into Annie and kissed her deeply. She fumbled with the buttons on Annie's shirt and pushed the silky fabric off her shoulders, planting kisses on Annie's neck, collarbone, and breasts.

Annie gasped and felt her knees go weak as Renee's warm mouth captured her swollen nipple with a tantalizing possessiveness. Renee tugged at the waistband of Annie's jeans. Annie stepped out of them, and they stood naked body against naked body, slowly dancing to the soft music. When the song was over, Renee took Annie's hand and helped her step into the bathtub. Annie sat on the edge of the claw-foot tub, her back against the nearby wall, while Renee got into the tub and knelt in front of her.

The cold porcelain was a delicious contrast to Annie's hot skin. Her insides heated up when Renee slowly kissed the inside of her thighs, first one thigh, then the other, until Annie begged for more. She tossed her head back and held on tight to the side of the tub as Renee brought her to the point of no return.

Afterward, Annie and Renee soaked in the tub, reveling in the warm, quiet solitude that was a rare gift in their hectic lives.

Renee squeezed bath gel on a loofah and gently washed Annie's back. "If someone would have told me a year ago that I would be here with you, I would have told them that they were crazy."

"I know what you mean. If you think about it, just a short time ago we were living totally different lives."

"It's amazing," Renee said, "how life can change in an instant. All I know is that this must be something special for us to end up here like this."

Annie leaned forward and hugged her knees as Renee rinsed the soap from her back. "As painful as losing a dream or someone we loved is, it's almost as if we had to give up who we were to become who we really are."

Renee thought for a moment. "Yes, I guess you're right." A pang of sadness tugged at her heart. She knew she truly loved Tom and Dana or having to let them go wouldn't have been as difficult as it was.

"Reen, do you think we'll ever be able to live together?" Annie's voice sounded wistful.

Renee patted her leg. "Of course we will. Once the kids are out on their own, they'll be so involved in their own lives that we'll just be an afterthought to them. Maybe we can sell one of the houses and buy a little vacation cottage up by Lake Erie for just the two of us."

"Mmm, that sounds nice," Annie said. Then she asked a question that surprised Renee. "Do you have any regrets?"

"Any regrets? About what?"

"About how we got here. Is there something you feel like you missed out on?"

Renee kissed the top of Annie's head. Knowing that the kids were healthy and happy, that Annie was back in her life again, and that Dana had found love again, too, she had no regrets.

"Not anymore." Renee slid her arms around Annie's waist and pulled her closer. "I have everything I need right here."

About the author

Maria V. Ciletti is a registered nurse working as a medical administrator.

Her writing credits include "Don't Sing: Growing up Lesbian in Catholic School," which was published by Taylor & Francis in their *Queer and Catholic* anthology in July 2008. A nonfiction story, "Taking Care of Ellie," was published in the anthology *Voices of Caregiving* by La Chance Publishing in 2009, edited by the Healing Project.

Her first novel, *The Choice*, a 2007 Lambda Literary nominee for debut fiction, was published by Haworth Press in May 2007. *Clinical Distance*, the sequel to *The Choice*, was published in May 2009 by Intaglio Publications and was a 2010 Lambda Literary, as well as a GCLS, nominee for romance.

Maria is a member of the Golden Crown Literary Society. She lives in Niles, Ohio, with her partner, Rose. She can be contacted through her Web site at www.mariaciletti.com.

You might also enjoy:

Clinical Distance
by Maria Ciletti
ISBN: 978-1-935216-03-2

In the sequel to The Choice, Clinical Distance begins six years later with Mina Thomas, who has finished medical school. After divorcing her husband, Sean, and losing Regan Martin, the love of her life, Mina sets out on a quest to make her way in the world and to find the love she lost. Mina dates—a lot—but after many meaningless rendezvous with nameless women, Mina decides to give up on finding love and devotes her time solely to her career as chief resident at City Hospital.

However, one night after having dinner with her best friend and confidant, police Sergeant Rosemary Rosetti, Mina discovers that the love she was searching for might possibly have been right under her nose all along. That's when Regan steps back into Mina's life.

Will Mina sacrifice her heart for another chance at love, or will she keep a *clinical distance*?

Sea Of Grass
by Kate Sweeney
ISBN: 978-1-935216-15-5

Professor Tess Rawlins spent the last twelve years teaching agriculture in California, away from Montana and her heart. When she's called back to the sprawling Double R cattle ranch and her ailing father, Tess is thrown back into the world she had nearly forgotten since the death of her brother two years earlier.

Unsettling memories boil to the surface for Tess, and her only pleasant distraction is the new cook Claire Redman and her son Jack. However, there is more facing Professor Rawlins than dealing with the memory of her brother or her attraction to Claire. Tess must figure a way to save the Rawlins's five thousand acres of rich grassland. It has thrived for five generations, when her great-grandfather started the dynasty in the 1880s; now she may lose it all to an unscrupulous land developer.

Set in the foothills of the Bitterroots, Tess and Claire find themselves in the fight of their lives—for love and the *sea of grass*.

You can purchase other Intaglio
Publications books online at
www.bellabooks.com or at
your local bookstore.

Published by
Intaglio Publications
Walker, La.

Visit us on the web
www.intagliopub.com